Resurrection

Kiára Árgenta

OPENING CHAPTER

First Printing, 2017

ISBN 10: 1-904958-67-2
ISBN 13: 978-1-904958-67-3

published by

Opening Chapter
Cardiff, Wales

www.openingchapter.com

Cover photo elements by Noel Dacey

Kiára Árgenta

Kiára Árgenta grew up in Paris before moving to Wales where she studied Russian at university. She worked as a journalist before leaving to live in Spain and then Hungary. She currently lives in Milano and is a full-time writer.

RESURRECTION

I am floating and I see Lilla, my stepmother. She is there waiting for me in such a beautiful red dress. I wonder where we are going as she is so dressed up; maybe she has come to see me in the Opera. But as I get closer, I see that it is not Lilla, although she looks so much like her. This woman is younger, softer, sadder and I remember her from photographs; my mother. I am delighted to see her so alive, so real after a lifetime without her, so why is she not so happy to see me?

"Mama! It is you! I know it's you, I waited so long, but why do you look so sad? Why? Don't you want to see me?"

And then I realise. She killed herself because she was depressed. Maybe because of me.

So my fears were right. She really did hate me. Like everyone else. She really does not want to see me. "Did you really hate me so much, mama?" I say reaching for her hands. "Please tell me the truth. I waited so long to hear it from you. No one else could answer my questions so please just tell me. I'm sorry if I made you end your life. I am so sorry."

She is real to the touch as I gently reach for her arms, her hair and her face and she is wearing the same beautiful red dress I have seen in her photos with its elaborate beading and sequins and I have longed for this moment all my life. She is so pretty but barely older than me. How is that? She has aged well. But I don't let this spoil the moment I wanted so much.

She embraces me and says, "No, my Natalija. I loved you. It was me I hated. Me. You were and you are so lovely. You are everything to me. You would have been." She touches my face with her cool hands but she still looks so unhappy.

I look into her dark eyes, so pretty and yet so haunted and say, "I'm sorry if I made you do it. It has followed me through my life that you killed yourself because I ruined

1

your existence. I am not a good person."

"Natalija, my darling. I never died because of you and I have spent my whole existence since regretting what I did. I have watched you and broken my heart every single day I didn't spend with you. I burn with the pain of not being with you, like being every day in Hell, but don't you know why I am so sad? I have watched you for so long; your wonderful career, your beauty and also your pain. Your double life where I watched you killing yourself with bulimia left me heartbroken and you still don't know why I am so sad to see you?" Her hands are holding mine tightly.

It then hits me. We are both dead. I am not dreaming. She has been watching me my whole life, watching me from above and longing to be with me. And now I am dead too. I remember, they killed me. Stabbed in my Opera, *Carmen,* for real. Someone had traded the prop knife for a real one. I remember the shock as the blade was jammed into my back to the sound of the toreadors, and the pain and blood. I remember dying on the stage as the applause was deafening and someone was shouting to hold the curtains. I remember Luca, the Italian tenor who was my Don José desperately trying to stop the bleeding, shouting for help and Krisztyna, my lovely Krisztyna holding me in her arms saying, 'My Natalija, what have they done? What have they done to you?'

Her tears were falling on my face as I tried to point to her necklace where I had inscribed on the back: '***Krisztyna, Un bel dì.....***'

But the one fine day never came for Krisztyna. Or me.

But I am here now, I am here with my mother, this one beautiful day and I want to stay. I never want to return to that place on Earth, not even for my Krisztyna. It got so painful I cannot go back. I want to stay here. Nothing is hurting here, not even the knife wound. My throat is not sore from singing and vomiting and I am not tired and run down.

I feel so alive. I am dead and yet I never felt so alive.

I am not dreaming. I am finally happy, finally at peace after years of torment.

"You are not dreaming, Natalija, my darling girl," my mother says reading my thoughts.

"But there is so much of your life to live. You have Italia to go to; to sing and be successful again and it will save you from hurting so much. There is someone in Roma so special waiting for you every day, so special you don't even know they exist but they are waiting for you. Yes, you have to go because you have so much to live for, so many years of talent to give to the world. I cannot let you stay with me although I want to so badly it hurts. I miss you like a living Hell every single day."

"Then let me stay. It is too much pain, I can't deal with it. Life hurt too much and I was already dying, mama. I was killing myself because life hurt. I might as well be dead. They only stabbed my body but my soul was already dead. I hated myself; my illness, my inability to love, to accept love."

"No, Natalija. You have to deal with it. I can't let you be here with me. You are going to be happy one day, famous beyond your wildest dreams. My darling girl, you have your voice, you have to get to Italia. Don't stay in Hungary, dead or alive, it is no longer safe. And I won't let you stay here with me, I won't let you stay even though I want you with me."

And she is pushing me away gently at first and I cling to her and beg her to keep me with her. So she pushes me away harder and I scream, "Don't leave me again, don't leave me! Let me stay! I don't want to live, I don't want life any more, it hurts too much! Please come back! Please take me with you! Mama, don't leave me! Don't make me go back!"

I see her gentle face so full of anguish as she pushes me

far away from her. It is hurting her so much to see me go.

"Goodbye my beautiful girl. You need to return now. I am sorry." And I see her outstretched arms, the tears on her face, her eyes closed as if in prayer. The red of her dress glows in the light and she seems like an angel, so pure and I am desperate to be with her.

And the jolt as I am back in my body and the nurse is holding the oxygen to my face; the doctors are telling me to stop fighting. My body has just been in the operating theatre where I died and am now brought back to life. My stitches will burst, I need to stay still and breathe the oxygen. I feel the pain and I don't care because I want to be with my mother. I don't want to be here, in life with all the suffering. I have had enough.

"Let me fucking die! I want to die! Let me die! I was with my mother, so let me go!" I thrash around and they hit me with a shot of something in my vein and I am gone. Only this time it is black and dreamless.

The next time I open my eyes, I am too tired to move. They have drugged me. A dull throb runs through me despite all the morphine. I am attached to morphine. I should enjoy the morphine but I am alive and I don't want to be.

There is Krisztyna. She is sitting there crying. Why is everyone so sad around me? It is like being at my own funeral.

"Krisztyna….." I try to hold out my hand but it won't move. "Tell them I want to die, tell them to let me go back."

I feel her hand grab hold of mine. My body is fuzzy and heavy. She is so beautiful but so sad and she cries to see me awake and alive. Last time I saw her on the stage, she was crying over me as well, as I thought I was dying in her arms to the applause of the audience behind the curtains. And then nothing.

"Natalija, they told me you died in there. Don't say you

want to die, it is killing me. The blade missed your heart by a millimetre. You died in the operating theatre, they told me you died and I didn't know if you would make it. I have been screaming in the corridors until they gave me some Valium. I was so hysterical I nearly got admitted myself until the staff came to tell me you were managing to stay alive. The Opera House has closed for investigation. It is a crime scene. My prints are everywhere because I ran on stage to hold you and I shouldn't have, they tell me. I contaminated the evidence; the stage manager was trying to hold me back. But I couldn't stand there and watch you on stage bleeding to death.... I thought if I hold her one last....."

She weeps into her hands. "And in the ambulance they wouldn't let me hold you, I had to watch them try to keep you alive."

"Krisztyna, I am here. Please don't cry. I just saw my mother and she was just like she is in the photos; so lovely and wearing red and we talked and....."

Krisztyna's eyes open wide with fear and she says, "My God, you really did die and you still want to. What about me, Natalija, what about me? What would I do without you?"

And as she cries, I can't reach her to stop the tears.

I don't even know what day, month or year it is. All I know in my last performance in *Carmen*, I was stabbed by a real knife and not the fake knife it should have been. All the cops have to go on so far in the investigation are Krisztyna's and Luca's prints on the knife and a faint print from the prop master who would have laid out the knife on the table. Luca was my Don José and Krisztyna who was playing Mercédès rushed onto the stage when they tried to hold her back. No one knows anything else. So far there is no more evidence. The company have had to close the Opera; there are no performances, right in the middle of our season for the first time in history. The Opera House is taped off by police. There are no visitors, no staff in the building, nothing. It is a shell, an empty shell, Krisztyna says. So strange.

She is being questioned for attempted murder as is Luca and the entire cast of *Carmen* is also under investigation.

But right now she is first in line. She has motive, they say. People have stepped forward to say Krisztyna has more motive than anyone else. How? I had so many enemies. How can they think my closest friend in the Opera would hurt me?

My Krisztyna. My love. But only I know what she really means to me.

There is a policewoman standing outside my room, arms folded. I see her through the glass. Krisztyna is not allowed to be alone with me. They are taking her straight to the police station for questioning. They have come to get her after she has waited all night in anguish in the hospital corridors when I was in surgery. She is lucky that she managed to get in the ambulance with me, lucky they have not dragged her to the police station before I woke up, but now they have come for her. The policewoman is watching us closely as though Krisztyna is going to hurt me. She doesn't take her eyes off us, not for a second, this pretty blonde cop, one of the few women cops around. There are so few that I remember this one from seeing her around Budapest, usually accompanied by three or four 'don't mess with us' male cops. But from her eyes, this pretty woman looks cold and hard and I know time is running out for us.

"It hurts me so, Natalija. They are going to question me over attempted murder and all I ever did was love you. Right now the police are going through our apartment, pulling it all apart, looking for clues to find my motive. The police are horrible. This cop has told me I am going straight to the station; she has told me what I could be facing. Even my ex-husband has been questioned and I know that he will say everything bad about me; that I resented you because he

6

threw me out of my home. My children don't want to see me as they now know what really happened to our marriage and they are so angry. They only see my ex-husband's side, they don't know how he beat me every day. How could I tell them the truth?

Now my nightmare continues as I could go to prison, Natalija. They could lock me away and I think someone in the company told the police they saw me near the prop table before the finale. Someone nameless and faceless. I will die if I go to prison. God help me when I meet all those male cops. Natalija, they will rip me apart, I am so afraid. When they know I am your lover, they will crucify me. I am so frightened."

Her dark eyes are lost, rimmed with black circles through lack of sleep. She strokes the side of my face and I feel bad for her pain. From her reactions, the cop does not like to see this display of affection. She is clearly disgusted with Krisztyna and she steps into the room. It is time.

"I will tell the police everything. We will leave this place and go to Italia," I say.

Krisztyna is silent and she gazes at me with such sadness.

"My children, Natalija, I can't. ... and my mother, she is not so healthy, I can't leave. Luca, he too is being held in the country. He can't go home to Italia as he was the one to stab you. How will anyone know who really swapped that prop knife? We all talk of back-stabbers but how many could be capable of this? I will die if I go to prison for 15 years, I will die."

The cop is gripping her arm, telling her firmly it is time.

"Krisztyna, you did nothing........" I turn to the cop. "Please, she would never hurt me, please understand."

The blonde policewoman doesn't look at me. She is gripping Krisztyna's arm telling her they have to leave right now and touches the handcuffs on her belt. I think she will snap them on her.

"Please don't hurt her," I tell the policewoman. "Please."

She ignores me and pulls Krisztyna's arm behind her back hard and drags her out of the room.

"No, no, no!" shouts Krisztyna and her eyes are wide with terror.

"Krisztyna, don't you know how I feel? What I was trying to tell you on the stage? I remember you held me as I blacked out. Krisztyna........"

I am too weak to shout and my words are lost to the air.

I watch through the glass as the cop grips Krisztyna more tightly and pushes her along the corridor. Krisztyna looks back at me with such sadness, but the cop shoves her ahead as if she is a criminal. She is now too far away to hear me.

"It's on your necklace, remember that. You have it on now. Please remember when you were going to sing in *Madama Butterfly* in Roma, that you still will and then one fine day...." But she has long gone when I say this.

I fall asleep, realising she is Krisztyna now to me, to everyone when she was Kriszta, only yesterday or the day before or whatever day it was when I was performing in the fatal Opera. She told me the night we first met, 'Only if you are in love with me do you call me Krisztyna', which is why I engraved it on her necklace. But she seems to have become Krisztyna. I don't understand and the morphine is giving me insane dreams and maybe I die again, maybe I don't because my father, Lilla and brother are there when I wake up. Fiamma is on a flight from Napoli. She should be here any moment. Fiamma, the girl who also loved me, who thought she had my heart when it was really Krisztyna's.

My father tells me he called Fiamma who was hysterical and got the first flight out of Napoli.

My father, brother and stepmother sit there as if I have already died. I tell them, "For God's sake, I am not dead. Anyway I saw my mother....."

8

My father looks at me and begins to cry. Lilla shakes her head at me and whispers for me to stay silent. My brother Levente just doesn't know what to say.

In the end, Levente gets up to go to meet Fiamma. She has texted him distraught as she is lost somewhere in the hospital entrance, bewildered by all the Hungarian signs.

She makes her full Italian funeral entrance holding a bunch of enormous flowers, openly sobbing and reaching for my hand and crying into her rosary beads. My father cries more. She is dressed in black ready for the funeral she thought was imminent.

"Fiamma, say something, please. You are wearing black because you thought you were coming to a funeral?"

I just need someone to act normal.

Fiamma nods and cries harder and this makes my father go over to the window to hide his tears.

Finally she speaks to me when my family go for a walk to give us time alone.

She doesn't look at me but says so quietly, "I know, Natalija. I know about Kriszta. She called me too to tell me what happened. I know everything. That what we had between us was a lie. That Kriszta was the one. Maybe I knew all along and I was lying to myself. I wanted to see you as they told me you might die. It tore my heart out and then I find out everything else from Kriszta, which I really knew all along and I die twice."

She raises her head and her beautiful green eyes look at me and I see all the hope she ever had disappear in that look.

I try to tell her it is okay, I am coming to Italia soon.

"No, Natalija. I died twice. You only died once. I have been living this lie since we met. I knew even before Kriszta told me. I knew before she said it that she had your heart. She even said she was so sorry but that was how things were, had always been." Fiamma looks at me, so full of sadness and regret. I know nothing can make this less harsh for her. I can't tell her it will be okay.

"In my heart, Natalija, I always knew you never loved me."

She holds my hand until my parents and brother return. She is going to leave but they tell her to sit down. She can stay with them for a few days, as long as she needs because she can't be alone in a hotel like this. Their home is open to her.

She thanks them and accepts the offer. She is broken.

I am left alone in my hospital bed. Everyone leaves together as though it is my funeral. I think of Krisztyna. What if they do hold her? She is terrified of prison. She said she will kill herself.

In the end the police do let her go after breaking her down by interrogating her viciously for two days and nights. Until further evidence is found in the Opera House and she is set free.

I look out of the window.

"I wish I had died," I say to myself.

It is darkening outside and a nurse coming in to check on me hears me and tells me that is terrible. No one wishes they had died, they should be glad to be alive. She rolls me on my side to change the dressing on my back and jabs her needle in roughly.

So what, I like the pain. Doesn't she know by now? I am a masochist.

"Doctor says to give you more morphine but you don't seem to be grateful to be alive."

"Just give me the shot. My father paid you enough, no doubt."

Bitch, I think. *Money grabbing bitch. She has no idea what I went through. Am still going through.*

I fall into dark sleep, full of twisting dreams; me and Krisztyna when we first met running through the trees in the summer evening in Margitsziget, me and Fiamma in

Napoli, me and my mother unable to talk. We look at each other and I want to say so much and she looks at me and the tears just fall down her face. Her touch is so real that when I wake up, I can't believe she is not here with me. She sits and watches over me in the hospital, her face so sad. I look under the bed and my insides pulse with agonising pain with having to twist.

I stare at the ceiling and wonder if I will ever sing again. I certainly won't be throwing up any time soon. I can just imagine how much that would hurt.

Maybe this will stop my eating disorder as I can break the cycle of bulimia and keep it broken.

Even before I left Hungary, it was over with Krisztyna. Neither of us said it but we both knew. She would visit me until I left hospital, sitting silently and sadly telling me everyone had gone from her world. The only good was the police had found the real suspect, that she will get years in prison. I tell her I do not want to know and I knew it would be a she. The men would never hate so much. I am all that is left for Krisztyna right now and her mother. All her friends dropped her, she has no work. The police tried to get her to confess to trading the prop knife for a real one. They were nasty, laughed at her when she said she loved me, humiliated her by asking in detail about her sex life and told her she was a cheap little whore. Even the pretty blonde cop had muttered something about her being 'unnatural'. *Just obsessed with someone more famous than you*, said the cop.

That opera star, Natalija, you just should leave her alone. Go home to your family, lady and be a real woman.

Krisztyna had turned to the lady cop for support but found none. She either was too afraid to challenge the male cops or genuinely disgusted by Krisztyna's confessions. Even alone in the room when the men had gone to get cups of tea, Krisztyna had said, *Please help me. I did nothing. I cannot go home, my husband beats me.*

The tears had run down her face and she had wiped them away with her sleeve as the female cop just stood and stared at her unfeeling, not even offering her tissues. She watched Krisztyna broken and crying as she popped chewing gum with arms folded and eyes like ice. Then the male cops returned, pushed a cup of dark, barely warm tea and a sullen, dry pastry across the table to Krisztyna and went over and over the same questions until she was exhausted and locked up in the cells for the second night in a row.

Once they found fresh evidence in the theatre which led directly to the real attempted murderess, Krisztyna was suddenly released, no apology or explanation.

She was lucky, they said. The blonde cop had unlocked her cell, given her a tasteless paper cup of strong coffee and said, *Go home. Go home to your husband and children, lady.*

He beat me, he beat me every day of our marriage, I had to leave, Krisztyna said again. The cop said nothing, just got her to sign a form saying she was free to go. *My husband beat and raped me every day for 20 years*, Krisztyna repeated in front of several cops as she signed her release form and collected her coat and bag. They shrugged. So what? They didn't care for investigating wife-beaters; there was no justice for Krisztyna. She wandered out hungry, exhausted through lack of sleep and so traumatised until I returned to our apartment.

But from then on our relationship was strained. She couldn't tell me she loved me and I couldn't tell her. She couldn't touch me as I was still healing. She would change my wound dressing on my back and sigh as I said it hurt. Even trying to hold me in her arms, I was as fragile as crystal. I would say, "Please Krisztyna, you have to stop holding me, my body is hurting."

She would get angry and say that I didn't want her any more. She was impatient thinking I would heal faster.

"For God's sake, just kiss me at least," she would demand when I turned off the light at night. My nightmares woke her up. I kept having to take painkillers in the night and she whined I was disturbing her sleep but not in the way she wanted. "I'm a passionate woman, Natalija. I have needs!" she would shout at me and we would lie next to each other worlds apart.

We would sit in silence on the sofa in front of the TV, her with no work and me recovering. She did her best to look after me; made us dinner every day, took me to the doctor but suddenly all our conversation had dried up and we had nothing to talk about. We were not performing, we had no Opera House or productions or gossip from theatreland. There was literally nothing to say.

Something had died on us in *Carmen*.

When I booked my flight to Roma for the end of April she wept.

"Krisztyna, I want you with me. Please can I book two tickets?"

"No," she said. "No, Natalija."

"Please, Krisztyna. You will be rehearsing in Roma for Butterfly in May anyway. Come with me now, don't stay in Hungary alone. You have no work and I don't want you to sit around the apartment staring at the river. Come and enjoy Roma. You can wander alone if you want but be alone in Roma and do your thinking there. It is beautiful this time of year as you can admire the city and enjoy the spring without tourists."

"No," she says. She will go crazy looking at that river. Cold, dark Hungary. It is no longer my country and she should feel the same. I have decided that I will become a citizen of Italia, even if I have to renounce my Hungarian nationality.

My own country has stabbed me through the heart.

"Krisztyna, why are you now Krisztyna to everyone? It

was always Kriszta. You said once, *Only if you are in love can you call me Krisztyna......*"

"Maybe I need the love from myself, maybe I am not getting it from you...." She looks at me sadly.

"That is so untrue. Why do you say that?" I cannot understand her. "Tell me what I can do."

I look at her, and she still looks at me with such sadness as though I broke her heart.

"It was Krisztina really without the 'y' but there was another Krisztina when I first started with the Opera, so I was Krisztyna to be different. Then it was easier just as Kriszta. Hard cold Kriszta, the bitch." Her eyes flicker with tears and she leaves the room and returns, her bag packed.

"You are not the bitch you acted in the Opera. It was not the real you, Krisztyna. I want to know everything about you, about the real you. Where are you going?"

"I have to go, Natalija. Please don't try to stop me," she says but her step is cautious as she edges towards the door. Her words are bold but her movements are not.

"It can be Krisztyna forever. And that Kriszta who was so cold and bitchy was your mask for the world," I say.

Krisztyna stands with her back to me, tears on her face, hesitating with her hand on the door frame.

"Don't, Natalija. Don't make this harder for me," she says. She doesn't turn round but she doesn't make that final step out of the door.

"You have always been Krisztyna to me ever since the night I met you at *Turandot* in the open air theatre. You were so lovely, so exotic and sensual," I tell her.

I need her. I don't want to be alone.

She wipes a tear away from her eyes. "I need to be alone, Natalija. I am going to my mother's apartment for a few days," she says turning to face me.

I walk over and try to hold her. "My Krisztyna, don't go."

"Natalija. I have to go, don't you see? Please just let me go," she tells me and she cannot look into my eyes.

14

I let go of her and she picks up her bag and walks out of the apartment.

It felt like the last touch we ever had and it was because we die that day. It is one of the saddest days of my life because I know. Despite her coming to Roma soon after me, we are already finished.

I stare out of the window at the Duna River with the warmth of spring coming through the windows. I feel so alone. Why is she rejecting me after all we have been through? She will be flying out in a few weeks so why not now. She has nothing here.

I wish I had died. My career in tatters, my body weak, my throat ruined and now I lost the only person I ever loved.

I cannot even cry because it hurts my insides. The pain of living is more unbearable right now than the pain of death.

Why didn't you just let me die, God? Why?

I would have been remembered as a great talent, life brutally cut short. I would have died knowing that Krisztyna loved me.

I would have been immortal, like an Opera heroine. Now I am nothing.

ROMA

I arrive in Roma and Marina meets me at the airport to take me to her old apartment. I cannot lift my baggage. I need airport staff to help me both sides and I really shouldn't be travelling but I have to get out of Hungary. I remember my mother's words and I am going crazy sitting around in the day and having nightmares every night about *Carmen* in the Opera House. Marina was the first diva I ever met when I was 23 years old. She was performing in *Tosca* in London as I sang my first role as Rosette in *Manon*. She liked me immediately and we stayed in touch after I met her again, as I guested at Roma Opera.

Faces of my haters and rivals have been haunting my dreams. They are laughing at me, all of them. I need to leave the city and my home country to stop the bad dreams because I do not want to stay in this dark place. Even my beautiful apartment overlooking the river in the spring warmth is not as it should be.

I am still in the shadows.

So I feel relief when I see Marina waiting in the arrivals hall. She rushes over to take my suitcases and drive me to my new home. Her embrace lasts a long time and she says she was worried sick. I don't tell her even her hug is painful as hell. She says in the car on the way out to the city, "It is every opera singer or actor's worst fear, some stage accident happens. You fall from a height, or some scenery falls on you. I nearly fell in the orchestra pit during one love duet. I forgot the space and that is bad enough. Once I missed the mattress when I jumped as Tosca. I didn't look when I leapt off the parapet. It was not high but I twisted my ankle badly. I know male singers usually have it worse as they are more often than us at the other end of a gun, and there is always that fear what if ..... But for some deliberate attempt on your life. God, you are brave, Natalija. You are so brave to come here so soon."

"I was going crazy; I can't sit around in Hungary with so many bad memories and I can't sing, Marina. I have to rest for the first time in my life and I am going mad," I say. "Roma Opera told me just to sit in on rehearsals. I will make sure no one forgets me for when I am recovered. God knows how I will get back to where I was."

This is on my mind constantly. Nearly at the top and now nothing. What if I am forgotten or lose my ability by the time I recover? I might never get back to a fraction of who I was.

"Nothing would ever happen to you in Roma Opera. You are going to be well looked after, Natalija. But Krisztyna? Where is she? I thought she sings in May so why isn't she with you? I thought she was coming to stay in the apartment too?" Marina looks at me.

She looks at me constantly as she drives as though I am resurrected or a ghost. Each time she takes her eyes off the road, we nearly crash into the car in front or she curses as we shoot a red light. I am afraid of dying again as her driving is atrocious, like most of the Roman drivers. I say nothing but my insides scream with pain when we screech to a violent stop and the seatbelt digs into me.

I tell her that I think Krisztyna is gone to me, that she won't even stay in the apartment in Roma. Marina is so sorry but she says brightly that she knows just the girl for me. She pats my hand and her face lights up. She is confident she has the answer to everything.

"Yes," she smiles. "I know just the lady from our company. Very beautiful, very sweet and very talented. And she is Hungarian too. Marina will fix your broken heart. Don't you worry now. You will love her so much. You can cook Hungarian food together. It is perfect." She seems happy she has instantly fixed my love life.

I haven't the heart to say, 'Please don't. I am not over Krisztyna, Marina. I don't want some nice Hungarian girl, I want my lovely Krisztyna back. I don't want anyone else.' I rarely eat Hungarian food let alone cook it. I hate the thought of spending my time with Marina's set up date cooking our national cuisine in the Roman heat. I imagine this Hungarian girl in an apron, probably short and stocky and called something like Zsuzsa or Judit.

I also never liked introductions as I am used to choosing people myself so effortlessly. But I am too broken to argue and think it is kind of her to try to make me feel better.

I know I will not like this Hungarian girl. Just because she is Hungarian; why would I? I hated most of the company in Budapest and they hated me. And if she is a mezzo she might hate me anyway. So I don't even ask is she soprano or mezzo, what she looks like, how old is she. Right now I do not care. All I care about is that I have lost my dear Krisztyna.

I imagine a young Hungarian singer, maybe pretty but so dull. Someone young and inexperienced since Marina calls her a 'girl'.

And maybe I am still clinging to the tiny sliver of hope that my Krisztyna will be back to normal when she arrives. There is still hope for *Un bel dì*......

I go to see the company doctor of Roma Opera the following day and so I think maybe I could try to sing. I asked the doctors in Budapest when can I rehearse. They told me that I am crazy and not to even think about it or my stitches will burst.

In Roma, the company doctor tells me not to even try to sing a note, how dangerous and stupid it would be.

"Natalija. Listen to the medical advice. You are not talking about singing as you wash the dishes, but heavy diaphragmatic singing for an opera. You could rupture your insides and that is before you feel that pain. No, don't even try; not here, not in the shower, nowhere. Don't even think about it because I see you are thinking about it."

"Not even a minor role or a concert soon?"

"Do you really think you can reach the chandelier?" he asks me.

I doubt if I could reach the front row.

"No," I say and I cry because I know full well September is the earliest I will be ready and I will have slipped so much by then; my voice will not be as powerful, my performances won't be as good. Even then they are telling me September is too early. I say that it has to be 6 months or I am out of Opera for good. Even taking 6 months out could mean the end of my career.

Give me 6 months and I will have healed, I tell the doctors.

One specialist in Hungary told me the time resting will work out well in the long run. My throat will have all that time to recover. Without the stab wound, singing before the summer on my damaged throat would definitely cut short my career. The doctor in Roma is concerned about my throat which has been damaged almost permanently by my eating disorder. He looks at the abrasions with a light and says, if I had not been injured and carried on with my bulimia, by the end of this year I would be finished. By December at the latest, my voice would be ruined, maybe even if I had stopped throwing up. My throat is a mess.

"Give it until September. Your throat will have healed. Unless you start throwing up again in which case you might as well pack up and go back to Hungary and retire," the doctor has told me.

"I am never going back to Hungary," I say. "It is no longer my country."

"See, even the horrible accident has a good ending," Marina tells me full of Italian optimism as she is waiting to take me for coffee. I have a prescription for all kinds of medicine and supplements to help my throat heal. This is on top of all the painkillers. I am a walking pharmacy.

I am full of Hungarian gloom. Marina cannot understand this. I am crying so she takes my arm and says Italian gelato will heal anything, so soft and gentle on the throat. We sit in the pasticceria and she orders tiny scoops of coloured ice cream and says I will soon stop crying when I meet my new love she has ready.

All I can think of is that the Italian doctor didn't waste his words. The directors have already told me I arrived too early when they see how ill I look. But I couldn't stay in Hungary. I stayed a month after my stabbing and left. I needed to just get away. There are bottles of heavy-duty painkillers lining the shelves of my new apartment. I am on the maximum dose.

I do not want the new love Marina has ready for me. I do not want to be touched by anyone, I am so fragile.

I have to drop La Scala's *Carmen,* which they understand, and promise me I can be easily slotted into next season. They tell me to come and see them. We can talk about next season's schedules. Napoli also ask me to discuss next season and invite me to go and host some concerts over the summer. I have to drop Roma Opera's *Nabucco* in the outdoor setting in July even though it is only four performances. They already know that the doctors in Hungary and their own company doctor say September if I am lucky.

All I do is say sorry. Sorry to everyone and they are so nice and it makes me feel worse. The fact they say I can take as much leave as I need, I don't even have to sit in rehearsals, it was just an idea.

"No, I do," I say. "I have to keep the music alive in my head."

The Italian doctors who examine me every week in the hospital tell me I would be insane to try to sing. If I don't rupture anything, I will wreck my career by a lousy weak performance which will ruin my reputation too. Whichever way I turn, I reach the same conclusion.

"Do you really want to be catcalled off the stage in La Scala, Natalija? Is that how you want to be remembered? That's if you even made it through one rehearsal? Don't be so stupid. If you were in a car crash, they would not expect you to sing. You keep coming every week and asking the same questions. You are so lucky to be alive. Think of that, Natalija."

"Think of it as a resurrection," one tells me. He is very religious and touches his crucifix as he says this. He would say that since we have just had Easter. He spreads his arms to the imaginary heavens.

Small consolation. Resurrected for what?

So I do any publicity and promotional work I can. I do interviews for magazines with photos where I am glamorous and gorgeous and draped over Opera stages. I tell my story to all the media; 'How I nearly died as Carmen, how I survived and will return.' I do interviews for television, for Rai Uno just so the Italian public do not forget me. The Italian media love this kind of thing. They see me as some kind of phoenix rising from the ashes.

I tell my story over and over again and the Italians can't get enough of it. It is getting more and more dramatic each time I tell it. I wear low cut dresses, full flowing evening gowns. I look like an Italian glamour model. I am getting more and more extreme each time I am on television.

I am seen as a miracle, a heroine. The real life Carmen who survived and will make a comeback. I do tacky talk shows where I am fully critical of Hungary and everything about it. I don't hold back, I need to get the poison out, my hatred of my homeland. *Such a thing would never happen in Italia,* I say. Italia is my home now. I also need the money and the fame. I am hungry for fame since I am not receiving it on stage right now.

I do a television advertisement for *La Bella Diva* parfum which involves me in a sensational designer dress sitting next to a fountain as I trail my hands in the water, looking every bit a movie star. I hold the perfume bottle up to the sky in my outstretched hands as though I have found the elixir of youth. It pays me very well and I look so beautiful, it makes me feel like I have some success. I am so anxious to remain in the public eye. My father said he would help out and not to worry about a cent. But I am so used to earning myself I don't want to ask. He wires money into my Italian bank account every month and I feel very guilty. He retired early due to ill health so already gets less pension than he should and here he is the bank of Hungary for me and my spendthrift stepmother.

I watch my perfume advert over and over and over again obsessively even when I see it on TV every commercial break.

I am the Diva. I am recognised in the streets. Everyone loves me here.

I am Natalija, Queen of the Opera World.

The rest of the time I am sitting in rehearsals with sheets of music. I sit in the corner and cry over the music sheets. Everyone is very kind, seeing me as the brave girl who nearly died.

Krisztyna is performing Cio-Cio San in Roma Opera. I will get the chance to see her one night and she will be magnificent I am sure, but it is so frosty between us on the phone, I doubt our relationship is salvageable. She has pre-booked theatre digs saying she cannot stay in my apartment. Marina had kindly said she could stay for free.

Krisztyna is angry with me for leaving her in Hungary despite the fact that I told her a thousand times she can leave Hungary and stay in Italia. I am sad that the stabbing and investigation by the police dragged her personal life out into the open. She now has a strained relationship with her children and instead of the leading solo roles she was getting in Hungary, her reputation is tarnished.

She has been dropped from most of the schedules for the autumn season in Budapest.

She was down to play leads or supporting solo roles and virtually overnight, they changed her schedule. Now between September and June she is back to even less than before. She tells me this on the phone and there is resentment in her voice directed at me.

You are responsible, she might as well have said.

Krisztyna, if you do well here in Butterfly, there is an opening for Tosca for the autumn. Marina is not taking it as she is abroad and she has already heard such great things about your Butterfly audition, I tell her.

All Krisztyna says is she doesn't speak very good Italian off stage, she is not sure about *Tosca* or future roles with Roma.

She cannot imagine a life in Roma. *My home is Hungary,* she tells me.

Despite everything that is dark and sad, she still clings to her homeland.

When we do speak it is full of angry silences. She doesn't even seem happy to be coming to Roma Opera in ten days or so to play the role of Butterfly, or even the chance to sing Tosca in autumn.

You just left me with all the mess, she tells me. And hangs up.

I know we are over forever. The glimmer of hope was just an illusion.

I just walk the streets in the warm air looking so depressed. Even strangers ask me am I okay. They are puzzled by Hungarian sadness.

In Roma at the end of April, I sit in on the last of the rehearsals for *Lucia di Lammermoor,* and this is where I see this glittering diamond. She is playing Lucia but she doesn't meet me in the final week of rehearsals as they are already on the stage, this being a big première. I am sitting in the dark of the auditorium, crying into the sheets of Donizetti so the musical notes are blurry. Anyway, she is so absorbed in her role, she wouldn't see the roof fall in. It is a Hungarian name, Anasztázia and I look at the cast list again and realise that she is the great Anasztázia, the international superstar who left The Royal Hungarian Opera before my time. I was so absorbed in my own career, unless my path crossed someone else's in an opera house, I never really took notice. And the company was so large in Budapest. Divas, superstars, I was one myself. But I know of this soprano's reputation across Europe, her wonderful voice and I had seen her in something before, but long ago when I was 18 years old. Anasztázia is not a common name in Hungary; it is too Russian. But this girl looks too young to be the soprano I saw ten years ago. The famous Anasztázia who left Budapest, the one I saw once as Tosca, was much older than me. I guess she must look older close up.

Anasztázia was always shrouded in mystery, the fiercely talented soprano who left Budapest before I started. She left behind memories of a great talent as well as all the Opera photos from past productions which still adorned the interior walls of the building. I would look at them and admire this elfin beauty who was so pretty but in an otherworldly way. She was one of their greatest exports. I never really knew why she left. Maybe she upset the directors or she was looking for more, as she had performed leading roles in all the big opera houses in Europe. No one talked about this shooting star who reached higher and higher across the world. Even Krisztyna never mentioned her.

I asked Krisztyna as I traced a photograph of Anasztázia as Tosca in its frame in the Opera House, *What happened to her? Where did she go and why did she leave?*

Krisztyna had shrugged and walked away leaving me looking at the photo of the great Anasztázia.

Leaving wasn't common amongst even the best and most senior Hungarian soloists. Many worked abroad and came back to Budapest to perform even if it was only a couple of times a year; there was a magnetic pull for the homeland.

Now, I wonder if Marina knows her well as on the cast list for *Lucia di Lammermoor* she is listed as one of Roma Opera's soloists, not a guest. She also speaks fluent Italian, like me, so she must have been here for some years. Most of the Hungarian singers including Krisztyna could only sing in Italian unless they were seniors who had worked in La Scala.

I could read more on the internet about this diva, but I haven't really got the heart. I go home after watching rehearsals and go straight to bed. Yes she is beautiful but then I remind myself, I am an observer now, one of the audience. It changes the dynamics completely.

I think, *I bet she is a right diva too. Even though she is a Hungarian soprano, I doubt if we would get on. To be where she is, she must be an accomplished back-stabber.*

And no doubt she is married to some handsome Italian lawyer and has two perfect dark eyed children and lives in a wonderful apartment in the best part of town.

She has everything. I already do not like this woman, in fact I cannot stand her. I make my mind up never to speak with her.

I am too wrapped up in my own heartbreak to work out this is the girl Marina has in mind for me as I have dismissed Anasztázia and her perfect imaginary life to match her perfect career. I am constantly obsessing about Krisztyna, since I have no singing to take my mind off my emotions. Now we are no longer speaking on the phone, I am unable to let go, praying she will be Krisztyna again once she arrives in Roma. I am still living in a traumatised fog.

IL DOLCE SUONO

When *Lucia di Lammermoor* opens a few days later in May, I attend their glittering première. It is an echoing and eerie modern version, the stage space all metallic industrial pipes and swirling smoke, evoking the mists of Scotland. The performance is amazing, and Anasztázia as Lucia is out of this world. I don't think I ever saw such a performance; she takes everything to a level I never even thought existed. Sure, I have seen many singers I think are perfection but this totally redefines the word.

She is so magnificent, her fragile appearance so deceptive as she unleashes her supple beautiful voice which stretches aching notes of pain seemingly through the Opera House roof. I can only wonder at the incredible power in that voice and her descent into madness is terrifyingly real. I am completely absorbed in the Opera as Anasztázia spirals in graceful balletic circles, before finally collapsing on the stage. Her applause for 'Il dolce suono' aria lasts five minutes alone. Instead of jealousy, I am in awe of this beautiful Hungarian soprano and her incredible performance. I am proud to be from the same country. She is magnificent.

My pride doesn't last because during the curtain call she places her hand on her heart and blows a kiss to the audience after she is presented with a bouquet of roses. I think, *Diva, so obviously staged.*

I make up my mind I will avoid her in the première and she won't want to speak with me since I am nothing now. I also do not do well with others having the attention I crave. She may be hauntingly beautiful but definitely not my type. She is too girlish, too fragile, too ice-maiden pale as though her skin has never seen the sun. Too unreal full stop. You might as well be with a china doll.

I like dusky, dark beauties like myself, like Krisztyna; women who smoulder with sensuality and passion. This woman has no sensuality. She is gorgeous but as cool as ice.

I head backstage afterwards and I am popping painkillers like candy. It aches so badly even to stand up in high heels but I wanted to look my best, so I am wearing a glittering gold dress with its metre of train and a gold tiara. Really all I want to do is lie down on the stage as my insides throb with pain. Marina takes me gently by the waist like a mother figure, through the swelling crowd and I am suddenly face to face with Lucia/Anasztázia. *Goddamn*, I think. *I have to talk to her now.*

"This is Anasztázia," says Marina as this girl stands before me. She is so tiny close-up; a delicate beauty with innocent wide blue eyes and layers of light brown and dark honey coloured hair and skin like porcelain. She is so doll-like, she doesn't look real. Anasztázia is dressed in a blue flowing silk evening dress with metres of train, which fall around her like a waterfall, giving her the appearance of a child dressed up in her mother's evening gown. She seems so dreamy, this delicate as crystal Anasztázia, that it is impossible to believe she is 44 years old, having just had her birthday a day before the opening night, Marina tells me with her hands on the elf's shoulders. She is nearly 16 years older than me and yet so ethereal my immediate thought is that she seems to have wandered in from the pages of a fairy tale book. She kisses my face gently like a child would and tells me in Hungarian she is so happy to meet me. She is anything but the arrogant diva I expected. She is so pretty I cannot help but stare at her and wonder at her beautiful alabaster complexion.

She is even more striking given that virtually everyone on the stage tonight, me included, is dark haired, golden skinned and very Italian-looking. This woman stands as a polar opposite to us in every way.

"I am Anasztázia. Always Anasztázia. Sometimes people shorten it to Ana but I tell them anyone can be Ana. And no, there is no Russian link, I am pure Hungarian blood." She holds her hand tightly in mine as she says this. "I have heard so much about you, Natalija. I have seen your photos on our theatre walls when you performed here in *Werther*." She smiles so genuinely. She isn't just saying this to be sweet, she breathes it almost with a sigh of wonder.

I tell her how outstanding she was, that I never usually say this and she is flattered, so timid as she graciously accepts the praise that it is hard to imagine she is Anasztázia, the international superstar.

"You redefined perfection tonight, Anasztázia," I tell her.

"Thank you," she says and her spoken voice is as delicate as crystal. So soft, so fragile when she speaks.

She is very shy with me, this fairy-tale princess. She can hardly look at me after our first introductions. She lowers her eyes and I see her eyelashes are long and sooty black, naturally black without the aid of mascara. They flicker like a china doll and I look at her, waiting for her to meet my gaze again. I expected her to be confident and attention-seeking, since we are both Hungarian and she is the star performer, especially as she commands the European stages with her powerful spinto soprano voice and extensive repertoire. She seems lost for words. Am I so intimidating or is she just uncomfortable out of character?

"Go get us the drinks, Anasztázia, and then I will leave you and Natalija to get to know each other," Marina says with a laugh, seeing Anasztázia is suddenly very timid.

Anasztázia turns to walk away, her dress cascading behind her in a wonderful trail of shimmering blue. I watch her make her way towards the champagne table as people stop to congratulate her on the performance. She pauses a few times to talk but I sense she is not someone who adores adulation, unlike me; she seems unsure of herself out of the Opera role. This gives Marina time to tell me this is my date.

"Her last relationship ended badly. She really likes you, Natalija. She says you are so beautiful. You would be good for each other. You both do so much crying alone, it is not good." Marina is determined to fix my love life and her friend's in one night.

"This is Italia, you need to stop that gloomy Hungarian spirit and love life like we Italians do."

"Marina, she is very beautiful, but maybe Anasztázia just needs a friend from her own country. Surely she has a man here?" I say.

"No our Anasztázia does not want all the men in Italia. They try, poor souls and they do not realise they will never be what she wants." Marina waves her arm across the stage, swelling with faces and designer frocks. There is no loud-mouthed smoky Krisztyna in sight, flirting and flittering through the crowd like the glittering social butterfly she was. It makes me feel sad.

"Besides you will perform mainly in Italia and Anasztázia is based in Roma, although she sings all over Europe. Anasztázia has no one. She gives her heart completely. She remembered you from when you performed in *Werther* for our company. She was away both times you were in Roma, but she saw the photos and asked, *Who is this beautiful raven-haired Hungarian girl? So exotic, so talented. Didn't she perform as Amneris in Budapest with Giacomo, in the open air festival?*

She seemed delighted you were transferring here. She was so horrified about your near-death, she actually cried. Just trust me. She feels very lonely as not many Hungarians pass through Roma."

Marina rests her hand on my arm and inspires confidence. "This lovely Anasztázia waits for you, Natalija. At least give Anasztázia a chance if you and Krisztyna are over."

Now as I look over at Anasztázia, I wonder is this my special person my mother told me about, when I died and she told me someone waited for me. I stare at her. She is certainly special but I cannot imagine a relationship with her. She is too unreal; I just want to look at her all night.

"Natalija! You cannot take your eyes off her. She is so pretty, no? Can I call her back now? She is waiting." Marina breaks my thoughts.

"Yes, please do," I say. Anasztázia is watching us, holding her champagne flute and the two for me and Marina. Her huge blue eyes are fixed on us, the gold streaks in her hair are catching the stage lights giving the illusion of a glowing aura; someone or something very otherworldly.

I think of wild, jealous Krisztyna and my needy Sicilian lover, Fiamma who never had my heart. The Opera World has stepped up a level and I need so to be with someone who is not mercurial. I have nothing left to give and I need someone who is gentle, not volcanic or demanding.

I look over at Anasztázia as Marina goes to fetch her and the crowds of mortals stare at this Hungarian beauty, so ethereal as though she froze time and held it powerless under her spell. She looks overwhelmed on the crowded Opera House stage amongst the glitterati. No longer am I driven by passion and cheap one nighters, I want stability and affection. Mostly I just think about music and getting well enough to sing again at 100%.

She is so delicate both in appearance and with her spoken voice like tinkling glass, it is hard to imagine she unleashed notes of such incredible sky-splitting power just half an hour earlier, performing one of the most difficult arias in the soprano repertoire. As Marina talks to Anasztázia, she loses her dreamy expression and smiles radiantly. Marina pushes her way through the crowd, with Anasztázia stepping regally behind her in a flow of blue water. Everyone watches as she floats along. Many people admire me too; glamorous, gorgeous and golden, but I am in so much pain I am finding it so difficult to enjoy it. I am not the star and for once, I do not care. Marina hands me my champagne glass and leaves me and Anasztázia alone.

I think of the wild Krisztyna who wanted me as her

possession. Krisztyna was so brash, so loud and smouldering with sensuality. She dragged me into the trees the very first night I saw her at her *Turandot* première in Margitsziget, drunk and laughing in the summer heat. Anasztázia is the polar opposite; shy yet full of positive energy as she talks to me. It radiates from her and I am trapped in this wonderful bubble of Heaven. Maybe my new character is bringing me a different sort of person, the kind who will not make me crazy and unable to deal with emotions, which all exacerbated the eating disorder. Removed from Hungary, I can see what a vicious spiral my life was.

Anasztázia tentatively asks me back to her apartment as I feel dizzy after one glass of champagne on my super strong painkillers. She says that she is too full of adrenaline to sleep and would love to talk more if I would like to. I am holding tightly on to a table and she rests her arm on mine concerned.

"We need to get you home, Natalija. You are hurting. You can rest at my apartment and we can eat. Come on, baby," she says guiding me out. Her touch is just a ghosting of a gentle little hand on my waist but enough; a tender, tentative ownership of me. She has already claimed me as hers and I didn't even say yes. I smile as I walk ahead of her up the steps and off the stage as I recognise the invite only too well; going back to someone's apartment after a show means only one thing. Although she doesn't seem the type to seduce me, she gazes at me in the taxi home as though I am the prettiest girl in the world and leans against me in the elevator wrapping an arm around my waist, to hold me up. Her perfume is sweet and flowery unlike the heavy scents I favour. The rest of the night's events have a dream-like quality. In my hazy, drugged state, she leads me into her bedroom by the hand. I am delirious with pain and exhaustion, so Anasztázia lays out a soft mass of pillows and helps me to get comfortable. She leaves a tray of snacks and a pot of coffee on the bed and goes to shower. I open my bag and take out the painkillers. Tonight has taken it out of me. Her apartment is enormous and beautiful; full of echoing spaces and chandeliers as she is very wealthy.

So I guessed right about her wonderful home and career but not the husband and children. I can see how lonely she must be in this big apartment and she is clearly not like I was, taking lovers all the time. Marina said she gives her whole heart which must make her cautious. I can see beautiful views of the night sky of Roma from the window since we are on the top floor and the bedroom leads onto a pretty balcony. I decide there and then, she can have all of me and more. I pour the coffee as I have no adrenaline to keep me going and I don't want to fall asleep on her. I try to eat a little.

Once Anasztázia returns to the bedroom, she seems to have become quiet again. She gets into bed cautiously in her silk dressing gown with her drink and sits towards the edge of the bed. She says once more how good it is to speak Hungarian. She hates and loves our country in equal measure, like me. She misses it and yet when she visits she loathes it. Her fame also isolates her. She travels a lot, has few close friends and she is alone. She chatters away waving her hands around, occasionally picking at some of the food from the tray. Then she lowers her eyes and becomes sad and reflective.

"I am so lonely, so lonely at the top of the world, Natalija. The loneliness is the hardest thing for me," she says and her eyes gaze up at the imaginary heavens way beyond the confines of this room as though she should be up there in the clouds. It adds to the feeling that she has fallen from the Empyrean. But she feels real enough; soft and warm. She doesn't need to be alone and I can make sure of that.

I understand Anasztázia so well. "This world gets lonelier the higher we go. But it doesn't have to be so," I add. I put down my drink and kiss her and she is barely there; a true fairy-tale princess. The painkillers have put me in a fantastical twilight world where time has stopped and some strange magic seems to be at work. Anasztázia strokes my hair. Her blue eyes are light and clear like calm water. She smiles at me, then laughs a lovely laugh into her hands, making me think of ice crystals falling.

"I asked Marina's help to set up this date," Anasztázia says.

Someone so famous and gorgeous needed her friend's help to arrange a date? She speaks as though she sees me as some kind of goddess. Maybe she is just very dramatic. The theatre does make us like that.

"You looked amazing tonight all dressed in gold like a queen," she says spreading her hands out.

"I was totally lost for words when I saw you. You won't hurt me, will you Natalija? My heart is very tender," she continues shyly.

"I used to take anyone who was beautiful," I tell her. "But it was so empty and it was no way to live. I never even loved anyone. I broke so many hearts. Only I thought I loved....."

I don't say it. Marina has told her I am fresh from a break-up. Still raw. Anasztázia nods understandingly.

"I would never hurt you, Anasztázia. I am different now," I tell her. As I say it, I even believe it myself.

"Who would say no to you, Natalija? You are so beautiful." She gently removes the grips from my hair, freeing the springy black ringlets.

"Where did you get all this wonderful hair, baby? Your mother?" she asks in admiration, running her hands through the full length of the jet corkscrews as they cascade down my back.

"No, my father has the same hair," I say.

Anasztázia's hands travel softly along my spine. Her fingers which massage my shoulders are like fairy dust, so soft they put me in a trance.

Marina did say Anasztázia was only a diva in her

performances, not so once she stepped out of role. If I was thinking clearly and not so drugged, this should make me uneasy; that I am Anasztázia's dream. I am someone she worshipped before even meeting them, a dream she has held since she first saw my photographs.

But I am not thinking rationally. I am too lost in the magical moment, my own fairy-tale fantasy.

She asks to see my scar so I let her take off my gold dress and I lie on my stomach.

"It still hurts really bad," I say. "I am on so many painkillers tonight. I get exhausted easily. But I can't sit at home without people remembering me, my career will be over."

"Baby, that will never happen. And I will make sure it never will, but you should be resting more. Tonight must have really taken it out of you," Anasztázia says.

If she was a mezzo, I would not believe her; that she would make sure my career wasn't over. I am younger, a threat. But she is a soprano. I am no threat.

Her fingers ghost down my back like balletic spiders putting me in a wonderful sleepy state and then she traces the scar of the knife wound. Her salty tears and her lips brush against it, as if she can kiss the damage better and her silky golden hair against my skin makes me shiver.

"They nearly killed you too, that company," she says. I feel her tears drip onto my back but I don't ask her what she means, I don't ask why she cries. Maybe her performance is still with her; the sadness and the madness of the role of crazy, beautiful Lucia clinging to her soul. I know that so well myself, being so dangerously absorbed in the Opera that you cannot let go, even long after the curtains close on the final performance.

Sometimes it clings to you until you are absorbed in the next role, sometimes even longer, snaking around your dreams and twisting your reality in the daylight hours. You become the Opera.

The resurrected Natalija lies back and drowns. I close my eyes and surrender. Some wonderful magic is at work; she is healing my damaged body with her own sweet tears and her butterfly kisses. I drift away and fall deeply asleep face down in the pillows. She must be from another world.

"We are fire and ice, baby, we belong together," she says. Or maybe she doesn't but I think I hear this in my dreams.

As golden light splinters through the window, I wake up feeling that I must have dreamed last night but this elfin beauty is still there, serene face lost in sleep. She is draped elegantly across the sheets, as if someone placed her beautiful white limbs in a stage-like pose. Her dark honeyed hair falls over the pillow and there isn't a single line on her face. The world seems like a fairy-tale place after so much darkness.

"I love you," I tell this sleeping Anasztázia.

As soon as I say this I regret it. I turn away from her and think how stupid I was.

I should have kept my mouth shut. I feel the dream vanishing and I am back to reality. What did I go and say that for? I don't know her and I hardly even remember the night only jigsaw pieces; the wonderful Opera, the stage of the première, her in a blue evening dress, me in gold and then her lips grazing my scar as I fell asleep in her bed. I am just intoxicated by the moment, only loving for the moment like the Carmen I was and then restlessly moving on.

And how many people have I said 'I love you' to in my life and not meant it? Hundreds I think. Men and women, all left devastated by me.

I hurt so many hearts and walked away without a backward glance. I am not a good person.

I will hurt this delicate diva, just like the rest.

This is crazy. The Opera World has coloured my consciousness. You can run away and swear undying love in 40 minutes on stage and it seems to infect our own lives too. We live hard and fast and it seems to have got more intense over the years as the theatre became my world. Reality is only some buildings in the street you pass going home at night. There is no holding back, no waiting, just all emotions exploding. And now I am telling someone I only met last night I love her. I just hope she hasn't heard what I just said.

I look at my gold dress on the bedroom floor and my back and insides suddenly ache with pain.

I sit up and reach for the bottle of pills.

Anasztázia's eyes flicker open like a doll, long lashes fluttering and she doesn't seem afraid of the comment that she must have heard. I can't take it back now.

"How about some coffee?" I say wanting to change the subject. I try to get out of bed and double over with pain. I collapse back on the pillows.

"Natalija, you are hurting. Please lie in bed and rest," she tells me getting up. "Last night was too much for you. Just rest and I will be back now." She is cocooned in her silk robe and I wonder why she sleeps in it. It is so warm in Roma right now. Maybe she feels uncomfortable showing her body, although she seems perfect to me. I rest as she goes to get the breakfast.

She probably didn't hear me. I could always pretend I said 'I love you' in a dream I was in.

I hear the clattering of cups in the distance.

"What happened to your love in Hungary?" She traces her fingers lightly on mine and I look at those eyelashes and think how I never saw such wonderful dark lashes on someone so fair.

"I wanted to say how much I loved her as I was bleeding to death on that stage, but I couldn't speak. Her prints were on the knife as she was performing as Mercédès and she ran onto the stage when I was stabbed. It contaminated the evidence. She thought she might go to prison for up to 20 years until they found the real murderess. The Hungarian legal system is so flawed. All the stress tore us apart."

"I'm so sorry to hear that," Anasztázia says turning to look at me. "Very sad for you both."

"But she is coming here for Butterfly. She is singing Cio-Cio San. She arrives in Roma in less than two weeks for rehearsals." I sigh and look at the ceiling. "And now I wish Krisztyna was not coming."

Now after wanting her back so badly, I don't want her to come here at all.

"Natalija," says Anasztázia putting down the coffee cup. "You didn't tell me......Marina told me you that you had split."

"It is over. Don't worry, it is all in the past." I feel a deep twinge as I say it. The sadness is still with me.

"Are you sure you don't still love her?" she says so softly as she looks at me, her eyes searching my soul for the truth. I sense she is afraid that I will hurt her.

"It is no more, I promise you, Anasztázia. I died and I am now resurrected." I smile at her in the golden light but she looks unhappy.

"Don't say that, Natalija. Please don't talk about death, I can't bear it. It is so dark and morbid." She gazes at me with her lovely clear eyes. Strange how she cannot bear talk of death despite dying herself on stage every night she performs.

But then I am dark and morbid.

She says nothing as she pushes the sugar from her pastries around on the plate. She pours more coffee and looks away. She gazes out of the window and I feel the sudden chill.

I must have said something I shouldn't.

"Did I say something?" I ask. "Sorry if I upset you about the death talk. No more."

She turns to look at me. Her eyes are sad and I wonder

what the hell I did, maybe I shouldn't have talked about Krisztyna.

"Did you say her name is Krisztyna? Not Kriszta from Hungary? Not wild Kriszta who drinks so much and is abrasive, insulting and has affairs with everyone? But she was married....surely not her?" Anasztázia says. "Not her."

"You know her?" I say, although I should have worked out that Krisztyna had been with The Royal Hungarian Opera years longer than me. She would have known Anasztázia although Krisztyna had shrugged and said she didn't know what happened to the great Anasztázia when I asked her in Budapest.

She would have usually said, *Oh she was a right bitch. Glad she left.*

But Krisztyna hadn't reacted at all. I thought nothing of it then.

As a soprano, Krisztyna would have hated someone beautiful who got the leading roles, sang in the finest opera houses in Europe and returned to Budapest to grab the best roles again.

"I hardly knew her, she was not friendly," Anasztázia says. She won't look at me and I wonder what I did wrong. I definitely should never have said the 'love' word. I have scared her already. Or maybe she really is thinking if Krisztyna comes here, I will go back to her.

"She probably envied you," I tell her. "She was married but it split because of me, or more like he beat her for years. He hated her being successful. She started to get leading roles; Tosca, Butterfly, Turandot."

"She was talented. But Natalija it is still so recent, this break up. Krisztyna always got who she wanted. She must have loved you," Anasztázia says anxiously. "I don't want to lose you, Natalija. I waited so long."

"I promise you, Anasztázia. She doesn't want to be with me now. We no longer even talk." Anasztázia still looks as if she isn't convinced Krisztyna has gone. She toys with her cup and has gone silent.

I waited so long. Waited for me or just someone like me?

But Krisztyna has gone. From my life and from my heart.

Krisztyna has a vicious side though. She is a jealous woman. I am with someone else and she will explode. She hates others' happiness and success, always resentful.

I will just stay out of her way.

Anasztázia has erased everything and everyone in one evening. She has that spellbinding effect. On the stage and off it.

That morning she tells me about her life in Hungary and why she left. She was not popular as she was famous so young, forever abroad and returning to Budapest for leading roles. Married to someone for 11 years, 'a fake marriage' and after her official divorce at 32, she spent two years mainly working in La Scala, London, Paris, Vienna, dating women everywhere.

"Natalija I was such a tart," she says holding her hands up. "All those flings in opera houses all over Europe. I feel ashamed."

"I was worse, Anasztázia, believe me," I say as I finish up the coffee.

"Nothing lasted until one day in Budapest, I performed with a beautiful young soprano. I loved her. She was difficult but she was worth it. Then a few months later, management called me into the office and told me it was bad publicity. They said, *Such a famous woman like Anasztázia in this 'kind of relationship'.* I denied it, said we were friends, but it was no good. They cut the other soprano from the schedules completely. She hated me then, as she was based in Hungary full-time. She lost all her work overnight."

She pauses at this memory and looks so sad.

"I told the company to go to Hell, that I would never sing for them again. I left Hungary for Roma eight years ago. I arrived in Roma with one suitcase, I was so desperate to leave and I had a lot of work promised to me here and in La Scala. Everything else I owned was sent on to me later. I just ran away really."

Anasztázia says she cried for a month when she lost her love. She felt as though the world had ended. They never ever spoke again.

"Where is she now?" I ask.

Anasztázia looks out of the window. "I honestly don't know," she says quietly. "Maybe she moved far away. When I was in media interviews, I just said Opera made relationships difficult. But in truth, Hungary murders everything good."

"And here? What happened here?" I ask.

"She left me for a man and moved to New York to sing for The Met. Marina knows how much I cried. I married at 21 for my parents. They are rural people from the south. I can never forget my mother's anger when I finally divorced. She screamed that I was 'disgusting and unnatural'. My father sat down and wept at the kitchen table, with his head in his hands. I had never seen my father cry. He said he had lost his beautiful daughter. They have rejected me. It didn't matter I was famous, I couldn't love men so they don't want me."

Anasztázia wipes a tear away and this is upsetting her. I hate to see her cry.

"Honey, please don't carry on if this is painful," I tell her.

She shakes her head. She needs to tell me.

"My parents ask me, when we speak so rarely, will I marry again. I won't so they do not want to see me. I offer to pay their travel. It was one of the worst moments of my life when my mother arrived home from work when I was 16 and found me kissing a girl. She beat me senseless. When I married she said, 'Thank God you turned out normal'."

"Poor Anasztázia. People always talked about me but I had so many lovers. They suspected me and Krisztyna but as she was married, no one in management noticed. The singers were bitchy but I was such a bitch myself. Here, only Marina knows," I tell her.

"Marina is a good person," she says. "She is so kind and you would never be a bitch, Natalija. You are so lovely."

Hearing about Anasztázia's parents I feel sad. My father and stepmother didn't seem to see any difference between my lovers, I was still Natalija to them, whoever I was with. My father did say once that I broke too many hearts.

So did I once, Natalija. It is an empty shallow life to be so good-looking, he had said sadly. *It is not the road to happiness having whoever you want, hurting your lovers.*

I only wish I had been everything Anasztázia wanted. But I was still Natalija the selfish diva underneath, the one who craved attention. The cruel and ruthless girl was just waiting to re-emerge. And maybe I expected way too much from this ethereal being who was after all, just flesh and blood. The first week I was with Anasztázia, I felt as though I was touched by the hand of God, as though I had found an angel dropped out of the sky. Dying and then being resurrected had intensified this feeling.

And we had just had Easter, after all. It was, as the Italian doctor saw it, a resurrection.

I too saw it in a religious fashion. I am like Christ, risen from the dead, my life full of wonder.

As I felt I was no longer mortal, it stood to reason I would meet angels in this new world.

It was a magical place. Nothing compared to that feeling I had after the *Lucia di Lammermoor* première, almost floating through life in the spring air. Despite the pain, I had such soaring hope.

I spent the rest of my life chasing that elusive first high, like a crack addict.

Nothing compares to that first hit.

Un bel dì

I decide to go and meet Krisztyna at the airport. She has been so depressed and I feel very sorry for what she went through in Hungary. I am afraid she will turn up and say she wants to be with me and I know that I can't. It is too late for us.

Because I cannot hurt this fragile Anasztázia.

Krisztyna has booked her own apartment just as she told me, saying she needs space.

The last thing I want is a clingy needy bitch. I am here to perform and not act as a nurse for you. I am the star now. Her eyes flash fire as she says it. No sadness; she is beautiful, cold and cruel. She looks as if my presence at the airport is an irritation, as though she thought she had already buried me. She is not the careless, wild Krisztyna but cutting and bitchy as she hurls out comments which she knows will dig deep. As if she rehearsed the cruellest words she could find and lets them all fly at me like daggers.

She says this spiteful comment about not needing a clingy, needy bitch as she gets into the taxi and the distance between us has turned into a ravine.

I don't need you dragging me down in my moment of glory. You are damaged and I don't need that in my life, Natalija. It is my turn now. She looks at me triumphantly as she says this.

I am not the love she saw only weeks ago, the one she wept over when she thought I would die. I reach for her hand but she wrenches it away with an exasperated sigh as if she is thinking, 'God leave me alone.' She hates me.

We ride in silence and drop her at her digs. I ask does she want any help? Does she know how to get to the Opera House tomorrow?

I am not stupid, Natalija. No, I do not need help from you. She slams the taxi door and thinks it is down to me to pay the driver the full fare despite my apartment being in a different district.

Fine. Let her go.

I could not forgive Krisztyna now.

The old Natalija would have shouted at her for her hateful attitude. If I needed proof our relationship was dead it is meeting her again. I am so grateful I didn't wait in hope for her. Krisztyna has decided it is over and just not told me. She is heartless. She knows I am an observer in some of her rehearsals as we are in smaller rooms, not yet on the Opera House stage. She stalks into the room a minute before the rehearsals start, full of attitude and gives me a look of defiance as I sit in the corner with the sheets of Puccini. As soon as there is a break she goes out alone, not speaking to anyone. When I see her in the Opera café one day she says, *I am busy, please leave me alone.*

She says this without looking up.

I walk away and she calls after me. "Natalija, I hope you are coming to my première."

I turn to face her and a smile slides across her lovely face but it is a smile full of spite.

I am the diva now, it says.

I know from her expression that she wants me to see her success. Even her invite is motivated by malice.

I say nothing and walk out. She knows I will be there.

At the première of *Madama Butterfly* I watch Krisztyna perform and the famous aria, 'Un bel dì' is astounding. The auditorium is deafening with applause after her aria and during the curtain call. She smiles and gathers the bouquets of roses up. She looks happy and relaxed and I hope this has made her feel good and less bitchy.

I join everyone on stage for the première post-show. Krisztyna is attacking the champagne table with a vengeance. So nothing has changed there then. This is Italia and she is a guest here. In Hungary she was an obnoxious party girl, but in Roma she still needs to make a good impression once the curtains close. Her smile which lit up the stage for the audience is gone. She glares at me with the same hatred as the day she arrived.

"You were fantastic, Krisztyna, everyone here thought so too," I tell her.

She is wearing the silver heart necklace from me: '*Krisztyna, Un bel dì....*'

I don't mention it as she would only say something sarcastic. She just accepts a kiss without a word. She is flawless in French and Italian for Opera but at a social gathering she struggles. Italian is the language everyone is using tonight which is making her feel isolated and angry. The only sparkle is in her glittering silver dress and the diamond tiara crowning her flowing dark hair. She is hauntingly beautiful but she doesn't smoulder with sensuality; she radiates darkness and rage. Many people want to congratulate her but she doesn't care, even when they turn to English. The only time she manages a smile is for the Opera House director. She knows she is in with a chance to perform as Tosca in September, as Marina has turned it down and Anasztázia who would be the other top choice, is performing in *Norma*.

Krisztyna looks every bit a Tosca. She wants that role. She is greedy for it.

As she speaks to the director with her fake snake charm, I go to talk to Anasztázia. She is very busy but said she loves Puccini, couldn't miss seeing the new première. Krisztyna sees me talk to Anasztázia and I feel her death stare from across the stage. Once the director leaves her, she is back to rude and abrasive. This cold Krisztyna is not the one who was hired for Butterfly although her performance was a sensation and looks set to sell the house for the whole run.

I tell people who ask me why she is so cold that she is very shy. *Like hell.*

Overall, the mainly Italian company are nice people and

cannot comprehend this Hungarian beauty who has sung Cio-Cio San to perfection. Even if she really is tired, she could give half an hour and then go home. Many performers do that, but she is too intent on drinking. As usual.

"You're not the person I knew, Natalija. You are so boring," Krisztyna says. She is clutching her fifth champagne flute and has started to show signs of angry inebriation. She hasn't eaten and pushes the plate of canapés away.

"You want me to get fat?" she says in an accusing way. "Now you are cured of your eating disorder, you want to feed me? That's fucked up, Natalija!"

I used to think she was beautiful when she was angry. Now I see her as aggressive and intimidating.

"No, I want you to eat because I care, Krisztyna. Please be warmer towards everyone," I say quietly. "We are in Roma, so don't drink so much. Maybe we should have talked more about *Carmen,* when I nearly died. It must have affected you."

"Oh, it's still Krisztyna, is it, my lovely lady? And dying? I just slit my own throat in my Opera. Dying is what we do for a living, Natalija. *Con onor muore.* Only you didn't. You are weak."

She looks away after this remark. She is being as vicious as she can manage; making the reference to the inscription on Butterfly's hara-kiri knife. My anger rises and I have a vision of dragging my ex-lover to the floor by her hair, claws grappling, biting and screaming. In a moment of rage I would lose Anasztázia, my reputation and all my future work.

I just say, "Krisztyna, not literally dying. Look, I know this is difficult but please talk to me."

She is glaring at Anasztázia. "And why are you hanging around Anasztázia? She seems sweet on you, but that's no surprise since she always did go after vulnerable girls. Vulture. She is circling your dead body right now, looking to rip it apart. Finish off what *Carmen* didn't. Looks like a pretty doll but she is not so sweet. She will shower you with gifts, then throw you away. I knew her once, baby," Krisztyna laughs.

But as Krisztyna's eyes flash with fire, I know she is jealous.

Anasztázia keeps glancing across the stage as she is talking to one of the cast and she appears troubled.

"That bitch always hurt her lovers and she had loads!" Krisztyna waves her arms around emphatically, spilling her drink. People are looking. In Roma, a drunk woman is not attractive and Roma Opera of all places.

"She is 16 years older than you! Old enough to be your mother, Natalija! That's rich given she walked out on her own daughter. Heartless bitch," she says full of venom. "I stayed with my family."

"And just look what it turned you into," I say. "Take a good look at yourself in the mirror. You are so bitter and twisted."

She just ignores the comment.

I don't know what Krisztyna means about Anasztázia. I just want her to shut her mouth. I am glad she is speaking Hungarian because I would hate anyone to hear her poison.

"I am so ashamed that you are Hungarian, you make us all look bad, Krisztyna. You are an embarrassment to me tonight." I turn away and walk off the stage.

Krisztyna follows me and grabs me roughly in the dressing room corridor.

"Ashamed, how dare you? I was the star tonight! People want me! Your diva days are over!"

Her long nails dig into my wrist. I try to break loose but she grips tighter.

"Krisztyna, stop it! You are hurting," I tell her. Her dark eyes are full of fire.

Anasztázia has followed us. "Krisztyna, let her go, please stop with the anger."

Krisztyna lets go and turns her vitriol on Anasztázia. "And you won't hurt her, Anasztázia? She is nothing anyway, just a faded star at 28! And you were always a back-stabbing bitch!"

She steps closer to Anasztázia and points at her.

"You remember what lies the company fed you, Krisztyna. Look at what you went through; they let you nearly take the blame for *Carmen*. And Natalija nearly died. She is recovering from a serious injury." Anasztázia remains so calm but she anxiously looks around even though no one speaks Hungarian. She wants this scene out of the corridor so she gently takes Krisztyna's arm.

"Let's go in your dressing room, come on, Krisztyna. Let me get you a hot drink."

"I told her I loved her," Krisztyna says."I told her."

She is splintering with Anasztázia's words, unable to deal with the gentle concern of her rival. Shouting and screaming are fine but Krisztyna is more upset by Anasztázia's sweetness. The vulnerable Krisztyna is breaking through the hard, arrogant front and her tears start to fall.

"Krisztyna, don't let anyone see you cry," Anasztázia says as she helps her off the floor where she has fallen, crying champagne tears. I take the key and open her dressing room. Anasztázia places her on the sofa and goes to get her a coffee from the machine. Krisztyna's hands shake as she holds the cup. Anasztázia hugs her, tells her it will be okay tomorrow. Krisztyna clings to her tightly and weeps.

"Just drink this coffee and we will take you home, Krisztyna. Everything will look better in the morning, I promise you."

"Krisztyna, I asked you to come to Roma and you rejected me. I don't understand why you hate me. Hungary is so bad for you. I wouldn't want to stay in my own country now," I say to this hopelessly lost love of mine. "Why do you stay there?"

Krisztyna is crying as she turns to Anasztázia. "I don't have the choices you two have. I have to take what I can get. I have my mother, my children in Budapest."

Anasztázia says, "Natalija told me how much she loved you. She gave you that necklace, so why don't you look at it and remember, Krisztyna? Remember how much she cared about you."

Krisztyna plays with the necklace as her eyes stare into the distance. Then she starts up her sobbing again, crying like the end of the world. Her mood is the most erratic I have ever seen it and it scares me.

She clings to Anasztázia and won't let go. Her tears stain Anasztázia's cream and blue dress but Anasztázia is more concerned about the emotional Cio-Cio San than her clothes.

"Natalija, we need to get her out of here. Can you call the taxi to your apartment? We can't leave this girl alone tonight," she says.

The last person I want in my apartment is Krisztyna. I want her to go back to her own digs but Anasztázia is insisting we cannot leave her.

"We will take you home, okay? You gave so much of yourself in your wonderful Butterfly role." She wipes Krisztyna's face gently.

"I am sorry," Krisztyna says quietly. "I am sorry for acting the way I do."

She looks at Anasztázia and says, "And I hurt you too once......I had feelings, I wasn't the bitch....I still do care."

Anasztázia looks afraid and tries to move away but Krisztyna is hanging on tight and she can't prise her loose. But Anasztázia's gaze as she looks away is depthless and full of secrets.

Krisztyna rummages with one hand in her handbag for her make-up and mirror and a small bag of white powder falls out. She tries to grab it from the floor but Anasztázia has seized it first. She is relieved to have a distraction.

"Cocaine? Krisztyna what the hell are you doing? No

wonder your mood swings are all over the place. How much have you taken?"

"Krisztyna. When did you start doing all that? You don't need to do this," I ask.

She isn't the first singer I have known to take drugs but I am still shocked. She was just a drinker. No wonder her moods are wildly spiking up and down. Even when I was on the phone to her, she was so erratic. I just put it down to anger. This is career suicide.

"Natalija, I had to do something since you left." She looks at me with such sadness.

Anasztázia just puts the cocaine back into Krisztyna's handbag. She can't deal with drugs.

I can't be cruel towards her tonight. "Krisztyna, please don't worry. We will talk tomorrow, I promise," I lie.

Krisztyna nods sadly and says, "We are not the same people now. Those careless bitchy divas. Well, you are not. Forgive me, please," she says her dark eyes lost and sad.

If it wasn't for Anasztázia, I would be weak. I still have feelings when I see Krisztyna like this.

Together we get Krisztyna in a taxi and safely into my apartment. Anasztázia says she doesn't want Krisztyna to know her address. After all, Krisztyna was so full of hate. I am still in Marina's old apartment, but I have been in Anasztázia's place so much. She has asked me to move in.

I think that it is crazy to move so fast. And I promised Marina rent until September at least.

It is way too soon to live with Anasztázia.

The only time I lived with anyone was Krisztyna. When her husband found out about us, he threw her out so she had to live with me. To be dependent on anyone scares me. I am cautious with my heart and already I have opened it to Anasztázia.

Krisztyna slumps against Anasztázia in the taxi. I ride in the front. I glance in the rear-view mirror and the two of them so close messes with my head. Anasztázia is stroking

Krisztyna's dark hair and whispering comfort. Their faces are almost touching and I suddenly have a feeling of deep unease. I turn away trying to reason that Anasztázia is just kind. I watch the golden lights of Roma glide by. My emotions are not rational. I am very tired.

Anasztázia drapes Krisztyna on my sofa, gently removes her tiara and shoes and covers her with a blanket. I just think how sweet she is, there was nothing between them. Anasztázia has such a forgiving heart, even for a rival. She doesn't carry any hate in her heart.

"We cannot have this cocaine around, Natalija. When did she start?" she says as she removes the drugs from Krisztyna's bag and tips the powder down the sink.

"Honestly, she never did. She only liked champagne. I would have known," I say.

I look at Krisztyna already passed out on the sofa, her face so unhappy in sleep.

I go to the bedroom. I am beyond exhausted.

"She is beautiful. Fucked up but so beautiful," Anasztázia sighs climbing into bed

I am too tired to think.

I want to get rid of the emotional Cio-Cio San from my apartment and forget all about tonight.

"Anasztázia, what did she mean when she said she hurt you too once? And you never told me about your daughter," I say resting my aching body.

Anasztázia looks at me as she is about to turn out the light and a flicker of fear ghosts across her face before she answers.

"She probably meant from years ago, when she was jealous in The Royal Hungarian Opera. Maybe she got me mixed up with someone else. We didn't really know each other," she says and turns away. She snaps out the light. But I sense she is not giving me the full truth.

"Natalija, a girl like her, you don't know if someone like that will even be there in the morning," Anasztázia says.

And as I drift away, something deep in my soul latches onto the remark about not being there in the morning. Krisztyna would often leave before I woke up. Back to her husband and fake family life.

You don't know if someone like that will even be there in the morning.

I pass out still in my dress and shoes.

I wake up and my make-up is stuck to my face and it reminds me of the days I passed out on my bed in Budapest, sick with tonsillitis and bulimia, exhausted and broken.

I totally forgot Cio-Cio San who was draped on my sofa last night. Krisztyna is standing in the doorway watching us with a look of total desolation. Anasztázia is asleep with her back to me.

I instinctively lie. *This is not how it looks. There isn't a spare bedroom, Krisztyna. Honestly. We were worried about you....I mean I was worried.......*

But Krisztyna's dark eyes just stare at me as she knows this is exactly how it looks. Krisztyna knows I am lying. She can see right into my soul.

Krisztyna looks so beautiful and so broken, a total contrast from the cold diva from last night, as though the terrible demon which possessed her has gone. She turns and with a shimmer of silver and a cloud of dusky perfume, Krisztyna vanishes.

It was over before she came to Roma. She knows she caused it. She was cruel.

I hear the front door close quietly and she has gone.

We both played games in Hungary, we both were careless, reckless and wild.

But this time, I could not trust her again.

Anasztázia sighs, turns over and I look at her beautiful face. She is too lovely to have me betray her even if I wanted to.

Marina even said about Anasztázia as she handed her to

me, 'She is yours now, look after her.'

I think this is the last I will see of Krisztyna, hoping she won't get the role of Tosca in September.

I wish it was the last memory of her.

I avoid Krisztyna for the rest of the Butterfly run. She doesn't contact me and I make sure I am not walking the corridors or in the café before and after she is due in. Anasztázia has to sing in a concert in Vienna and I can see she is anxious because I am here with Krisztyna still in Roma. Some nights she has said she is too tired for me to go to her apartment, which is fine but why doesn't she trust me? She is hardly in Vienna for a long run.

It is the first shadow of darkness; the fact she cannot trust me with my ex-lover in the same city. She even says, "Krisztyna is still here. I don't want you alone with her in Roma."

I know exactly why. She doesn't trust me.

So I book myself a ticket to go to Vienna. This is not the Natalija I was. Following someone around. I tell her and she is so happy, I see the worry leave her face.

Anasztázia hugs me and I feel that I am losing myself. The once fiercely independent Natalija is becoming someone else's toy. Just like everything, in my life there are only extremes. I feel if I lose Anasztázia I will die. I have lost control just like I did with bulimia, with overwork, with anything. I have fallen in love and run away with someone in one act. It will burn right through me and by Act 4 one of us will be dead or broken-hearted. There are no happy endings in Opera.

I lie awake in bed with this dark thought spinning through my head. When I sleep, I have nightmares. Anasztázia never has nightmares.

My nightmares get worse. I keep dreaming of Krisztyna every night.

'I will never leave, Natalija,' she tells me. 'You thought

you buried me but I am still here. Remember us in the taxi, you remember, don't you, baby? Your girl and me.'

Yes I do. In the dark of the taxi after the première, Krisztyna resting her head on Anasztázia's shoulder, her tiara shimmering in her dark hair, eyes closed. And Anasztázia, elegant and regal in her cream and blue evening dress with her arm gently wrapped around Krisztyna.

Something about it has branded it on my brain.

I dream of my mother. She looks so sad and in the dreams I am searching for her, or she is in the distance gazing at me with her lovely dark eyes but never speaks. One night it is so real, she is in the room; Anasztázia's bedroom. I think I am awake as I look at Anasztázia sleeping and actually sit up in bed and say softly, "Mama, why are you so sad? You were right, she was here in Roma; my Anasztázia. Look at her; she is beautiful. But why are you sad?"

My mother gently takes my hands. She hands me my snake bracelet, the one Krisztyna gave me with the jewelled rubies for eyes. It was on the bedside table.

"Why are you giving me this?" I ask. The blood drips through her hands and I say, "Mama, are you hurt?" The bracelet is wrapping around my wrist tighter and the snake eyes weep blood and there is a bite in the palm of my hand. I am terrified. The poison is flowing through my body paralysing me. I cannot move my left arm, the paralysis is setting in. Soon I will die.

I am screaming, "Mama! Help me!" But she is gone.

Anasztázia is shaking me and saying, "Natalija, wake up. It's a nightmare, darling. It's okay."

The light is glowing gold in the distant sunrise and I am holding the snake bracelet on my wrist. "Snake bite! Please help!"

"It's just your bracelet. Look." She holds my wrist and turns the bracelet round. I look at my hand and the bite is not there. The snake's eyes are rubies again. I am going crazy.

"Maybe you shouldn't have such jewellery. It is kind of morbid." She looks at the bracelet and the silver spider ring which is a poison ring; its back opens and I would pretend to drop poison in people's drinks by putting flour inside. No wonder everyone hated me. One memorable event was the première of *Il Trovatore* when I dropped flour in the lead soprano's champagne during the speeches as she had just taken poison from a ring as Leonora in the Opera. *God, I was a bitch*. She dropped the glass to the floor.

Anasztázia sighs and says, "I'll make some breakfast, Natalija. It is nearly time to get up anyway."

I clutch hold of her, still traumatised.

"Anasztázia, it was so real. My mother was here and she looked so sad. She died when I was a baby. She jumped into the Duna River and survived the fall, but her heart was damaged. She died a year later."

I look at the gold in Anasztázia's hair in the morning light, no wonder I see her as an angel. Especially after all the dark yet wild beauties I was with who were so passionate, but so volatile.

"Natalija, you poor girl. You have had so much pain in your life. She was Hungarian? We are so suicidal as a race. It is terrible. The Italians never understand."

"No, it is my father who is Hungarian. My mother was Welsh, Sicilian, Icelandic. She was beautiful, Anasztázia. She spoke to me when I died in hospital. I was so happy to see her as I always thought she hated me and I made her attempt suicide."

Anasztázia blinks a tear away. "That is so heartbreaking, Natalija; that you went through life thinking that. I didn't know about your mother."

"She said she regretted every day she spent away from me, she said you were waiting for me in Roma and I had to go back. I was shouting because I wanted to stay with her.

Then I woke up and the doctors were holding me down."

Anasztázia traces the outline of my face and her eyes gaze into my soul instead of looking heavenwards and she says, "That is the saddest story. And she said I was waiting for you?"

She seems disturbed by this. I thought she would like the fact my mother told me this special girl waited in Roma for me. There are tear-drops on her black lashes. She is so affected by tragedy and sadness. She tells me it is her Hungarian spirit.

I worry that instead of her lighting my shadows as I thought when we first met, I am pulling her into mine, into the blackness. The darkness which has haunted me my whole life is still there in my dreams and now it is starting to bleed back into my waking life.

I don't realise that Anasztázia has her own reasons to be sad. That she has many secrets she hides from me.

STORMS

Krisztyna has impressed the Italian audience, so they are giving her the role of Tosca in one of the early season events which means she is here again in August for rehearsals. I was hoping for everyone's sanity that someone else would be chosen.

But she is outstanding. She always sells the house, the Italians love her and given Marina and Anasztázia are not available, the directors want Krisztyna back.

I am worried this could lead to more roles in Roma. This is her second in only a few months.

It was something I dreamed of before, when I knew I was transferring here. Me and Krisztyna in Roma together, both of us performing in Italia.

Now it is the last thing I want.

For the whole two week run of Butterfly after her première, I avoided her. We had nothing more to say and her heart which was cold and icy was broken and shattered. Anasztázia says she didn't see her either, but she doesn't want to talk about her, so I leave it.

As soon as Krisztyna returns to Budapest the phone calls and the texts start up. Butterfly absorbed her sadness and she focussed all her pain on her performances. Roma Opera was so impressed with her hauntingly painful broken-hearted arias. What they don't know is the pain is so real. They think she is a chilly Hungarian who is amazing on stage.

But without work until August and in our old Budapest apartment she is left reflecting on everything. Everything she did and didn't do.

In the texts she begs me, other times she is angry but always obsessive. I try to be kind and not hurt her. No wonder I never grew up all the time I was with her. It wasn't so clear, but the pattern was similar. My bulimia was terrible when I was with her and although she tried to help me fight my illness, the volcanic domestics didn't help me grow.

The last text before she returns to Roma for *Tosca* is horrible.

> **She doesn't love you, Natalija. And she cheated on you during Butterfly. I am going to see her in Bregenz. She cheated on you many nights. Why do you think she came to my première, Natalija? You didn't figure that out? You gave her your heart, didn't you? You are finished in the Opera World. Your voice has gone.**

I am so angry as she is just stirring me up over something which cannot be true and I am so chewed up with angst about my career, I respond.

> **You are a liar, Krisztyna. She would never go with you. She hates you. One day I will be star of the stage again. Anasztázia is everything you are not. Leave me the hell alone.**

A few minutes later her worst comes through.

> **I wish you had died.**

I am alone and there is no Anasztázia to tell me it is okay. Seeing a text saying that I should have died makes me cry. If Krisztyna had shouted it in anger it would have been different. And I realise Krisztyna is absolute poison now.

I am afraid of asking Anasztázia the truth.

I put the phone in a drawer and don't look at it.

Natalija what were you thinking?

I feel kind of uneasy, as though the reality I created is actually an illusion, that I am living some kind of new life but it is a hall of mirrors. Nothing is what it seems. Reflected in the glass is Anasztázia and me and I turn to face another mirror and the two of them are together, mocking me; Krisztyna and Anasztázia. I dream of it so much. A fairground funhouse and it starts so sweet and ends with me waking up in horror twisted around the sheets.

Anasztázia is in Bregenz Festival in Austria for *Otello* from early July until middle of August. I am to host a few concerts where I do not sing, but introduce the performers in Napoli in an open air theatre over a week in August as I am still not able to sing until summer is over. I am asked to introduce the opening night of *Carmen* at the open air festival in Roma, speaking as the reincarnated Carmen, the girl who is brought back to life. The Italians are loving it, just like they did when I first arrived with my opera gowns and sad story. I am still wanted, not forgotten. I should be happy about this because it sure as hell would not have worked in Hungary. If I wasn't singing they would never have me. Especially after the corruption, the flawed investigation, all the lies.

Italians are so open, so enthusiastic and loving this drama. They are still not bored of the story. Even singers in the company or taxi drivers want me to tell them the story again. They have heard it but they love it. Right now, I would be too afraid to sing in *Carmen* even if I was well. I agree to introduce the open air festival but really, I don't feel good about it. I don't like concerts either. I need to lose myself. The talk shows for TV, the perfume adverts were fine. I was in a role. Hosting a concert pushes me out of my role. I am uncomfortable in my skin.

I am down to sing roles from September onwards starting

with minor roles leading up into Amneris in *Aida* in January at La Scala and I worry I won't be ready. At the end of July I take two weeks to go to Bregenz to stay with Anasztázia. She is performing in this huge floating stage in Lake Constance. I want to see her but I also want to see this legendary Opera stage. When I do see it, I don't know if I would even want it. I never even thought about going there before now even though it pays well but the set is so epic, it overwhelms the singers who appear as dots to the 7,000 audience. You really could be anyone on stage. And people are not here for the names, just the awe-inspiring spectacle of the sun setting and the enormous set.

There is also the risk of falling in the lake itself. One dress rehearsal, both Iago and Emilia fall in and Anasztázia says she is terrified of falling in. She cannot swim especially in a heavy embroidered opera costume. Another good reason for not taking the role. For three of the performances I am there, there are violent storms over the lake which means only the top price ticket payers get to move to the smaller indoor arena and see the show. I get to see both the outdoor stage and then the indoor theatre performance on the night of a wild storm. Afterwards, when the Opera is finished and we go back to the hotel, the epic storm carries on. The whole lake is split by lightning, great jagged forks of it. I watch it out of our hotel window and it is amazing. Way better than the storms in Hungary although they were always dramatic too, splitting the sky with lightning, turning it dark green, dusty pink and unnatural colours especially in July and August.

Anasztázia is afraid of storms. I laugh and say she shouldn't be in Bregenz, as the storms here at Lake Constance are renowned for being otherworldly and besides *Otello* opens with a violent storm and some wonderful stage magic, so why should she be afraid? She says I am cruel. I tell her I am only teasing her but she says, "It isn't funny, Natalija. Storms terrify me. You are not nice to me, not nice to me at all here." Her face loses its lightness and she puts the pillow over her head.

I climb into the bed and she won't come out of the pillows.

I wonder why the hell she has come here anyway. She can't swim, is terrified of storms and is not visible on the epic set. She says from under the pillow she will never come here again. She could be anyone on that huge set singing Desdemona. She feels so small.

"You are small and doll-like, Anasztázia. So pretty, like a porcelain doll I would buy in a toy shop." It is meant to make her smile.

"I am not just a pretty doll, Natalija. You seem to think that you can parade me around like an ornament on your arm. That is so like a man, owning me like that. I am so sick of it here in Bregenz; too much German around, harsh and ugly language and you are not helping," she says miserably.

"I need love. Krisztyna never calls me a doll and leave that light on, I can't stand to see the awful lightning in this room."

"Come on, now, baby. I don't mean you are just a doll, and I came here for two weeks just to be with you. Oh forget it." I turn over away from her, and I am about to go to sleep and then I turn back.

"What the hell did you say?" I ask her. "What's this Krisztyna comment?"

"Nothing," she says. "Forget it all."

I grab her shoulder and pull her over to face me. "What did you say about Krisztyna? She said she is coming to Bregenz. Has she been here? Have you seen her? What is going on?"

There is fear in her eyes. "I meant she calls me a bitch, a diva, everything else. She hates me, she always did. And no way would she come to see me here. That's crazy, Natalija. She hates me!"

"When did you last see Krisztyna?" I say.

She tries to turn away again and not answer and I am

mad so I pull at her arm roughly and make her face me.

"Look at me, baby if you are going to lie to me! Just look at me!"

She cries out, "You're really hurting me. Natalija! What is wrong with you tonight?"

My hand is gripping her so tightly, I have left red marks on her arm and I let her go. She sits up in bed, rubbing her arm, afraid. Afraid of me. Her blue eyes look at me with sorrow.

I say, "Baby, I'm sorry. I didn't mean to hurt you. I am so sorry."

She just looks at me and says nothing. Then she lies down again and puts the pillow over her head. She won't speak to me.

I try to sleep through the storm. She cocoons herself in the sheet, wrapped so tight I can't touch her.

She looks like a corpse.

The storm clouds are moving in on us too. I fell too quickly, too deeply for this elfin beauty. Now seeing her mortal side; that she has not wandered into my life from a fairy tale book, it is all burning up like a fire. I have also watched her and she is so flirtatious with pretty women. Anyone from other opera singers to waitresses to stage managers. It could just be nothing; she is a very gracious lady, but knowing how flirty I was in the past, my instincts are telling me otherwise. Everything about her cries innocence and purity yet she is not an angel dropped from the sky, the one Marina says gives her heart completely. Anasztázia has made out her heart is true but I sense in reality a different story. She doesn't flirt with Marina or any men; she is crafty and chooses her prey carefully just like I did. And if she doesn't trust me entirely, it suggests she is also not to be trusted. I try to live in hope but Krisztyna has put doubt in my head and now Anasztázia has slipped up over some comment and didn't reassure me at all with her answer.

Her moods are also way more volatile than I first realised. She radiated a magical serene calm when I met her, but the real her is actually living up to the tempestuous diva I guessed she would be.

Except she is not demanding, more desperately insecure, childlike in her behaviour, craving attention and love and no one can provide enough. When she doesn't get it, she cries, says no one loves her, that she is dying without love. Probably her parents didn't help, rejecting her so callously.

I also blame Bregenz. Anyone would feel small on that set; it is epic and a 7,000 audience is nearly double the size of the biggest Opera stages. The run is too long, made worse by being trapped in the place, totally unlike performing in Milano or Paris where you have the city outside the theatre. Bregenz is existing for the show and very little else. She had the option of a shorter run but took the extra shows as it pays well and is now bitterly regretting it. There are alternate casts but she says the days off are even worse, nothing to do and nowhere to go.

I return to Roma and I am totally lost without her. I do not like this feeling of needing. She calls me every day and she senses I am not feeling good. "What happened?"

"It's the start of *Carmen* and I am having to introduce the Opera. I am really scared, Anasztázia. It is only a few shows and it is bringing back horrible memories."

"You will be fine. They will show you the props every time. You won't be near the stage. Don't watch the ending. Leave before Act 4. No one here would hurt you, Natalija. You were right to tell them you are not well yet, and they are paying you to introduce the Opera Festival. I've seen all the TV coverage and magazines and it is so Italian. They love you and your story because they love a drama."

I don't tell her about my ex-love and her horrible texts, which are carrying on.

I don't tell her I have lost my control and all I want is

Anasztázia. Not working is killing me. It is making me obsessive, jealous and paranoid.

Anasztázia calls me after my first *Carmen*. I don't want to talk about it.

"My brave Natalija, you are doing so well. I had to be strangled again tonight and I really hate Otello. He has bad breath and he eats hot dogs and ketchup before the show. I tell him, *Please, chew gum*...."

Despite my anxiety, I laugh at her story.

".....I nearly threw up on Thursday when he was leaning over me and I am trying to be asleep. I say to the stage manager can she please ask him to do something about his breath."

"Oh, Anasztázia," I smile. "I feel so much better to talk to you."

"Why do British men like these hot dogs and sauces? He has a stomach, this fat stomach, Natalija and he is all sweaty and his stomach is sticking in my chest when he holds me and his make up has slid down his face by the final act. He is orange and all I can think of is to shut my eyes and think I kiss you."

"Is it working?" I ask. "Did it work when I was there?"

"No," she says. "In any case, there was a different Otello. The one you saw got sick with tonsillitis. Thank God I didn't catch it. And besides, you don't eat hot dogs. And as for ketchup, it is so disgusting!"

She hesitates. "You are okay with food when I am not there, Natalija?"

"I see the eating disorders specialist tomorrow again. Every week. I haven't thrown up once, Anasztázia. Not since Budapest, I swear. But honestly, I am better than I have been in my life. It would hurt like hell anyway. I can't even think of it."

"I am so pleased. I know it is hard...."

"You helped. I would have been tempted but after my

injury, God the pain was bad enough without throwing up. I probably have lost my touch by now," I laugh.

"The reviews of Bregenz are good, but they do say 'this huge Otello is matched by the tiny Hungarian soprano Anasztázia with her doll-like appearance belying a voice to split open the Heavens with her pain, more than a summer storm over the lake'."

"Well you are, like an otherworldly little creature. That's what I said when I was in Bregenz. It came out all wrong about being a doll."

"I know, you meant to be nice. I was just stressed, Natalija. I have your photo from *Aida* with me and I look at it every night. I cut out the photo from a few years ago because you as Amneris in Margitsziget is something truly magnificent. All black and gold; a perfect Egyptian goddess you were. I was so proud you were from my country. Even the Italian press carried the photos, as Giacomo, one of our company played King of Ethiopia," she tells me.

I never knew that. All this time Anasztázia has been at Roma Opera, I had only heard about her reputation across Europe. I didn't really care to find out more, just knew she was a pretty Hungarian soprano who dominated the schedules of the biggest opera houses. I was such a diva, I never revered anyone back then. I met people occasionally such as Marina, when they were famous and I was starting out, but I never idolised anyone. That was my trouble. I thought I could rival Maria Callas, I thought I could be better than anyone. I was arrogant and deluded.

So it is very touching Anasztázia kept my photo from *Aida*, but that was the Natalija she never knew. I was Amneris, glittering golden Amneris. She worshipped an image of beauty.

"My last lover was so jealous. No wonder she left me in the end...."

"But Anasztázia, you honestly cut out my photo and kept it? For three years?"

"Yes I did. I was so sad when I missed seeing you in *Werther* as twice you were in Roma and I was singing abroad. I ripped a photo of you off the wall when no one was around. Maybe I shouldn't have," she sighs. "I thought you were the most beautiful thing I had ever seen in my life."

There is a long silence. I don't know what to say. The dead air just hangs there as we are on the phone. We all do strange stuff but to idolise photos of someone you never met? And all this as she was performing as the star across Europe.

She saw me as the embodiment of beauty. She fell in love with my looks, not me. I did more or less the same with her; I adored her after watching her as Lucia, when she floated across the stage in a waterfall of blue silk at her première. But I was nearly hallucinating on my painkillers so I was in a dream-like state, I had just been resurrected, so no wonder it seemed unreal and magical.

It was a total set-up date, arranged by Marina. The hall of mirrors opens further, reflecting our images, twisting reality.

Nothing is what it seems.

"I shouldn't be telling you this, Natalija," she says. "Please don't think I am strange. I love beauty, that's why....."

"Anasztázia, listen. I wondered why you went to that première of Butterfly, to see Krisztyna. You never have time for other Opera performances."

"I love Puccini and I had to support a Hungarian lead. It is good to show support for Hungarians, we don't have many in Roma." She sounds so convincing and says it without hesitation. But I cannot see her expression. Easy to lie on the phone.

"But with Krisztyna......did you...."

"I have to go now, Natalija. I am so tired and I have to sleep. I am back in a week. Don't worry now," she tells me and says goodnight quickly and hangs up before I can ask her any more questions.

I couldn't bring myself to ask anyway. Krisztyna was lying about Bregenz for sure.

But I still sense that Anasztázia is not telling me the truth. I know she loves Puccini but in my heart I feel there is something I don't want to know.

I try to rationalise that I am anxious, that maybe Bregenz and having all that time free was just not good for me. After all I have been working myself to death for years and I am still only 28. I half think about an eating binge but I know I am strong and I won't. Besides the pain in my back and insides with throwing up would be terrible.

I am in control of bulimia now.

My old love turns up on my apartment doorstep in Roma saying she needs to talk and I tell her it's not a good time. I have just arrived back on the train from Napoli, after working for the Open Air Theatre and I am tired. I am worried about her state of mind. She seems so desperate to come in. So desperate I have had 20 texts today, pleading to meet.

Since she saw me with Anasztázia her texts have been constant.

> *Tell me it isn't true, tell me how I can win you back, tell me you forgive me for how I was. I need you, Natalija. Your only Krisztyna.*

"Please let me in," she says. "Please, Natalija."

"I can't forget those texts, Krisztyna, the comments after Butterfly about me not dying 'with honour' and then to send a text saying you wish I had died. How can I forgive you now?"

"I am so sorry, I was drunk and angry both times. I didn't mean it. You remember me at the hospital, Natalija? When you died in the operating theatre, I screamed so much they nearly had me on the psychiatric ward. I felt like I died. What I said after that was really unforgivable but I am begging you now. Please?"

So I unbolt the door. She steps inside dark, beautiful and smouldering. So pretty, in her black dress, so calm, even smiling gently at me. It is the dress I bought for her once from a designer boutique near the Opera in Budapest. I am about to ask her about it but as I close the door and I turn to face her she smacks me hard across the face. I am so shocked. Krisztyna never hurt me in her life.

"That's for everything I took for you, with the cops and the company treating me like a criminal. And for running off with her," Krisztyna says her face cold and angry, dark eyes full of hate. "Anasztázia, *my* ex-lover." She taps her chest as she says this. "She was mine, Natalija."

My Anasztázia was Krisztyna's. She can't have been. They hate each other.

My face burns with the force of her smack. I hold my cheek.

"We are opera singers and you should never hit anyone on the face. Even your ex-husband knew that and he was a bastard. You can damage the jaw," I tell her.

"Yeah, baby. That was nothing." Her haunted lost look from before, after her Butterfly première, is now a look of hatred. The Krisztyna who smouldered with rage when she arrived in Roma stands before me only now she is more than just angry, she is violent.

"You say all this, then you plead the next time you are sorry. You are so full of venom. Are you on cocaine again? Why are you taking that stuff, you don't need it..."

"Maybe I do. As you say, alcohol affects the voice." She tosses her dark hair over one shoulder.

Her beautiful eyes burn with hate and she shoves me into the wall, hurting my shoulder. She pulls me towards her and kisses me roughly and I push her away.

"No, Krisztyna, stop it," I tell her. "I don't want this. Don't kiss me. I do not want you."

She is still beautiful, she is still the image of the woman I adored but she is dead inside. Even her touch is aggressive, her speech harsh. I thought Krisztyna had gone, that she had admitted defeat. But she is back, angrier than ever.

She reaches for me again and pulls me against her, dragging her hands through my hair.

"Stop it, Krisztyna. You have to leave now!" I tell her. "I don't want you! You disgust me!"

"Fine!" She shouts. "Fuck you, Natalija!"

She shoves me into the hall mirror and it shatters and falls to the floor with a crash sending splinters everywhere. Pain shoots through my arm and my elbow is bleeding from the impact.

"Seven years bad luck, baby," she says her eyes full of cruel mischief and she folds her arms.

"Seven years. And you can't deal with it."

"Krisztyna you broke the mirror, not me. That seven years is superstition. What did I ever do to you? I loved you only you rejected me first."

She is silent for a moment and just looks at the blood running through my fingers.

For a moment I think she is going to say sorry, help me bandage up the wound, beg forgiveness.

But she looks at me coldly with no emotion.

"You have to even ask? You pick up with her as soon as you get here. Maybe you planned it and cheated on me before; you have been performing in Roma twice before and you probably met her then." She is full of fire and despite the blood dripping down my arm she seems not to care she has hurt me. She just stares at me as I hold my cut arm and no emotion registers on her face.

"I never met Anasztázia until April," I say.

"Liar!" she says and steps closer to me. "You must have. I saw you in bed together and you looked like you had been with her a long time."

"I was asleep on the bed in my dress. You saw nothing, Krisztyna! She is just my friend. You never made it easy for me or you. You are so full of hate for everyone including yourself."

I feel tears ready to fall. I watch the blood seep through my fingers. I feel sick and my head spins, as to see blood on my hands brings me back to that awful night I was stabbed in *Carmen* and saw my hands wet with my blood.

"Now you want to cry. After all the crying I did over you. And don't forget she was mine before you. She loved me once! You saw her in the taxi at that première of Butterfly, you didn't hear what she whispered to me as you were watching us from the front. You still don't get why she came to my première? She even called me before I arrived in the country, for God's sake. Said she had waited eight years to see me again!"

"I don't believe you; I don't believe you about Anasztázia. She despises you. I asked you to come to Italia and live with me so why are you so violent and angry when you rejected me?"

"I am mad because you pick up with the first Hungarian and it would be Anasztázia. Trust you to want better. Don't let her innocent elfin beauty fool you. She is so cut-throat and she wrecked my career in Hungary. They slashed me from the schedules because of her and it took years until I got back to where I was, only now you made it happen again after dragging me into *Carmen*! You want to know what she's been doing the nights she told you that she was tired and needed to sleep? And Bregenz was amazing this year and I am not talking about the stage, you know."

She throws her head back and laughs.

I feel sick and taste blood in my mouth. Krisztyna never lied before, she was brutally honest.

"No one liked you or me in Hungary, but that doesn't mean anything, Krisztyna. I don't want to hear what you say Anasztázia told you. I don't believe your lies and how can you say I dragged you into *Carmen?* I was the one who nearly died. What happened to you in the police station was not my fault. Can't you see that?" I say and the tears flow. I am as fragile as crystal.

"Your precious doll was with me the nights she stayed home alone! She threw me away once and she will throw you away too." She wrenches at my hair and pulls out a piece.

A smile crosses her face. "I have a piece of you baby. Black magic on this and you will be mine again. That's once she has wrecked your career because she has to be the diva. Always."

"Why do you even want me back, Krisztyna? You obviously hate me," I say.

"Because I cannot stand to see you with her. She loved me and so did you! I lost work for years because of her, the company cut me from schedules as punishment for being with their most famous soprano. I had to take work in provincial theatres until they started to throw me scraps of roles again and she just got on a plane and came here!" she says angrily.

She pushes me back against the wall again and bites my neck.

I scream, trying to push her away. She looks at me afterwards, licks her lips and says, "Still sweet."

I fall to the floor.

I hold my throat. It is bleeding. "You crazy bitch, Krisztyna. You are a fucking vampire! I'll tell her what you really did."

"When she comes back from Bregenz next week, I will tell her. That you invited me here, bored with her. But Natalija you need to know that she has cheated on you with me, that she still will. You need to open your goddamn eyes because your love is so blind."

She laughs and I wonder what else she will do. But she

just gives me her Turandot death stare at the doorway and leaves, slamming the door so the glass shakes.

Krisztyna; she was the soprano cut from the schedules, the love Anasztázia talked about when we first met. No wonder she hates Anasztázia. She had to scratch around for work until Budapest finally started giving her some roles back. I feel sick. Mostly I feel sick that Anasztázia never told me.

If she only had told me the truth. It would still be insane if we had both dated Krisztyna but I could have tolerated that. But now; the lying, the cheating, not knowing what is real or illusion. I sensed it and I should have trusted my instincts. I am so stupid thinking my life is now a fucking fairy tale with some fairy-tale princess.

It is just splinters, fragments of glass. Like this fucking mirror.

I pick up the pieces of the mirror, cut my fingers on some of the shards and worry about the seven years bad luck.

It is just a superstition but I am very superstitious.

Seven years bad luck.

Marina stops me in the corridor and points at my neck the following day. "What the hell are you doing?" she demands grabbing my arm.

"Marina, it isn't what you think...."

She says in a low angry voice. "You would cheat on her? She's fragile. What are you going to say when she sees that neck? It is Krisztyna, isn't it? You just can't keep away from her while Anasztázia is singing her heart out in Bregenz. It would kill her to know. And Krisztyna of all people. She is not a good person, Natalija. She behaved like such a bitch at her Butterfly première."

"I was attacked. I swear to you Marina, I am not lying."

"What by? A Hungarian vampire bat? What is wrong with you? I thought you would never hurt Anasztázia."

"Marina wait...."

She is already walking away. "Save the lies, Natalija. You are cruel. Underneath it all, you will hurt that gentle woman."

When Anasztázia returns that weekend to Roma she will be straight into rehearsals for *Norma* which plays alongside *Tosca*. I have visions of all my dreams, my new found life falling apart. The bulimia once masked anything that hurt. *So they don't want you? So what.* That was my approach then and I am afraid now, because I can't throw up my feelings. I have to speak with Anasztázia and she has to tell me the truth.

I need to know even if I have to leave her. I hate living this life of illusion.

The mark on my neck has faded to a dark purplish bruise by the time Anasztázia is back. She asks me what happened. I say someone hurt me, that Marina is angry because she thinks I am cheating.

Anasztázia traces the bruise, the teeth marks are still there.

"Who hurt you, baby? Tell me," she says. "Some horrible man? That technician who is always hitting on all the females? Please, Natalija."

"You know who." I don't want to look at her.

"Krisztyna did that? And this?" She touches my arm which was cut by the mirror.

My elbow is taped up. "That too, the mirror in my hallway. I was bleeding. I thought she came to talk, I swear to you. I pushed her away. She hit me. She was violent."

Anasztázia is raging. "I comforted her when she was upset. We took her home the night of her première because I felt sorry for her."

"But I never knew you were her lover too, Anasztázia, I never knew you called her before she came to Roma and spent nights with her during Butterfly," I say. I look at her and she avoids my eyes. "She was the soprano you loved wasn't she? The one they cut from the schedules and then you walked out on Budapest and came to Roma? And worst of all, I find out from her not you!"

"She's lying," she says waving her hand dismissively. "I was just telling her it would be okay that night in the taxi. And now she is spreading all these vicious lies."

Anasztázia behaves as if the thought is crazy but she does not reassure me enough with this. Krisztyna is right. For such an actress, Anasztázia is a terrible liar.

I tell her not to say anything but she has marched up to Krisztyna when she sees her sitting in the Opera café. Krisztyna is looking out of the window toying with her coffee.

Anasztázia yells at Krisztyna and I am grateful that we are the only three people to speak Hungarian, even though not many people are around.

Krisztyna doesn't say anything at first, just smiles like a cobra. She stares mockingly at Anasztázia, calm and amused.

Then she says, "Don't you remember begging me, Anasztázia? Begging me to come back and forgive you after I lost my work because of you. The crying, the phone calls, even turning up at my family home like some desperate schoolgirl. And then you just forgot me. I'm the one you threw away to come to Roma. What will you do to your sweet little Natalija? Don't you remember only the other night with me? You cheated, Anasztázia, you are cheating with me since Butterfly. Tell Natalija the truth, tell her about Bregenz and the hot summer nights......" Krisztyna sighs.

"Tell her about us," she says and she stares at her hard and coldly. "Us."

Anasztázia picks up the coffee cup. I know she will throw the liquid on Krisztyna.

"No, don't. Anasztázia," I say. "Let's go, please." I try to reach for the cup.

"Do it, baby. Can't wait to see you jump to your death in the flames in *Norma*. You are such a diva even your own daughter hates you. You threw her away too," says Krisztyna so full of venom.

After Krisztyna's last comment, Anasztázia drenches Krisztyna in coffee. Then she grabs the sugar bowl and dumps that over Krisztyna's hair. Krisztyna closes her eyes and instead of flying at Anasztázia, smiles with a look of satisfaction. She has got to Anasztázia and she loves it.

"Even a bowl of sugar wouldn't make you sweet, Krisztyna! You were always so poisonous!

I didn't lose your work in Hungary, you did it yourself for being such a bitch! Everyone hated you! I hate you!" she screams.

Krisztyna still has the smile on her face. She licks the coffee and sugar from her lips and she looks at us with total contentment.

"You have to love to hate so much, Anasztázia." Krisztyna smiles. "Don't you? I can see right through your angry facade, I always did, baby."

She is unnerving with her calm as the coffee drips on to the table, her dark hair full of sugar.

Anasztázia drops the sugar bowl on the table and runs out of the café.

Krisztyna is losing it. The few people in the Opera café stare at us and I am anxious to chase Anasztázia out. They don't understand a word, but they don't need to; Krisztyna covered in coffee and sugar is enough.

"Anasztázia, wait!" I call. She is running fast down the stairs to stage door. She doesn't look back or answer me. I run after her.

I ask Anasztázia when I catch up with her further down the street what Krisztyna meant by her comments. *Anasztázia. I know Krisztyna was the soprano you loved. Krisztyna has again said about your daughter. Why does she say this when you told me she was lying? And Bregenz? Tell me! I can deal with the past but not now, just tell me the truth! Tell me! I hate these lies!"*

"No, I have not been cheating on you with Krisztyna and I will throw more coffee over her. She is evil. Don't believe the lies, Natalija. Hungarians are full of lies."

Anasztázia is walking ahead of me down the hot street and the noise of the crazy Roman traffic is frenzied. She doesn't look at me. She is avoiding my questions about the past, about this daughter of hers.

"No way would I ever be with her. I hate her, I really fucking hate her," she says.

I grab her arm. "Stop walking away and tell me the goddamn truth!"

She stops and turns to face me.

"Shut up about it all, Natalija!" she says so full of rage. She pushes me away from her.

"Why don't you know when to stop asking? You know nothing about my past life! Nothing! Are you happy now you have seen your china doll lose it? Is that what you wanted? To test me to see if I am real?"

I am so surprised by her extreme reaction, not just a snappy 'stop asking me' but really incensed that I am digging into her life, the one she hides from me. I step away from her.

But she scrapes her sunglasses through her hair and looks at me, her blue eyes soft again and she puts her arm round my waist.

"Sorry, Natalija, I am so sorry to get mad at you. I will talk about it all soon and I am sorry but my daughter......it is so difficult..." She looks so sad again, looking past me into the distance and sighs.

"It's okay, Anasztázia," I say. "Tell me when you feel ready, okay?"

She turns away from me and buys us a small pot of ice cream each. I don't like ice cream, even Italian but it breaks the darkness as we sit down by a fountain to eat the pistachio, meringue and chocolate pots. She has forgotten I don't like ice cream. I told her enough when I first met and she kept buying it for me. She has already forgotten. Or she is confusing me with someone else.

She starts to talk happily about how much she loves Roma, changing the subject entirely, waving her arms in the air and resting against the bench as she inhales the city which is her adopted home.

But Anasztázia has dark secrets and stupidly I have already left Marina's apartment, moving everything into Anasztázia's. My rental period was up and not earning much was the main reason for deciding to move. Anasztázia wanted it, but I was hesitant. My instincts were right.

It is too late now. My head was telling me not to be so stupid, to wait, to ask my father for some help with my rent and stay independent but I did not listen to the voices in my head as I do not know what is real any more.

I fell in love with an illusion because I wanted to believe in a new life here, leaving the darkness of my past behind. Only it has followed me like unclaimed baggage on the next flight in the form of Krisztyna. Marina gave me the reference, reassuring me that Anasztázia was gentle and sweet. I should have been more cautious.

I am resting until I have to fly to Milano the first week of September for *Rigoletto* rehearsals. I will fly home every weekend. It is a small role and I cannot be away from Anasztázia as Krisztyna is still here for *Tosca*. I know Krisztyna; twisted and angry but if anything she was brutally honest. She told people things they didn't want to hear such as they were fat, ugly or couldn't sing. She never held back especially after a drink. She was bulimic when I first met her and never denied it, even laughed about it and said she only did it now and then. Which she did. She told me she loved me first only last December, that she always had.

It seems like a lifetime ago. The time she played

Turandot.

And I don't want to stay in Milano alone. It is a role I have played as Maddalena and such a tiny role at that. I know as I get well, as I have to take roles away from Italia or Anasztázia does, it will push us apart even more. I am already feeling the distance; I do not know the real Anasztázia with the dark undercurrents which flow like dangerous riptides under her calm surface. She is 44 years old and I have known her for just four months of her life.

TOSCA'S KISS

I go see *Tosca* although it is Krisztyna singing Floria Tosca
and common sense is telling me to stay away, but I have no
common sense right now. Everything is shot as far as my
judgement goes. I go one Friday night after I return from
Milano for the weekend, mainly because Anasztázia is being
distant and quiet. I am angry with her and we are not
talking very much. She knows that I sense she is lying;
about God knows what and certainly about Krisztyna. But
the feeling just hangs there in empty space. So we don't
talk. We sit in separate rooms in her big apartment.

I watch *Tosca* from the company box. Then as I exit
backstage past the dressing rooms, one of the costume
ladies tells me my Hungarian friend who sang Tosca wants
to see me, she seems upset, could I go and talk to her? This
lady speaks only Italian and cannot understand why
Krisztyna was so sad as she helped her with her costume. I
hesitate. I shouldn't go near Krisztyna, but I think what can
happen in the theatre? I am safe here.

I will congratulate her on her performance and leave. I
won't even go into her dressing room. I will stand in the
doorway, briefly speak with her and then leave.

I don't want to go to her dressing room at all. I don't even
know how she knew I was here tonight unless she looked on
the box office system, unless she has been looking every
show for my name on one of the company tickets.

I knock on the door and think, 'I will tell her that I
watched her, she was sensational but I am not wanting to
speak to her tonight. She has to stop doing this. I am not
ever going back to her.'

The door opens and Krisztyna, already changed into a
low cut black silk dress, pulls me inside.

"Krisztyna, I am only here because your costume lady
told me you were upset which you are clearly not. I have

nothing to say other than to tell you that your performance was sensational, which you know already. Now, I really have to go. Anasztázia is waiting."

Krisztyna stands in front of the door blocking my exit. "She isn't here tonight, baby. She would have told me. I am not stupid." She smiles maliciously.

"She is meeting me outside and why would she tell you anything?" I say.

"She has a concert tomorrow night. I know her schedule. In fact she told me only the other night when I was with her." The look in Krisztyna's eyes is taunting.

I was with her.

I try to pass her but she holds me back.

"Don't tell me you don't still feel for me either, because you are lying. Look...." And Krisztyna turns over her heart necklace in her fingers. It expressed everything I never said and the promise of the beautiful day which was so close, it was almost tangible. Instead of hope and love, it has brought resentment and hatred.

"Krisztyna, Un bel dì......" Her dark eyes look at me and her perfume is the same dusky one as when we first met, her skin is almost touching mine. If this is what she thinks love is then she is twisted. The necklace meant everything before. The sentiments are now dead.

She destroyed it.

"Don't tell me you don't still think about me. Why did you come to watch me?"

"I did think about you, Krisztyna. But you murdered everything even before I came to Roma.

I came here tonight to see *Tosca*. But we are over. It was sad, but it never had to end this way. First you push me away, refuse to stay in Roma with me and insult me so horribly. Then you turn violent, attacking me in my apartment. You were beaten by your husband; how could you hurt me after all you suffered?"

Krisztyna turns the key in the dressing room door and

removes it, drops it into her dress.

I step back, "Open this door and talk if you need to say anything. Open it, Krisztyna. You need to let me go."

She ignores me and sits at the dressing table, takes out her little bag of cocaine and asks me to join her, loosen up and take some powder.

I tell her no way do I do that shit. If she gets caught in here, she is screwed.

"The door is locked, Natalija." She has tapped out some on her compact mirror and inhales a long line with a black straw. She has even got a little make up bag to store her portable drugs kit in.

"I hope you are not having drugs in my apartment. My father will go mad, Krisztyna. And let me out of this room," I say.

She looks at me, inhales deeply as the drugs go into her bloodstream and says, "You are alone, little girl, all alone in the world. Anasztázia is losing interest in you if she is calling me up, I told you. Listen to me over this. I wanted to tell you tonight. I am Tosca. That is what she wants and not some has-been diva, Natalija." She inhales another line and closes her eyes.

"That is such a bitchy comment. I am in recovery. What the hell has happened to you, Krisztyna? You are brilliant on that stage and such a psycho off it. When did you get so cruel?"

"After *Carmen*," she says honestly. She doesn't look up. She is quiet for a moment.

She is so beautiful but cold and she says so carelessly, "I wanted to ask you to come back to me. I still have feelings, Natalija. I'm not going to lie because I still think you are beautiful. I'm giving you the chance to save yourself from that arrogant diva you are with. Take it now while you still can. I am giving you another chance but I get to be the success for a change."

She looks at me with defiance, nothing soft or kind. Why

would I accept her offer when it is so unfeeling, just a 'take it or leave it'. She doesn't really want me.

"No. As you said, I am a 'has-been diva' to you. You do not really want me, Krisztyna. You want to get back at Anasztázia. You hate her so much you would even take me back just to hurt her."

She laughs and with one swift movement rips my dress down to the waist, tearing the delicate lace.

"Black silk underwear, baby. Does Anasztázia like that?"

Her eyes glint at me dangerously and her hair falls over her face as she just stares at me like I am some cheap slut.

What a bitch. I pull my dress over myself, mad at her.

"You like to be the submissive one, don't you, baby? You are a lazy lover, aren't you? Remember us? It wasn't so long ago....I bet she is rough too or maybe you haven't reached that stage with her yet. She is best when she hates you and her love turns to ice. Just like me; she hates me and her passion is invigorating. You will get there soon enough."

She smiles and there is satisfaction in her smile but she doesn't touch me again.

She settles down on the floor and takes out her powder.

She inhales deeply and sighs then she looks at me as I try to pull my dress together where she has torn it.

"What a bitch you are. This is one of my favourite dresses," I tell her.

"Shut up!" She screams at me."You broke my fucking life! And then you ran off with Anasztázia as soon as you got to Italia. She wrecked my career when it was going well! You both left me with all the mess in Hungary twice! Only this time was worse; I could have gone to prison for you! They told me I was disgusting and to go home to my husband! Even the female cop, when I was crying just looked at me like I was garbage!"

She hates me because the investigation wrecked her life. It threw up everything about our relationship, made her children stop speaking to her and the police were harsh. But why blame me? I was the one who nearly died.

"Krisztyna, they tried to blame you and no one deserves that. But think of everything you have now. They love you on stage here, your life can be so good so why the hell do you want me to come back to you?"

I slide to the floor, feeling tired, so tired of this Krisztyna, the cruel Krisztyna she has become.

"Anasztázia; you don't know her, Natalija! You don't know what you got yourself into. You should get out now. I will forgive you for messing up my life if you let me be the star. I want you to let me be the diva now." She taps out some more powder.

I look at her and tell her she is a liar, that I do not want her, that I would not go back, everything is over between us.

"Don't you get it, Natalija? She even called me before I arrived in Roma in May because you told her I was coming! For God's sake, girl, listen to me! You don't want to hear or see but you need to."

"I don't believe you! I stayed with her most nights."

"Most nights, Natalija, most nights. But there were a few you didn't, like when she said she was tired and now, you are in Milano in the week. Haven't you noticed her being distant? Like her mind is on someone else?"

Anasztázia is busy. She would never. She hates Krisztyna. They had history, that is all.

"You are not the woman I knew, the fiery gypsy girl." She looks at me hard.

"Did you really cheat with her?" I search her face for traces of the old Krisztyna. But she has snapped shut and only her eyes blaze fire.

"Ask her yourself, ask Anasztázia," she says and she looks away from me. "When you are in Milano, she calls me up......"

"You ruin everything that's good!" I knock the powder lines off the mirror and send it clattering to the floor. "You and your twisted mind, Krisztyna!"

"You goddamn bitch!" Krisztyna is scrabbling around scooping up her cocaine from the dressing room floor desperately.

"You are sick, Krisztyna, you need help." I watch her with disgust. Scrabbling on the dressing room floor for her drugs. Performing as Tosca only half an hour ago and now scratching around like a hopeless junkie for her precious white powder.

"I hate you and I hate her," she says. She is looking at me with her long dark hair loose, her face beautiful but so empty as though her soul left her body as she scrapes her powder from the floor.

As I get up to leave she just watches me, her eyes so dark they are almost black.

"Next time I see you, baby you will be alone," she spits at me. "The moment you are out of town Anasztázia will be calling me again. She always begged me for love, said she wanted love not my passion. She has that tiny tattoo '*Vissi d'arte*' on her left hip bone." She half closes her eyes in memory and then looks at me and licks her lips. "Sweet," she says. "Honey sweet she is."

She must have been with Anasztázia, how would she see a tattoo? I haven't even seen it. She hides her body in the dark.

"Krisztyna, I would never, ever go back to you."

She just stares at me and her face betrays anger that I won't give in to her.

"You should have died and then I could have grieved, Natalija, you should have died."

She is still kneeling there, with her black silk dress loose on her golden shoulders.

"Maybe I should, Krisztyna but I am alive and you can't deal with that. You just hate and hate because no one loves you."

"We'll see," says Krisztyna. "I killed your love. Your love for Anasztázia is dead now. That is Tosca's kiss, baby. I murder love and hope."

Her smoky eyes stare at me with no emotion. Krisztyna turns everything light into dark like a sorceress.

She throws me the key and goes back to searching for the remains of her powder with her fingertips.

"You were best as Turandot," I tell her. "Because you were Turandot, Krisztyna, you were her or more like you are. Only last Christmas yet it seems a lifetime ago. No one can give that death stare to 1700 people and make them shiver but you did. I thought it was because you were so good; now I see it is because you have a heart of ice."

"Get out," she says in a low voice without looking up. "Get the hell out and don't go to her tonight looking like that. You look like trash with your ripped dress."

I step into the corridor hoping no one will see me. I run out, down the steps and out of stage door. The stage door men are calling after me, but I don't stop. The world is spinning and the warm air of Roma is still and holding its breath. My new life is over, as I know it. My fragile new hope and love destroyed. I run around to the side of the building in the darkness and I call a taxi and the driver asks me am I okay when I climb in the back.

I say, *Love breaks your heart.*

I could have gone to the stage manager, could have told them Krisztyna was doing drugs in her dressing room. I could have had her thrown out, blacklisted by Roma Opera. But I don't want to give her more reasons to hate.

I don't want her career ruined and her full of vengeance.

I just want her gone from my life, I want her to find a new life and stop ruining mine.

I go home to the apartment shared with my false love. I do not want to see anyone tonight, especially not Anasztázia. Thankfully she is already asleep looking so innocent with her body sprawled on the bed, her lovely face soft and peaceful. *Treacherous heart*, I think. *You and your lies.* I quietly climb into the bed and turn away from her. I don't want her near me tonight because I will beat her, hurt her, slap her and I am not violent. I fantasise about holding her down and smacking her until she begs me to stop and admits to everything and I am disgusted with myself and my violent thoughts.

I have nightmares. Krisztyna is laughing as I lie there pulling my torn clothes over me trying to cover my dignity. I am on the stage in La Scala, my dress hanging off me, my underwear on show and the crowd is laughing and jeering and throwing oranges at me. Oranges like we always had in *Carmen.* Only now I am not throwing an orange at Don José as the fiery gypsy girl but being pelted with them by La Scala audience. Krisztyna is in the wings laughing. She is evil and I run from the stage and she catches me by the arm and tells me I am ruined. I am her possession. Now I have fucked up on stage and all I have left is her. She is so beautiful in the dream but so cruel and her dark eyes smoulder with contempt. Anasztázia is there in a flowing blue dress and she is laughing too. She stands in the dressing room corridor and leans against the wall and laughs at me. Her face is heavily made up and like Krisztyna, she is beautiful but cruel. She stands next to Krisztyna and asks me, *Don't we look good together, baby? Don't we, Natalija?*

Krisztyna laughs more and wraps her arm around Anasztázia. *She is mine now,* she says and I drop to my knees and cry. They both walk away and I am left by the side of the stage having lost everything. *You were useless,* says the artistic director as he passes me. *Your voice is ruined. Go home to Hungary, little gypsy girl. Go home and beg on the streets by the Opera for a living. That is all you are good for. That is as close to Opera as you will get now.*

When I wake up next morning Anasztázia has already gone

out. I don't care where. She says very little that day as I am
working on my music notes in the kitchen and leaves early
and arrives late from her concert. She doesn't ask why I
didn't go, she doesn't even seem very affectionate as I am
still up, sitting in the living room. As she sleeps, lost in her
dreamworld, I move her silk dressing gown to one side and
in the half-light there on her hip bone is the tiny tattoo;
Vissi d'arte. I touch it gently and wonder why she never
showed me before. I know it is her favourite aria but
Krisztyna wasn't lying. Oh false ice princess. Cheat and liar.

She senses something as I am looking at her, as there
seem to be faint white scars here and there on her skin but
it could be the light. She stirs so I quickly turn away and
pretend to sleep.

I take my flight back to Milano the next day.

I am in La Scala for *Rigoletto* and the rehearsals are
painful. My voice has lost its power and it still hurts to sing,
nearly 6 months later in September. It is a minor role,
Maddalena, but I am relieved as I cannot be any less than
perfect in this theatre. I am flying back to Roma every
weekend of rehearsals. Krisztyna is in for *Tosca* and
Anasztázia is performing in *Norma*.

But the idea Krisztyna has branded on my brain churns
around so much.

I get a few texts from Anasztázia that week but when I
try to call her she doesn't pick up her phone.

I know why.

When I return to Roma the following weekend I look around
Anasztázia's apartment obsessively when she is in the
Opera House. I am looking for signs of Krisztyna staying
here. Looking for anything. A piece of jewellery, anything at
all. I hate going through Anasztázia's stuff. I don't go deep,
not through drawers or cupboards only obvious places like
under the bed, even looking on the bathroom floor for signs

of Krisztyna's dark hair and I find one and my heart races, but I hold the long strand up to the light and it is black and wavy not the dark brown of Krisztyna's. It is mine. There is nothing. I have to stop. I am imagining it all. I am losing my mind. Looking on the floor for hairs. I must be going insane.

Then as I lie on the bed and stare at the ceiling feeling guilty hunting for evidence, I stare at a diamond earring stud in the bed. I pick it up and my heart races.

It is Krisztyna's. She always wore gold hoop earrings, never studs but I remember in the dressing room last week, she was wearing diamond studs because they would match Tosca's diamanté crucifix and tiara. It is virtually identical to the ones she had in her ears. She must have lost one here and then gone and bought another pair. The diamond stud is not Anasztázia's. She only ever wears some pearl earrings. She has others, but no studs. I have seen all her jewellery in a box.

I have proof. One night or more this week when I was in Milano, Krisztyna was here.

Anasztázia didn't even change her sheets after cheating. That is such an insult.

A dirty cheat, a dirty lying little slut.

She let me move everything into her apartment, giving up my own and has been cheating.

I actually hate her for not covering everything up and being so careless. I am even sleeping in Krisztyna's goddamn sheets.

When Anasztázia arrives home I show her the earring and tell her I found it.

"Oh, that's a relief," she says genuinely. "I thought I lost it ages ago." She takes it from me so obviously claiming it that I could believe her. If I hadn't found it in her bed.

"Where's the other one?" I ask.

"Oh, it's in the drawer," she says. "Somewhere." And she won't look at me.

"I found it in the bedsheets, Anasztázia," I say.

She has her back to me and I see her grip the drawer as she is placing it in a box.

"I don't know how I managed to get it in there, maybe it was caught in some clothes I was wearing," she says and turns round smiling and shrugs her shoulders.

She is a terrible liar.

Right. And I know everything I don't want to know. It is all true.

LA MALEDIZIONE

I am sitting in the living room ready to confront my cheating little elf because I cannot stand the atmosphere, cannot stand being lied to whether by her silence or her dismissive air. I have had enough. She needs to tell me herself first, she needs to tell me.

About everything.

When she walks in, fresh and beautiful and happy, she looks at my face and asks me what happened? *What is wrong, why am I sitting here looking so angry?*

I just look at her calmly and say, "How many times, Anasztázia? How many nights? I know, I saw your tattoo. And I found that earring. It wasn't yours. They belong to Krisztyna because I found the earring in the fucking bedsheets and Krisztyna had diamond studs for *Tosca*. She lost one here and bought some more so don't lie to me. You goddamn little whore! I can't even believe it myself. Tell me!"

Anasztázia looks at me with such sadness. She doesn't answer.

"Tell me!" I scream. "Just tell me or I am leaving you forever! Tell me about Bregenz or you will never see me again! I mean it, Anasztázia!"

She lowers her eyes and fiddles with her bracelets. She says so quietly I can hardly hear her with her gentle glassy voice, "It is all true. Maybe four or five nights during Butterfly, a few nights in Bregenz and maybe three since *Tosca,* maybe four. And yes, she was the soprano in Hungary, the one the company told me to stop seeing, the one they cut from the schedules and she said she would never forgive me. I also called her before she came here, when you told me she was going to be performing in Roma."

She sits down and holds her head. "Natalija, I just can't find the words to tell you......."

I knew it, I knew Krisztyna wouldn't have lied. I feel sick

hearing about this betrayal, not just last week but the whole goddamn time I have been with this cheating little elf. Our life has been nothing but an illusion, a web of fucking lies.

"It had been eight years, Natalija. Eight years and I just wanted her to forgive me, I swear to you. We hadn't spoken since I left Hungary. All I wanted was to make her see I never ruined her career, that I had no say in the directors cutting her from the schedules but then when I was in contact with her and saw her again.....all those feelings came back..... I was weak. I met her in the café in the piazza just to talk, just to tell her it was never my fault she had her work cut, I wasn't a backstabbing bitch. She told me she forgave me, she missed me, she had never forgotten me......I am so sorry. I went to the Butterfly première to see her perform but I never ever planned all this. Natalija, I feel ill that I have done this, but I was afraid. I didn't know if you would stay with me....."

I look at her and I hate her so much. She won't even look up at me.

"Krisztyna told me that you left everyone broken-hearted, that you would leave me, Natalija. She said you left her too and broke her heart, you left all your lovers. I was so afraid because she told me you hurt so many people. Krisztyna, she was my first real love.

But I hated her this summer. She just taunted me all the time, telling me you would leave me, she was cruel. I hated her but I couldn't stop going back because she convinced me that you would leave me and I believed her. Forgive me, darling, please or I'll die if you don't. It is you I love, I swear on my life, Natalija!"

I want to slap her so badly, slap her hard. But instead I shove her to the ground and she falls like a rag doll. I would never touch that beautiful face. I would be just like Krisztyna to do that. She lies there at my feet as I look at her in disgust. She starts to cry.

God, you stupid woman, I think. *You stupid selfish tart.*

"You cheated with her during Butterfly? In Bregenz? And now when I am in Milano?" I scream. "Why? What is wrong with you? No wonder you have been so distant! If you had only told me yourself, only been honest, only told me what she had said. I never left her! She lied to you and you didn't even give me a chance to explain! She ended everything between us! You hate her and still you have her in your bed? Are you sick? Do you get off on hurting people, Anasztázia?"

She wraps herself round my knees. "Please, darling. I am so, so sorry. Seeing her again...it was such a mistake. All I ever wanted was to tell her I was not the one who wrecked her life in Hungary. I wanted her to forgive me, that is all, I swear. She twisted everything, told me you were cruel. I loved you, I do love you but I was so convinced you would break my heart."

She cries and the tears run down her face.

"Only it didn't turn into just her forgiving me. You are the one I love, I never thought you would stay, Natalija......"

"Anasztázia......." I sink to the floor and put my hands over my face. "You listened to her! Of course she would say that? Are you stupid, Anasztázia? She wanted to break us up!"

The shadows are there, monstrous and black and laughing in the corners.

"Your instinct was right, Natalija. I cheated on you and I hate myself. And in Bregenz she just arrived and I was so lonely, I missed you so much. I cheated on my Italian girl who went to The Met, which is why she left me, I cheated on everyone. I cheat and I hate myself and everyone leaves me. I loved Krisztyna....but you are the one, Natalija."

I push her off me and she lies on the ground crying.

"Thanks a lot, Anasztázia. And what am I? Light entertainment? Some dessert? You treacherous bitch, I really thought you were special, I really did. And now I have left my apartment to come and live with you and this is what I walked into!"

I sit down on the sofa as she lies there crying her heart out and I feel so angry. Let her cry. I am angry with myself for trusting Marina when she handed Anasztázia to me and for trusting this cold ice princess. I only saw goodness in her. I only saw a trick of the light.

"No, Natalija. I loved you ever since I saw your photographs but I messed up. Beat me if you want, Natalija. I can't forgive myself for hurting you. Beat me, hurt me if it helps you." She moves closer to me and tries to touch me.

I slap her hand off my arm.

"Save it and I never hit people. And that is really the limit; you missed me so much in Bregenz you had to take Krisztyna! You lied about the past and you lied about now. How can I ever trust you again? How can I trust you when I am in Milano? Why do you cheat, Anasztázia, if the people you love leave you?"

I look at her weeping on the living room floor like the fallen angel she is.

"Anasztázia! Why?"

"Because I cannot be alone, when I am alone I can't stand it......because I ruin everything that is good, because I am scared everyone will leave me. And you, the best thing that ever walked into my life....." Her eyes are closed and tears run through those long eyelashes I loved so much. And I truly hate her.

"I want to take it all back, Natalija. I hate myself for what I have done. Please forgive me!"

"Your mother was right, Anasztázia, you are disgusting!" I feel like throwing up. Marina doesn't know the real Anasztázia. Marina's gift was a poisoned chalice.

I walk out of the apartment leaving her crying like the end of the world on the living room floor.

I hate her for what she did.

"All lies, how could she? Unable to exist without hurting me. Cheating, lying, I hate her, I hate her," I say to myself as I leave.

I am glad to be in Milano in the week to get away from everything. I am so angry with Anasztázia, it burns. I want to leave her, I want to leave this little slut. But my bank account and my stupid heart won't let me. And maybe, I just cannot bring myself to do it, when she has pleaded for forgiveness, wept for hours and begged me to hurt her.

She has bought me all kinds of gifts; flowers, chocolates, clothes, jewellery. She sits and cries as I am unmoved by all her offerings. She sits at my feet gazing at me like some stupid puppy I kicked.

"Even wife-beaters buy chocolates and flowers, Anasztázia," I say and drop the latest beautifully wrapped gift on the coffee table and walk out of the room.

I go to bed and lie there and ignore her. Pretend I am asleep so I don't have to look at her or listen to her whining and pleading.

"I love you, Natalija," she says. She strokes my hair from my face. "I love you so much."

She wraps her arm round me. I move away from her as I don't want her cheating body near me.

"I don't love you, Anasztázia. I don't think I ever did. You are nothing underneath that diva image.

I loved Lucia, not you. Never the real you. You are a mess. A total fuck up." I am lying as of course I loved her but now I don't know how I really feel underneath all this bubbling rage.

I hear her crying softly and I just do not care.

We step out early in the morning, me still unable to talk to Anasztázia who is insisting on taking me to the airport. I don't want her to. She has been in the dress rehearsal this weekend for *Norma* but I refused to go. I had the evening free and didn't. She has watched me like a wounded animal as I ate breakfast in silence. I don't even want to discuss it so I don't say a word and she has the sense not to start her

I'm so sorry refrain.

I sit on my flight to Milano and think what a mess everything turned into.

My resurrection has gone horribly wrong. So much for a new life without pain and jealousy.

So much for being set up with a greedy diva I was reassured would be sweet and never hurt me.

So much for love.

Anasztázia calls me in Milano and just says that two more performances and Krisztyna will be out of here. She even says to me that Krisztyna has been under enormous pressure with some family problems back in Hungary. She is protecting this half-crazy Floria Tosca. Well, I don't care now. I don't care if she is still cheating because they can both go to Hell. Together.

I tell her this.

Then I hang up without saying goodbye.

I have lost patience. I wish I had never moved to Roma. I wish I had based myself in Milano and guested in Roma. I would have not been so swept away with Anasztázia. I would have dated her but I would never have fallen for her so deeply. But I am stuck in Roma.

September has melted into misery for me. Thank God I am back to singing because it takes up my energy and anger.

When I fly home the following weekend I ask Anasztázia what the hell is she going to do about Krisztyna. What if she comes back for future work. What are we going to do, more like. Because I cannot stand the thought. I would sooner try to transfer to Milano, or Madrid or anywhere.

Anasztázia looks at me with sadness. "She will never get roles here again, I promise. Marina said she will not allow it, she thinks she is evil. Marina is the most senior, she knows the directors so well, she will make sure."

"Well you sure as hell made it up to Krisztyna this summer, baby," I say sarcastically. "And how can you stop her, you and Marina? If she gets a role, what are you going to do? Then tell management she is crazy and does drugs?"

"Oh, Natalija," she says and I feel her hurt gaze on me. I can't bear to look at her.

I am so angry and so stupid.

I wonder if she is planning to cheat again when I am in Milano with someone else. Now Krisztyna is gone, maybe she is already scouring the stage for fresh meat. I start to think of her history, her past life with Krisztyna. Anasztázia continues to prepare the evening dinner, but she doesn't look at me. She starts to get plates and food out of the fridge.

We eat in silence. It is late, she is tired after singing and I am still mad. We go to bed and she falls asleep wrapped in the sheet, her back towards me hiding her secrets from me.

I lie awake worrying about everything. I lean over her and there are tears on her face, streaked through the make-up she was too tired to remove and I feel a little guilt. Her hungry diva heart just craves love constantly like an addiction. The darkness is moving in like a gathering storm in the distance.

Then the constant crying and begging me to forgive her. She is getting hysterical. The night before I fly back to Milano is especially fraught. Anasztázia weeping as though her heart is breaking, "Love me, please love me. I just want you to love me."

I take my flight back to Milano at some ungodly hour and Anasztázia calls me that evening and asks how things are.

Fine, I say.

Besides when am I going to see her in Norma? It has already opened. Can she reserve me a ticket for the weekend? The show is going well. She would love me to see it.

"Honey, I am busy with *Rigoletto.* I am sorry but I am

performing this weekend too so I will not be back. Besides, I do not want to even watch you leap to your death in the flames at the end. My career is starting up again. Please, I am tired," I look out of the window at the lively Milano street and get the urge to walk in the late summer warmth.

"Oh," she says and her hurt is deep and aching. "Oh, I am so sorry that you still feel like that, you obviously hate me."

"Stop saying that, it is grating on me now. And yes, Anasztázia I do hate you so can you quit calling me when I am busy in La Scala in my first role here. You are good at sabotaging everyone else's careers." I end this stupid call and leave the hotel for a walk in the evening sun.

Sorry, sorry, sorry.

Krisztyna is so intoxicating, it's true. She is about the most sensual person I ever met.

I wish we had never ended because Anasztázia is hopelessly flawed. Krisztyna was messed up too, but we had known each other for a long time. Ever since my first beginnings with The Royal Hungarian Opera when I was 25.

I was still coming to Roma but maybe Krisztyna might have transferred as well in time.

I blame the stabbing for turning Krisztyna into the cold-hearted angry diva she now is.

Another reason to hate the bitch who did this to me. She destroyed Krisztyna's life too.

But then my cheating diva would have forced her way between me and Krisztyna. She would have turned everything upside down anyway. What a fucking mess. Why did they have to have had all that history together? Damn the fairy-tale princess and her greedy needy nature.

I sit down with a gelato not because I like it but because sitting by a fountain with a gelato is something I did with Anasztázia in happier days.

I get dozens of red roses on my opening night of *Rigoletto*.

The stage door man laughs and says, "*A*. All signed with the letter 'A' and kisses. Who is A? Andrea? He is a lucky man. Lives in Roma?"

"Yes, yes he does," I smile at him and he helps me carry the flowers to my dressing room. "He's a surgeon." I don't know why I say this but anything other than someone theatrical and people won't ask too many questions.

It is one big problem here in Italia, what to say when people ask about your relationships or if you are married. In Hungary everyone was more reserved. The passionate Italian men are forever hitting on us. In the company, in the streets, in the supermarkets, anywhere. No one really takes in the fact I have gone to live in Anasztázia's apartment. I am new to the country, her apartment is big with three bedrooms so she might offer me lodging especially as I am Hungarian as well.

But she will not take a euro from me.

"No, Natalija. I do not want or need rent. You are here because I love you. Just if anyone asks, you do pay rent but really it is none of their business," she told me.

So if anyone ever asks me, I am renting a room in Anasztázia's big place. Oh, just casually. *Yes, I rent from her. It is good to cook some Hungarian food, speak Hungarian at home.*

Especially in the bedroom.

And now all I can think is, *I hope I don't get tetanus from those thorns. And her heart of thorns.*

The rest of the cast of *Rigoletto* are envious. I am playing a minor role and my dressing room looks like a funeral parlour or a diva's delight. There are red roses everywhere. Laura, the Spanish girl playing Gilda is full of admiration. "He must love you like nothing else, Natalija. Either that or he did something wrong and is trying heart and soul to win you back."

She gives me a sly smile and slopes off to her room. But I

don't think, *What a bitch*. I think she is perceptive. Her body language suggests she speaks more from experience than envy. She can't envy me now anyway. A tiny role with a lousy voice. She is the star of *Rigoletto*.

I don't even text to thank 'A'. I wonder about cheating myself but I am just too damn tired.

I don't answer her call that night to say it went okay. I am burnt out, I go to bed.

All that runs through my dreams is the leitmotif for 'la maledizione' from *Rigoletto,* the spooky sequence of notes. I keep dreaming I am Gilda and end up murdered.

That is what comes of being superstitious and believing in luck and curses. They come true.

I am also disturbed as when Gilda is stabbed to death, the lightning splits the multi-towered stage as 'la maledizione' comes true. I am not dealing with *Rigoletto* well, especially as it is so dark when she is stabbed. I am obsessed with asking the prop master is he sure the knife is always blunt and he gets sick of me asking every single night. *Of course it is blunt, it is a prop. I told you a million times.*

He doesn't know my history and *Carmen*.

Lilla, my stepmother calls me to see how my run is going. *How is Anasztázia?* she wants to know. But she is very concerned about Krisztyna.

She seems so sad, Lilla has told me. *She is just not the Krisztyna she was. She is thinner and paler. She is getting work but she seems very troubled, Natalija. She seemed nervous too when I visited to collect the money for bills. Did anything happen in Italia? Did you fall out? I know things fell apart between you after Carmen.*

No, I lie to Lilla on the phone. *Just I have a new life out here. Krisztyna wouldn't stay in Italia but it was difficult for her in Roma to see me with someone else.*

Especially as she knew Anasztázia from Hungary long

ago. Anasztázia was always the star. But I gave Krisztyna the chance to be with me when I left in April. She didn't take it.

I am lying so much I don't even know what truth is. Caught between a psycho ex-lover and a serial cheat and lying to people in work about relationships. I can't remember what lies I have told and who to.

Yes, that's true, Lilla says. *That and everything in Hungary. Awful that she was taking the blame at first. Poor Krisztyna must be hurting to lose you.*

I know, I tell her.

When I hang up, I wonder did she go with Anasztázia to show me what a cheat my new love was, or did she just want vengeance.

Krisztyna was always vengeful, probably still angry about her career being messed up years ago because of Anasztázia. The company wouldn't have cut Anasztázia from the schedules so they cut the lesser known singer. Then Anasztázia left anyway. Krisztyna was not a star. I thought Krisztyna was happy singing supporting roles, but it turns out that was never true. She wasn't even allowed to take supporting leads until she had earned the trust of the company again. Her husband was only part of the reason she never took centre stage. He beat her anyway, successful or not. Only this year did I know that for 20 years he beat her virtually every day.

Lilla tells me that Krisztyna has got some work lined up in the Opera House in Madrid in *Lucia di Lammermoor* and some concerts in Hungary. Occasionally this season, she will perform for The Royal Hungarian Opera. I worry that *Lucia di Lammermoor* will send her over the edge. Anasztázia says it is a role which takes so much digging into the soul for the dark side. It is not a role to be taken lightly. When my run in La Scala finishes, I tell her Krisztyna is playing this and she says angrily, "That fits. Crazy murdering bitch."

"You have played that role, Anasztázia," I tell her. "It is a role. And ironically I fell in love with Lucia or you as Lucia back in April. Krisztyna is never a murderess."

Yet she murdered love, with Tosca's kiss, I think.

"But that role is dangerous. And for Krisztyna, not one she should take. Turandot and Tosca, they are different in darkness but Lucia, Marguerite and roles like that. I have played those myself and I know how close to the edge it takes you. It is as though you are staring at this black hole of madness, it is very frightening when you get absorbed in such roles."

"I know. I have played Marguerite in *La Damnation de Faust,*" I tell her. "And you probably made her crazier, stirring her up again, raking up the past. You just couldn't leave the past alone, could you? Couldn't control your cheating little body."

I feel her hurt look but cannot face her. She makes me so angry it is difficult to be civil at the moment.

Anasztázia who seemed so sweet will cheat again, and again. And soon I will become the old Natalija. The bitchy, cut-throat ambitious bulimic who hurt her rivals and all her lovers because she didn't want to be hurt herself. And unlike my ice princess, I will not cheat because I am so desperate for love, I will cheat because I want to hurt.

I am an obsessive by nature. I know how bad obsession can be and I understand it even more since my injury because overwork masked it for so much of my life. When you work yourself to death, you can channel it, When I have periods of time without much work, it is terrible. I obsess and I cannot stop.

My throat is still not properly healed and I am still having to limit the roles. *Rigoletto* has been my first since March. It is so hard to turn down the big roles, but the opera houses have been understanding. They think my only problem is my injury from the stab wound which healed remarkably quickly. It is painful singing on it and every now and then I feel twinges which go right through to my core. No one has any idea my throat was damaged apart from the doctors. The stab wound is allowing my throat valuable recovery time. 6 months almost, without singing. I still hope to be taking on role after role like I did.

So when I am asked to sing Azucena in *Il Trovatore* with rehearsals starting February for early March by Roma Opera, which will follow on immediately from *Aida* in Milano where I rehearse early January for end of January shows, I take both. These are demanding roles but I accept as taking breaks and smaller roles now, is giving me time to get well. I know I can do it and later in March I will have some work in Madrid for *Don Carlo*. Not my favourite opera but it is an extra opera house. I turned down Madrid's offer of *Carmen* for next June as I still have stage fright over this ill-fated Opera, but I should be able to sing a new role in Napoli; La Principessa di Bouillon in *Adriana Lecouvreur*. It sounds like me; a vengeful angry role. A twisted love triangle. Maybe Anasztázia should be playing Adriana and ending up poisoned. I have not really done so much for Germany and my German language roles are not really down on my repertoire. But I don't really care. After my many bouts of tonsillitis caused me to drop *Die Königin von Saba* in Budapest after just the dress rehearsal and a below standard performance, I have not used German since Opera academy. I sang the part of Judit in *Bluebeard's Castle* with an arrogant vile moonface of a man which was my only Hungarian opera. That was below standard too and not one I want to repeat; intense and difficult. So I am limited to French and Italian. Which means more travelling to play the roles.

Maybe I should have gone to watch *Norma* after all.

I might have felt better watching Anasztázia leaping into the flames to her death.

I hate her so much I want her to burn in Hell.

AUTUMN CHILL

I obsess about Anasztázia cheating with Krisztyna. It is a double betrayal. I picture them together, like the intimate moment I saw them in the back of the taxi.

Every time I go to sleep, I picture Krisztyna lying across the bed.

I don't know why I stay other than for financial reasons. I have told Anasztázia that I never loved her and since then she has sat at my feet and virtually begged me for love. Saying she cannot believe I never loved her.

I am so angry my heart has closed to her.

I want to leave her but I am cruel and selfish and reducing her to begging is at least giving me some satisfaction for the hurt she caused. I have never begged for love like Anasztázia, the demanding insecure diva who needs love more than oxygen. She is begging me to love her and my cold heart gets some satisfaction from this. I also stay because I need someone in my life, if only for physical passion. I am rough with her and she takes it all. I know when I dig my claws into her and bite her, it is hurting her but she doesn't complain. She is grateful I am still here.

I still remember the magic I felt when we first met. How I saw this wonderful creature who captivated me like no one else. I lied when I said I never loved her. I did. But not this Anasztázia. Not the one who sits crying on the floor, reducing herself to the state of someone as desperate as Fiamma, my Sicilian girl, who wrapped herself round my legs and begged me to love her.

I loved the Anasztázia I first met, who held me in a bubble of wonderful fairy dust back in May.

Who seemed so lovely, so sweet and calm. Who had such promise of love and kindness.

But of course she is a diva. At her level, I don't know why I expected anything else. I was kidding myself and so was Marina.

Marina doesn't really know this girl. They say they are friends but in the whole time I have been in Roma, we have never met with Marina socially outside the Opera House. At most a quick espresso in the café inside and talking about work, not even a café down the road.

Anasztázia doesn't have any friends. She is horribly lonely. Her family never call her.

Her parents don't like her for being 'unnatural'.

They sound horrible. They have a superstar daughter who is rejected because she dates women.

Yet I still can't forgive her, there is no excuse for cheating.

The main reason I stay with her is the apartment. Marina's place was nice but more than I can afford right now on my payments from small roles and Anasztázia has a huge place, echoing and full of lovely ornaments and chandeliers. I love the apartment so I might as well get something out of this selfish lover. Anasztázia won't take any money from me. She probably wouldn't have taken it anyway. But she sure as hell won't take it now. I don't even offer.

I dream about Krisztyna. Sometimes she is cruel, hurting me, mocking me. In others she is the old Krisztyna, the magical radiant beauty who set the Opera House stages alight as Tosca, Butterfly and Turandot. Krisztyna is haunting me. As though she cannot have me in reality and has actually performed the black magic on my ripped out lock of hair like she said. I start believing that she has performed a binding spell. One morning I wake up from a bad dream so I go and get some coffee and sit in bed. It is still so early, 6am, but I don't want to wake Anasztázia although I feel like pouring the coffee all over her.

She is murmuring in her sleep. "Krisztyna, why?" she sighs. "You know how I feel." As clear as if she were awake. I can't listen to this. She is dreaming of Krisztyna in a very different way. Mine are bad dreams. Hers are romantic or at least pleasant, the way she sighs and looks so happy. I am mad at her. Me sitting here awake and her even cheating in her sleep.

"What did you say?" I shake her awake and spill coffee all over the sheets.

"Natalija, what the fuck? God, what is this; coffee all over the sheets? What the hell are you doing?" she says grouchy and tired.

"You have been talking for the last ten minutes about Krisztyna in your sleep. Why, Anasztázia? Do you really still love her?"

"No, it was a bad dream. Jesus, why did you wake me so early, Natalija? Shut up." She looks at the alarm clock and turns over and faces the window. She has a nerve. I feel like shaking her.

"You seemed happy. You even sighed her name while I have been sitting here," I say.

"Still cheating in your sleep."

She turns round again and says, "You spilt your coffee all over the sheets, damn you. They are my favourite; lilac. I only put them on yesterday. You are becoming so cruel towards me, Natalija. I am not cheating in my sleep!"

I can't face looking at her hurt and angry expression. I will hurl the rest of the coffee over her pillow if she doesn't shut up. She has no right to act hurt over anything.

"She is still in your heart, Anasztázia," I tell her.

"I cannot control it. I never...." she says.

Stupid, spoilt little diva.

I finish my coffee and get up.

"Well, maybe you still love her too, Natalija. Maybe that's why you don't throw her out of your apartment in Budapest." Anasztázia sits up in bed. She looks so pathetic as she says, "But I heard you, the first night you were with me. I heard you say you loved me."

"Maybe I was dreaming, Anasztázia," I say. "Just like you

are now because I cannot remember saying I loved anyone."

The chill is in the air.

"Anyway, Krisztyna attacked me. She isn't the woman she was but you were the one who cheated on me," I say. "Calling Krisztyna right after I told you she was arriving for Butterfly is the worst.

I had only just met you and told you she was my ex! Talk about a betrayal. I thought I was looking at an angel but I was wrong. I know you can't control the past and who you once loved, but you sure as hell can control your cheating little body right now."

I pull on my dress and comb my hair.

"Body of an angel and the heart of a demon," I say coldly looking at her. "I find her diamond earring in the sheets and you said it was yours. God, you must think I am really stupid."

"No, Natalija.....no, I never meant......" She reaches over to me and tries to take my hand and her eyes are so full of remorse. She tells me that she cannot find the words to say how sorry she is. She tries to hold on but my fingertips pull away angrily. It is October; the summer is slipping away and so are we.

Anasztázia is quiet for the rest of the morning. She even looks through one of my boxes and finds photos, of women and men from my past.

"Why do you still keep these?" she holds the photos up as if I have some dark secret.

"Because I can't erase my past. You had a life; you were even married. Why are you even looking through my photos? My family are in there, my Opera photos and you, many photos of you! Put those back! For God's sake!" I snatch the box away and put it back on the shelf. How dare she?

"I was alone before I met you, Anasztázia. You are the one who is in the wrong. Don't play the martyr!" I grab her

105

arms, force her to look at me. "And this daughter, Anasztázia. What the hell did you do to her? Murder her so your career came first?"

"Let me go! That's horrible, Natalija!" she tries to push me away. I hold her tighter.

"No! Where is she? Are you incapable of telling me the truth?"

Anasztázia just goes quiet and gazes at me with those blue hypnotic eyes and her face is so sad. She won't talk about the girl.

"Well maybe you should never have got involved with me," I tell her. "You should never have started what you couldn't finish."

Anasztázia goes quiet. For a few minutes she just kneels on the carpet and stares out of the window and I am waiting for her pathetic whining. She says quietly, "Natalija,.......I was going to tell you about my past life, more of it but you never seemed to want to hear....." Then she just throws up her arms and cries out. "Why don't you just leave me since you hate me so much? Just leave me today, stop torturing me. Just walk out of that door and break my fucking heart! Then it is done! And I will cry for eternity!"

She clutches her chest.

"God you are such a drama queen, and maybe you didn't act that enough for the audience sitting at the back of the gallery to see," I say looking at her. "Diva. Cry a few more fake tears."

Despite her fragility, I do not feel like comforting her one bit.

"But Natalija, I love you! Way more than anyone else, ever!"

The violence rises up through my body like lava and it burns. I want to hurt her; slap her and shake her but the thought of violence disgusts me.

"Where are you going?" she asks. "I will make us something to eat. Please don't go out."

"Stuff eating, Anasztázia. I need to walk in the sun," I say. "And how would you feel if I had been with *our* Krisztyna all those times here in Roma?"

"It would have broken my heart, Natalija," she says. "When I first saw photos of you, I really did love you."

That is just insane. You can't fall in love with someone from a photograph.

"Then we both fell in love with complete illusions then, baby. Photos? Come on. You cannot love an image! I wish I'd never met you, I wish I'd never taken this role in Roma. As soon as I can I am transferring to La Scala to get away from you," I say.

She stands in front of me and takes my hands.

"Please, Natalija, don't leave Roma Opera because of me. You don't even like Milano. I am still the Anasztázia you met."

She is so tortured, so sad, I feel a pang of sorrow. She is too pretty a lady to be crying her heart out without me feeling something.

"Natalija if you leave me I will die. I swear I will die. My heart will break......I am so lonely...." she says and she clings to me like a child. "I am so lonely, please don't go out! I will die without you!"

What can I say when she is so melodramatic? I sigh and look out of the window. I put my arms around her. Of course she won't die if I leave.

"Anasztázia, you are like a child. You say you are lonely with me and then go looking for passion elsewhere."

"I always needed so much, more than one person could give me. I hate being alone, I can't stand it! The silence, the emptiness even for one night. I go crazy! And Krisztyna was an addiction this summer, a terrible addiction. She kept telling me you would leave. Every day I thought my Natalija would leave me."

Krisztyna played on her weakness and her insecurities, taunted her, lied when she said I was heartless and left all my lovers.

I feel some kind of pity for the child-like Anasztázia, who is so terrified of people leaving, she makes it happen.

"No person can give you enough love, Anasztázia," I tell her. "You want the impossible. No one can love you so intensely every second of the day and night. And with this Opera lifestyle it is even more impossible."

Maybe this is payback for the hearts I broke in my life. God is testing me. God is sending me this challenge; leave and be sad or stay and accept what I cannot change. She will not change.

She cries so much that day she could fill an ocean. I don't know why she says she is so lonely when I am sitting right here. She will make herself lonely since she cheats on everyone. I spend the whole morning listening to Anasztázia's tears. They echo round the apartment and I consider calling her shrink. I just need her to stop as I am working on my music notes and I just have to leave her to cry. She will be ill at this rate, she will lose her voice. She is supposed to be writing up her work. She is convinced I am going to be gone after her concert so she begs me to go to New York with her.

"No, you know I can't, I am working," I tell her. "And I wouldn't want to anyway."

It has made her even more distraught.

"If you really can't get it together, baby, you should consider not going either," I tell her.

"Tell them you are sick and cannot go. Just cancel it if you are crying all the time. You cannot travel in your state. Your voice will be affected after all this crying and you won't be able to sing."

I also have no desire to go out of Europe even if I did have the time. I was offered work at The Met last year but I turned it down. It wasn't a lead. I just had no desire to go, despite its reputation and good pay. Many singers think I am crazy to restrict myself with my already restricted mezzo repertoire. I also turn down any comedy or britches roles.

Maybe one day I will go to The Met.

But not now, not for a long time.

There is a huge cloud over the sun. As I predicted we are in our fourth act, one of us has to leave or die. I felt as though I was touched by Heaven and now it is growing colder, darker, sadder. Under her delicate sweetness lie such deep currents of insecurity and a terrible fear of loneliness.

She ruins everything by chasing some shooting star.

Anasztázia is still crying in the shower that evening. She hasn't stopped all day and is coughing.

She is damaging her voice.

I go to clean my teeth and she is weeping as though the world will end curled up on the bathroom floor in a towel. There is a razor on the floor of the shower and some drops of blood and she says she cut herself shaving her legs.

I consider calling Marina and just asking her can she please help me deal with her distraught friend. Instead I just carry Anasztázia to the bedroom. I see some blood on the towel and there are cuts on the side of her knee.

"Don't, Natalija, please don't say anything," she begs me pulling the towel down.

She has not cut herself by accident. She is self-harming.

"Why here? It must hurt with a scratchy razor, why do it at all, baby?" I tape up her knee.

She looks at me and says, "It does, but it is small damage, no one will see."

"You want me to call your doctor, because I am actually afraid for you, Anasztázia? You are scaring me. This self-injury is not fair on me, you need help. Can I call Marina for you?"

"I haven't done it for so long. Please don't tell my friend, please don't call the doctor. But, Natalija, everyone leaves me."

"You left your husband, you left The Royal Hungarian Opera. You make your lovers leave you. Life doesn't have to be this way. You are making it all happen."

"My own daughter hates me. I could only deal with Opera...."

I make her swallow a sleeping pill with a hot drink. Anything to stop this terrible storm which has raged all day.

"When I was 22 with my c-section scar still healing, I was set to jump into the Duna River. A man and his brother hauled me off the bridge, but I was slipping in the rain anyway. The ambulance took me straight to the psychiatric ward. The doctors just gave me antidepressants and sleeping pills and released me two days later. They just said it was normal post-natal depression."

"You don't have to tell me all this now," I say. "Try to rest."

"Mária is 22 years old now. I miss her. My ex-husband moved to Geneva and my schedule never took me to Geneva."

Anasztázia rummages in the drawer next to the bed and brings out a photo in a silver frame of a really beautiful girl with dark honey coloured hair and deep blue eyes.

"She said I no longer existed when I last saw her two years ago, that I was 'disgusting and unnatural' which are the words of my ex-husband. She hates me! All I have is my voice."

"Stop it! Anasztázia she might one day realise...."

"No! I lost her! You see what being at the top does, Natalija? I can hardly breathe at the top of this mountain, the air is so thin. Mere mortals cannot exist and I am up here alone....." She stands on the bed and reaches up towards the chandelier on the ceiling, as though she is looking for the sky. If she won't sit down I am calling the shrink on emergency call out.

"Anasztázia, please just get down. Try to sleep. Please sit

down. You must be exhausted."

I am feeling further away each day. As though she is floating up in the clouds like a helium balloon and I am way below, unable to reach her.

"You are not alone," I say as she is starting to drift asleep. Thank God because I am exhausted too. I look at her sleeping and her body is twisted around the sheets and I see scars in different places, some so pale like fine white lines. Her lovely porcelain skin and I know that night that she is a self-harmer, that she has been doing this for many years.

I don't love her. I thought I did, but I do not love her now.

I think she is becoming more and more unwell, she needs help. Her work has masked depression for 20 years. The more she has given on stage, the more it has taken from her. The depression, crying, cheating compulsively and self-harm are not just her diva-like behaviour. We all go a little crazy in this world, but Anasztázia is sick. I can't blame alcohol or drugs because she never even drinks except the occasional first night champagne.

I arrange the covers on the bed and watch her sleep. She looks so fragile, so sad, so totally broken.

But as I watch over Anasztázia, I don't hate her any longer. I see her as a very sad, lonely and unhappy woman.

She just self-destructs. She never meant to hurt me.

I pull the duvet over all her scars and stroke her hair gently. I look out of the windows and wonder what the hell I am going to do. I watch her breathing easily, now so calm. I sit there for a long time.

The next morning she has got up early and gone out. I lie in bed alone and stare out of the window at the blue sky and the clouds drifting in the warm October air. Anasztázia is a wreck. She is too fragile for this world. So desperate for love, so desperate she hurts the people she most loves.

I never begged forgiveness when I hurt. I walked away from broken hearts without a backward glance. I was so cruel once.

One of the reasons Anasztázia became so successful is because like me, with my bulimia, she wanted to stop every emotion she needed to feel so she buried it all under her punishing schedule and performances. In the spring, in those early days in Roma, I thought it was the beginning of some wonderful new hope and now I realise it was all a complete illusion, performed by a stage actress of the finest calibre.

That night she begs me to hit her, take a belt and beat her to get the pain out of me.

I am shocked and tell her no way. I am not going to ever hit anyone. And how crazy she is; how would she explain the bruises in a costume fitting?

She even screams, "I was with her in this bed. For God's sake hit me." She tries to tie her wrists to the bedframe. "Take that belt from the chair and hit me until your pain is gone."

I pull her off the bed and she is struggling with me to get herself tied to the frame.

"Anasztázia, stop it right now or I am calling the ambulance and they will hospitalise you and you will miss your concert in New York!" I shake her and she lies on the bed broken and crying. Not because I hit her. Because I won't.

I go and sit in the living room. This relationship has turned into something really terrible.

I never heard someone cry so much in my life. She will have no voice left for her concert.

I call her private doctor and I tell him she has been hysterical, cutting herself. She is crying all day and she has to go to New York tomorrow. He comes over immediately and gives her a massive shot of Valium as she lies weeping on the bed.

As she sleeps, he hands me a prescription for

antidepressants, anti-anxiety pills and a small dose of anti-psychotic medicine for me to get her the next morning. He tells me she should not be going to New York. She is very sick, that she has suffered depression and some kind of personality disorder for years and he has been worried about her for some time. She is resisting taking pills but he tells me she must. Every time she takes a demanding role it gets worse. She is so ill at times he is worried she has psychotic episodes as she takes on the character of the role.

Like Lucia di Lammermoor, I say.

He says that she is giving too much, it is becoming her. The character takes her over so completely.

She needs to be in hospital or at the very least seeing doctors every day and she should not be alone.

I tell him that she refused to cancel New York.

"Natalija, Anasztázia should not be taking so much work. She needs to perform only in Italia, not be alone in strange countries. She is going to get much sicker if we don't help her but I guess you knew about her illness?" he asks, assuming I know everything.

"Yes," I say as I open the front door for him.

Of course I didn't know she was sick when I met her. I knew nothing about her.

Everything has fallen apart as summer has melted into October.

It is breaking her heart.

But she shattered mine, even if she never ever meant to. I cannot truly forgive her.

And I cannot watch her cutting her body, I cannot hear her hysterical crying for one more day or night. She is not well enough to be going to New York. She says she doesn't need the pills when I return with her medicine from the pharmacy the next morning, especially the anti-psychotic.

I am not psychotic! She screams. *No way am I taking that shit! These are crazy people's pills!*

I tell her, *Take the goddamn pills or don't go to New York. This is a small dose of a very modern anti-psychotic, more of a tranquilliser. Just take the pills, Anasztázia, you know you should not be travelling so far in this state.*

Don't you tell me what to do! She shouts.

No one says you are psychotic, but your choice of roles and refusal to treat your depression is pushing you into psychotic episodes, Anasztázia. You need to ease off the intense madness of roles like Lucia, take the pills, see the doctor and your illness will get better.

I am not sick, she tells me. *I am just going through a rough patch.*

Anasztázia, my father once thought he was the King of Hungary and he was always in a rough patch. He had much stronger pills than yours and you know why he didn't get better? Because he kept thinking he didn't need the damn pills. He just got sicker and sicker when I was a kid.

Do you know how many times he ended up in hospital? He regrets it all now, as it cut short his career.

Is that what you want? Because if you don't take it seriously, you are going to lose everything you ever worked for. Is that what you want?

She becomes sulky and reflective. She watches me silently as I have to pack her case for New York.

Anasztázia is still brooding as I take her to the airport in a taxi since I don't leave for Latvia until the next day. I am feeling sorry for her. But more in the way I would for a sick friend or relative.

I am reassuring her we can work things out but please, give me space.

Don't call from New York. And take the pills. If anything is terrible there, please go straight to the emergency at the hospital. But I cannot do anything from Europe. It is not fair on me.

She is not taking it well. I have packed her medicine in

her hand luggage and told her if she refuses to take it, I cannot stay with her a day longer. She looks at the pill bottles and reluctantly promises she will.

One week, Anasztázia. Just get through your concert and get help. Then call me from Roma. Just let me be alone for one week.

We ride to the airport in silence. Occasionally she gazes at me.

I am sorry she is hurting. But I have had enough.

I have told her before she left not to call me from New York but I know she will. One week, just focus on her work and call when she is back in Roma. I can't leave her but I need space so I just move everything out of the master bedroom and into the one furthest away. There is a pink pretty room and a lilac one, both with ornate stuccoed ceilings and chandeliers and ensuite bathrooms. I take the lilac one as the pink doesn't have a balcony and just hang all my clothes in the closet, place the books on the shelves. But Anasztázia doesn't know this yet.

I feel after the doctor told me she should not be alone, I need to take some responsibility. I cannot leave her alone in this state.

Marina has come to visit me the night Anasztázia is away. I am not in the mood as I leave for Latvia in the morning. But it is the first social call outside work and I do need to talk to someone about Anasztázia.

I make some coffee and Marina confides in me that she is very concerned.

"Natalija, listen to me. You have done so much good. I have seen the change in Anasztázia. She was sad before you, then so happy, only not so much the last few weeks. She isn't a diva. She really loves you. I am worried as she seems to be very sad."

She looks at me and I can't tell her about the cheating, about Krisztyna. That just isn't right. Why drag it all up, as it goes so much deeper than just tarting around.

"Marina I haven't got the energy. I am going to be rehearsing and I am shattered just dealing with her emotions. I can't really discuss it but she is sick and depressed. She needs a shrink. I didn't know how bad things were but she really needs help. I had to call her doctor out the night before New York and he told me she should not be working out of Italia but Anasztázia will not listen. Please help, please try to talk to her. I don't even know if she will take her medication."

"I know she has had some depressive illness, but she told me it was nothing, was years ago. I will try to help, Natalija. I will talk to your girl and she will smile again." She is full of hope that just one conversation will fix Anasztázia.

I doubt that.

It has been horrendous. Crying all day when she is not in the Opera House.

Marina doesn't understand.

The next day I leave for Latvia. I am going for the first time to sing for Riga Opera. They have wanted me for bigger roles in the past but I never considered it. It was too far north. They wanted me to perform as Carmen, a year ago but I still had a lot of commitments in Hungary then. Every opera company wants me as Carmen. Now, even the thought of playing Mercédès in Vienna in November scares me. My once favourite Opera and I associate it with bad luck and dying.

So I am taking this small role as Rosette in *Manon*. This was my first ever role, Rosette when I was 23 having just completed music academy in Italia. I performed in London and met Marina who was in *Tosca*.

On the flights to Latvia and when I change in Warsaw, I think about everything that has happened.

In Hungary I was free. I loved no one and belonged to no one; I was Carmen, I loved beauty whether it came in male or female form. Even when Krisztyna moved in with me after her violent husband threw her out, I still was repressing my emotions and so was she. It didn't seem so big a deal.

I have talked to my shrink who tells me it is never going to be easy; two divas living together. You give your life to this Art and it becomes your life. You only meet other opera singers or anyone theatrical. The theatre is your life. I need to stop seeing people as magical creatures who have walked out of fairy tales.

But the shrink is not understanding the Opera World. All of us who give so much to our roles feel so intensely, we cannot seem to function at a slow pace.

Only pain and hurt remain, glimmering dangerously on the horizon.

SNOW QUEEN

I have to get my career back to where it was. I am an opera singer. All the sacrifices I have made to perform; all the hard work and lonely peripatetic lifestyle for the first few years, no friends at university because my life was Opera. Nearly killing myself with overwork and bulimia and then the stabbing. I have to get my Opera life back or I feel I cannot exist. Anasztázia will have to be shelved for now. I need to work and I come first in my life.

I feel as though my dreams have slipped away. I have hardly sung, only *Rigoletto* last month and my voice has fallen from sensational to average. I am lucky to be getting supporting roles, mainly based on my reputation. I am afraid my career is ruined and I am not even 29 years old. My father once asked me early on in my career if I didn't make it, what was plan B?

There is no plan B in my world. I hate it when anyone asks me that. Plan B is for losers.

We land in a swirling snowstorm that October afternoon in Riga. I have never been so far north although my mother studied at Latvia University on a year out and spoke fluent Russian. She gave me my Latvian name. After this run I will have a few days in Roma, then Vienna and then a concert in Budapest. I am glad I thought to wear my midnight blue fur coat but snow in October after flying from the warmth of Roma? It was still late summer there. Riga Old Town where I rent an apartment is so chocolate box pretty. I can walk back in five minutes from the Opera House. The cold doesn't bother me, but I am told it can get to minus 37c in a bad winter. I would hate to live here permanently with this harsh climate. The theatre is set in gardens at the edge of the Old Town and is a traditional horseshoe shaped auditorium with a beautiful chandelier. The company are kind.

They ask me again about *Carmen*. It will return on 2nd

September next year, which means August rehearsals and they really want me for the role. They even say how nice it is in August and September. The weather will be good to me, they tell me. They are so nice in this cold country that I agree. The pay is not great but I would like to add another opera house to my repertoire. Maybe I can conquer my *Carmen* fear with this new place.

They inevitably ask me am I married. This is always difficult and constantly asked in Italia. I just say I have a love back in Italia, he is Hungarian. I make up anything, always, *He*. 'He' and 'she' are the same word in the Hungarian language so it always felt less like lying before, but now it is different. I am lying.

In magazines or any media interviews, I say I have a casual love now and then, or at times I say I am alone but my private life is just that; it is private.

I am missing Anasztázia, I can't deny that. Intense, draining, melodramatic but so beautiful. Even sad she is lovely but I can't truly forgive her. She has tried to call me several times from New York which irritates me. I told her not to, so I do not answer. She doesn't listen. I don't think that perhaps she is horribly lonely and she needs to hear my voice. I am selfish. I do not need her right now and I do not miss all the volcanic domestics.

Anasztázia returns to Roma and calls as soon as she arrives to ask why have I moved all my stuff out of her room and into the lilac bedroom. I am in my Riga apartment looking at the snow outside and tired after my week of rehearsals.

"Natalija, why have you done this? Marina called to tell me she spoke with you. I know it is because I am emotional and messed up. Marina didn't mention Krisztyna, so you didn't tell her?"

"No, your secrets are all safe with me but she is worried about you. She knows you are ill but not that you are a cheating little tart."

"Natalija! Please, I am sorry! Please tell me what I can do," she says.

"You forget I was so fragile too. I deserve better than this," I say.

"Natalija, I was in a bad place when I first met you but don't leave me now."

I am silent on the phone. I don't know what I can say. She is in a worse place now. She seemed fine at first, so calm and serene. A fairy-tale princess who radiated good energy and had an otherworldly aura.

"Natalija! Are you listening?"

"Anasztázia, I moved my stuff to another bedroom, I haven't left you."

I look at the spires of the Old Town outside my window. I am sick of her whining and pleading when I am tired.

"Please, darling. I can't bear life without you. Without you the world has no colour, without you it hurts to sing, without you my heart will break. Is it true you never loved me?"

God, will she ever stop? *Shut up*, I think.

"I thought you were ethereal once. As for love, I think intoxication is the word. I never gave my heart to anyone. Now you confirmed why. Anasztázia, go to your doctor, take your goddamn medicine, talk to Marina." And I hang up.

Our relationship has more melodrama than *Tosca*. What was supposed to be sweet is just as rocky as Krisztyna or Fiamma, more so.

She has a week off before *Cavalleria Rusticana* and *Pagliacci* rehearsals commence in Roma.

Leaving stage door after rehearsals the next day, the stage doorkeeper tries to tell me in broken English there is a friend here for me. I am puzzled.

Outside, he says. *Very pretty lady*.

So as I emerge into the chill, I see the Snow Queen standing against the white wonderland. She is wearing her white fur coat and it adds to the appearance of her as a mystical being. She looks so beautiful I forget for a few seconds how she hurt me. She throws herself into my arms and I look into her hypnotic blue eyes so clear but so sad. Anasztázia. So beautiful, so rare, so perfect.

Then I think, *Goddamn diva. Goddamn lying, cheating little tart. What the hell is she doing here?*

"Anasztázia. You came all this way?" My first thought is how sweet, the second how stupid and the third, *I can really, really do without this.*

She is dropping to her knees in the snow, asking me for the hundredth time to forgive her, hands clasped together in prayer. I think of the besotted Sicilian girl, Fiamma, in Budapest who clung to my knees one night much to the entertainment of everyone else.

Some of the other singers are exiting stage door. I do not need a scene so I haul the Snow Queen up.

I want to tell her to stop being so needy, she is the great diva. People should be begging her.

"Doesn't this tell you how I feel?" says Anasztázia. "Always my career was first until now. Two flights and in this freezing place just to tell you, my Natalija that I love you, I give you my life."

What a drama queen. You sure have a strange way of showing it, Anasztázia. Save it for the stage.

"Come on, we can warm in my apartment. You should have waited inside, you'll freeze here."

I take her arm and get us into a taxi. She is shivering despite her fur coat.

"It is so miserable and cold here, Natalija. Why are you in this frozen wasteland?" she asks looking at the white sky as we get out of the taxi. We walk five floors to the top of the building and she is still complaining, "And why is there no fucking elevator? What kind of country is this?"

I light a log fire. The glow is so beautiful and it warms the whole attic apartment.

"It's pretty in the snow, Anasztázia. I am a singer and I

was conquering the European stages. Now look at me. I am taking what I can get."

"Natalija, you can still be the best, but don't shut me out. You didn't answer my calls from New York," she says.

"Anasztázia, I told you not to call," I tell her. "I always thought love was just an emotion I could just act on stage. I am 28 and I never let myself feel. After this summer I realise why."

"Not even for her?" she says gazing at me so sadly.

"I did, but I buried it."

She looks away."What about me, Natalija?"

"I was intoxicated by you but I don't know if I can call that love."

"Natalija, I was lonely, I was unforgivable hurting you. But I always loved you more than anyone."

"Then why ask me for forgiveness?" I say. "Talk to God instead, Tosca, and go and give jewels to the Madonna's mantle. Maybe you love me now because you realise just what you lost."

I throw another log into the fire and feel her hurt expression fix on my back.

"I would give my life to take it all back," she says. "And I do talk to God. Every day."

"I hope you are talking to your shrink as well, Anasztázia. You need help for your self-harm. Did you bring your pills your doctor prescribed and have you even been taking them?"

She doesn't answer. I take her bag from the sofa and look through it. She lets me and sulks.

The pill bottles are in there and they have been opened. Some are gone anyway.

"They are not working," she says miserably. "Only the benzos give me a little calm. But it doesn't last and the anti-psychotics make me doped so I haven't taken those every day."

"The anti-depressants always take a few weeks to kick in,

Anasztázia and the drowsy effects will wear off. For God's sake, your illness is serious. Take it seriously."

"I am not crazy," she says. "Those are crazy people's pills."

"Do you really want to get sicker? Would you argue if you needed medicine for your throat or heart? You need these pills now. Maybe in time you won't but you sure as hell do now. If you don't take them now you could end up with a terrible depression, so debilitating you can't work. You are not crazy, you are ill, just like if you had a physical illness."

"Shut up, Natalija. I don't want to think."

She is maddening. Why people are so resistant to pills I don't know.

The fire crackles and the whole place is toasty. I get out some sushi I had ready. I start placing the sushi on some plates. I do have food in the cupboards now. I am not the girl I was. I might be cured of bulimia for good.

Anasztázia hangs up her coat. She takes off her blue dress in one sweep and looks at me seductively and climbs onto the bed running her fingers through her hair. She looks like a model posing in a studio.

"You don't have to do this, Anasztázia. You don't have to act the temptress. Why don't you sit by the fire and eat some sushi? You must be hungry after your journey. You are beautiful, you don't need to throw yourself around my bed in silk underwear."

"I am not some fragile little doll you put on your table. You always seem so afraid of touching me, Natalija," she says. "Maybe that's why I cheated on you." She gets mad and throws a pillow at my head.

"Don't you dare blame me!" I tell her angrily and slap the pillow back on the bed. "Don't you ever blame me for being such a little slut. Cover yourself up and eat some sushi." I throw her my robe and sit down next to the fire unable to look at her. She makes me mad.

"Natalija......"

"Put that robe on and eat," I say as I gaze at the fire. I am not giving in to her demands.

She stretches out an arm to take a plate and sits on the edge of the bed.

"What are these?" I say tapping some plasters on her left elbow and around her right knee.

"Nothing, forget those, cut myself shaving," she says, pulling the robe around them.

"Like last time when you cut yourself in the shower? Come on, Anasztázia. I know."

She eats the sushi and says she doesn't like it much. Too Russian. They eat a lot of it here.

She tells me to surrender as her soft hands caress me like silk, unzipping my dress and I shiver as they travel along my spine, tracing the scar on my back.

I don't want her touch but I am weak and my back is aching. I tell her to stop but I am tired and her delicate fingers feel good massaging my shoulders.

"It has healed so well, your terrible scar," she says.

"It must be all your salty tears," I say. I close my eyes as her body drowns me like molten honey. This is another problem with Anasztázia. I lose myself as if she casts a spell on me and I am powerless.

I wake up to her dark golden hair draped over the pillow, her face always calm in sleep it is hard to imagine she could get so hysterical. It is quiet because a ton of snow is muffling the world outside. I see it on the skylight. The snow blankets everything. I gently pull at one of the plasters on Anasztázia's left arm and it comes away. There is a slash which could only be done by a razor blade or knife. I pull off the other plaster and there are two more cuts.

They are self harm scars, I have seen them on girls before. I pull at the last plaster and I feel her long sooty eyelashes fluttering against my skin like silken butterflies.

She jolts awake and says, "What are you doing? What the

hell are you doing? Stop it!"

She cradles her arm and hides it from me, pulling the duvet around her.

"Take the plasters off your knee as well," I tell her. I reach for them and she pushes me away.

"I told you, cut myself shaving," she says looking at me, her eyes wide and afraid.

"You did this to yourself? Anasztázia, this is worse than the last time and you promised me you wouldn't do it," I say and grab her left leg and she curses me and tries to hit me away but I pull the plasters away. I see more cuts, not deep but still enough to make me so sad.

She turns away and says, "Are you happy now? Are you happy now you know the great Anasztázia is a total fuck up? That I am crazier than hell?"

"Anasztázia, I saw them when you were sleeping, after the doctor had given you an injection. I saw all your marks, new and old. You are beautiful, successful, so why would you do that to your perfect skin?" I ask her.

She covers herself with the duvet. "You were self-harming, vomiting all the time, damaging your voice. That's even more destructive. And you examine me for scars when I sleep? Why?"

"I had no choice, Anasztázia. Self-harm like this is way worse. Everyone in the theatre understands eating disorders but not this. When will it stop? You need to show your body for costume fittings. You will lose roles when they see all this."

"It's only a little bit. No one will know. That's why I did it in those places so no one will know." She buries her face in the duvet and is crying.

I say I will make us breakfast. This self harm, this is horrible. If she did it when she was much younger, I would understand but it is escalating. I am so worried about her.

"That is why I always prefer the dark, Natalija. I didn't want you to see the old scars in daylight."

"Just don't expect me to forgive you for cheating, because you do this, baby," I say.

"Please love me again. I just want you to love me," she says from deep inside the pillows.

I just want her to go back to Roma. I want her gone.

"Eat something and we can work on this," I say. "Come on, now." I haul her into a sitting position like a rag doll and place the breakfast in front of her with the pill bottles.

She looks with suspicion at the breakfast tray with beetroot juice. "That juice, it looks so dark, like blood, Natalija. It is very morbid. And this bread, what is this? It is black and unnatural. Why are you always drawn to the dark side?"

"Yes it is Russian black bread. Put some peanut butter on and I have coffee as you like it with this lovely creamy milk. You know they have blue cows here, Anasztázia? There is a rare breed of cow......."

She wants her sugary Italian breakfast. She doesn't care for the story of the rare breed of Latvian blue cow. She pushes the black bread around miserably, chokes on the beetroot juice and says it is horrible. She drinks the coffee with some biscuits and at least takes her pills.

I tell her her I am surprised she didn't like the beetroot juice since she likes to see her own blood.

She turns away from me angrily when I say this and doesn't say goodbye when I leave.

I have to get to rehearsals and when I get back Anasztázia is worse. She can't manage to light the log burning stove so sits under the duvet with the TV playing a trashy Italian game show.

"I moved to Roma for a reason and when I come here I realise why. The people are so cold, the place is cold. And I am Hungarian. I still hate the Russians. The regime I lived under where so many people died, my own relatives. I hate them, these Russians. So should you."

"Of course it is cold, Anasztázia. And half the people here

are Latvian, not Russian," I say.

I am younger, I don't have the animosity of the generation even 10 years older than me towards Russia.

I don't know how she has managed to travel the world. She seems so hopeless at life, as though the theatre world has stunted her development. It is not unusual, especially amongst ballerinas but I thought opera singers were more grounded.

Anasztázia is not Anasztázia. She is only the role she plays. Which is her greatest power on the stage but a terrible curse in her personal life. The real woman is volatile, needy and desperately insecure. She was still playing a role when we first met and I never saw the real her, until it was too late.

"It is warm in Roma, still end of summer. We should be there," she says.

"I am surprised given your alabaster complexion you don't like the snow," I tell her. "You look like you are suited to this climate. You don't even lie in the sun in Italia."

"Well I don't like it here," she says folding her arms and pouting. A reluctant Snow Queen.

She is leaving early tomorrow as she is rehearsing for Nedda in *Pagliacci* in Roma. It is an easy role in a short Opera which will only play over a week with *Cavalleria Rusticana. Am I coming? And why am I not in Cavalleria?* She knows I played Lola before.

"Anasztázia, I am working here, for God's sake. I will also take *Carmen* here next September. The schedules for Cav and Pag were drawn up before I joined Roma. Look I got you your Italian breakfast for tomorrow. I even got us some fresh pasta for tonight." I hand it to her.

She picks at the pasta, whines that it is way inferior to Roma pasta. Like everything here.

"Get in this bed, I've been alone all day, Natalija," she says.

"I told you, you don't have to play that temptress role. You don't need to......and stop with the lonely little me act. If you were so lonely why were you with Krisztyna in Roma?"

"Natalija. I'm serious. I am in Hell burning for my sins." She reaches out an arm and pulls me to her.

She has a fresh plaster on her arm, covering the soft skin from her wrist to her elbow underneath, as if that would fool anyone. There is a little dried blood on the cream coloured sheets.

I haul the duvet up.

"No, Anasztázia, no! You did it again, you cut yourself today? You are ruining yourself, ruining your body!" I feel ill. I can't even leave her alone when I go to work.

"I'm sorry." She closes her eyes. "I was hurting."

I pull the duvet away and grab at the big plaster she is hiding on her left arm.

"No, no please don't!" she is shouting hysterically. "Don't! Please don't, Natalija."

I stop because I do not want to see. I throw the duvet over her. I can't look at her injuries any more.

"You are sick, Anasztázia," I tell her. I wrap her in the duvet. "You are very sick. It is making me ill too, just dealing with you."

"I want passion," she says.

I tell her I will hold her later tonight and that's all, because it is a real passion killer, self-harm. She is too persistent so I go and sit in the chair by the fire.

"Anasztázia you are a world famous soprano. I could almost understand you harming yourself if you were not getting roles but nothing is going wrong," I say.

"Not on stage, Natalija. Only in my head once I am off it. And you left me," she tells me.

She scrunches up in the duvet, her sooty black lashes looking down, tears on her cheeks.

"Love me and the pain will go away," she says. "My

Carmen, please.....just love me."

"No, baby. No," I tell her. "Let me sit here. This is all too much. Please, I am tired, Anasztázia, I am so tired. Just stop it," I tell her. I wish she had never come to visit me.

"I saw photos of you as Carmen on your website, in an opera magazine. One day I will see you sing your famous seductive gypsy girl," she says. "Please show me Carmen tonight."

"No, Anasztázia, right now you need to let me be. I never felt less like Carmen in my life."

I stare at the snowy rooftops, the spires of the Old Town. There is a black cat statue, its tail on end and back arched on one turret. That is exactly how I feel. Tense, edgy, claws gripping the spire.

And the damaged beautiful Snow Queen lying in my bed.

Only it has turned into something sad and frightening.

"I am ashamed. I haven't harmed myself for over 20 years. Apart from the night in Roma I was hysterical, I swear to you," she pleads with me.

She is lying. She knows she is. She never really stopped doing it.

"Just hold me," she begs. "I need you!"

She is out of the bed and she lunges for me so I push her away. I don't push her hard, I just can't deal with her demands, but she stumbles backwards in the small studio space probably on account of the meds she is taking. She loses her balance and falls heavily, hitting her head on the glass coffee table with a horrible crack.

For a few awful seconds, there is silence and she lies on the floor not moving. I feel so sick and I think, 'My God, I killed her. We are in Latvia and I killed her. I will be in prison for life.' I am frozen in shock. She doesn't move from where she has sprawled, I don't move. Then she begins to cry, her hair falling over her face. I rush to hold her, kneeling next to her. "Baby, let me see. What did I do? Oh God, I am so sorry. I never meant to hurt you."

I lift her head up gently and there is a bad gash on the right side of her forehead, near her hairline. The blood runs from the deep cut and drips onto the white carpet.

"Oh, darling, that is a bad cut. Wait, I'll get some ice."

I open the freezer and I am so sick after what I did, I have to throw up in the kitchen sink before I do anything. I vomit and splash water on my face then trembling, I fill a cloth with ice and wrap it up. She is flopped over where I left her, crying softly with the blood running down her face. I sit next to her and press the towel to her head, wiping her face with tissues.

She lets me hold her up, I wrap my arm around her shoulders. I press the ice in the towel on her head. There is blood in her hair.

"Did you hurt your face, your teeth, your jaw?" I open her mouth, check everything but her forehead clearly took the full force of the fall.

"No. Just my head. My head hurts so bad, Natalija. It really hurts," she tells me.

"Are you feeling sick?"

"No," she says so quietly. "It just hurts, is it deep? Let me see in the mirror." She tries to get up but she is dizzy.

I hold the ice to her head and then look at the nasty cut on her head. "No, don't get up. But this is deep, baby. We need stitches. We are going to the hospital now, okay?"

I help her to get up slowly and into her blue dress and wrap a blanket around her as she holds the cloth to stop the bleeding. She tries to reach for her white fur coat.

"No, baby," I tell her. "Not your white coat. It might get blood on, we'll get straight into a taxi now." I stuff her pill bottles in my bag to show the hospital and carry her down all the flights of the stairs wrapped in the blanket. She doesn't weigh much. She goes quiet and is limp in my arms, her head resting on my chest. "It will be okay, baby. We are just going to check you out."

We sit in the taxi with me holding her, the towel pressed

on her forehead to try to stop the swelling.

She won't let go of me in the hospital. When the doctor examines her, he tells her that he will stitch her forehead. It won't show so much near the hairline and she will have a bad bruise but it will heal. There will be a scar but luckily it is not more serious.

Then he turns towards me, his face stony and his voice harsh and accusing. "I need to treat her alone. You can wait outside. Just don't let her sleep for five hours and if she is delirious or floppy or vomiting, bring her straight back. That is a nasty gash to the head. She is on medication so she will be very drowsy with the painkillers added to it. She needs a lot of care with her illness, not cruelty. It is not her fault she is sick." He stalks off.

He thinks I hit her because she is ill. That is even worse. I feel horrible.

It doesn't help she has plasters on her body which he noticed. The bruise is already coming up on her head. He also looked at my watch, seeing I am right-handed. If I slapped her face it would hit her left side, meaning she would fall and crack her head on the right. Except that didn't happen. It was an accident. I would never hurt her, I just didn't want to touch her tonight.

When she comes out she looks so sad and broken. She has a white dressing over the wound and she is holding a prescription for painkillers and a leaflet. We stop at the pharmacy on the way home. I tell her to wait in the taxi and I go in. I hand the pharmacist the prescription and look at the leaflet printed in three languages. It is a domestic violence helpline and I feel ill with guilt.

In the apartment, I sit on the bed with her in my arms. I make her drinks, tell her to keep telling me how she is. She rests her head on my chest, says very little and all I can do is stroke her hair, say it was my fault.

"No," she says quietly. "No, never. I was out of control,

Natalija. It was scary. I was crazy and you only pushed me away because I was too much. I scared myself with how I was. It was an accident. I tripped over that carpet, it's these meds, they mess up my balance. You never would hurt me, I know that."

She looks up at me. All I do is hurt people and bring bad luck. I am a curse. I feel like a bad luck charm.

"That fall could have killed you, Anasztázia or you could have damaged your teeth, your jaw. Your beautiful face is scarred, I feel so terrible."

She looks at me and takes my hand. The bruise is coming up purple underneath the white dressing.

"No," she says. "It was an accident. I was having a meltdown. It wasn't fair on you. And don't worry, my jaw is fine. I only hit my forehead. The doctor checked everything for me."

"What about the rehearsals? You only have five days and you can't fly like that, Anasztázia."

"I will see how I am in a few days. If I miss the first week it is okay. I know the role inside out."

I know that Anasztázia is very sick. But it would destroy my career to care for her. She also needs time out; she can't keep working like this when she is so ill. The opera houses she works for think she is calm and immensely talented. No one knows, apart from her doctor how sick she is.

That night I am too afraid to sleep despite it being hours after the injury and she is not dizzy, or nauseous. I light the candles next to the bed and I watch her sleep, the warm glow casting a flickering light over her sad face. The world suddenly seems so cold and wintry.

The next morning Anasztázia wakes up and says her head hurts like crazy. She goes to look in the bathroom mirror and I try to stop her but she has to go to the bathroom anyway. I hear her cry out. She comes back to the bed in a panic. "Natalija, I forgot for a minute what happened. The bruising is purple and blue and this dressing is covering the wound, I need to see it. I need to see how bad it is. Please." She starts trying to remove the dressing from her head.

"No, Anasztázia. It needs to stay on. The stitches will dissolve but please, keep that dressing on.

It will look bad today. Listen to the doctor and wait. The bruising will fade in a couple of weeks, please don't worry." I help her to lie down again.

"My face is a mess," she says crying. "I am ruined. I ruined everything. I always ruin everything."

I tell her, *It is okay, it will be okay. In a few weeks it will all be okay. It was a bad fall.*

Actually I am not sure anything will be okay. It is all a fucking mess; the head injury is only a part of it. I open her pills and make her take the morning meds as she is so distraught. It will calm her down.

I will make sure she is taking these pills twice a day.

I give her a painkiller and bring the tray of sweet breakfast pastries, freshly squeezed juice and coffee. I thought the Italian breakfast would cheer her up. She eats it silently, as if I broke her heart not split her head open last night.

She looks like a domestic violence victim. I look at the leaflet next to the bed and the pill packet. "That doctor thinks I beat you, doesn't he?"

"Yes," she says sorrowfully. "He never believed me. He told me to seek help. He said it exists everywhere. Gender is irrelevant. He said you hit me because I am sick."

"Promise you will stay in bed? You promise to call an ambulance and go straight back to hospital if you feel ill or have any self-harm thoughts? And please don't take off the dressing."

"I promise," she says looking at me with those beautiful eyes. She is already calmer after her medicine. And she thinks she doesn't need it? Her eyes are closing, that is good.

"I will call you in the break, okay?" I leave the TV and fire on for her and go out of the door quietly.

My bag rattles and clanks as I go downstairs. I have removed everything sharp when she was in the bathroom, even forks. She has only got spoons and butter knives. I don't know what to do with all this. I can't be walking around with a bag of deadly sharp kitchen blades. Outside the apartment block is a big snowdrift. I check no one is looking and take the plastic bag and stuff it deep into the snow.

Anasztázia misses the first week of rehearsals for *Cavalleria Rusticana* and *Pagliacci,* and calls them to say she had a head injury falling in her apartment on the marble floor and she will be back for the second week of rehearsals. The ten days she is in Latvia she is calmer. She is too broken and she is taking her pills. I go to rehearsals and come back to see her and she is calm and seems so much better. I almost think we can work things out as she is so undemanding.

She asks me what happened to all the knives. There was nothing to cut her bread, only butter knives. She looked everywhere.

I tell her why but not where they are. She probably thinks I took them to the theatre.

"Oh," she says. "Oh, Natalija." She looks at me so sadly.

But the third day she is alone longer as I return late. I have brought her some blue balloons; her favourite colour. She is happy to see me, the fire going and the TV on but next to the bed is a cigarette lighter, the one I use to light candles.

"Show me your arms," I ask her.

She shakes her head and won't look at me.

"Show me!" I shout. She slowly pulls her arms out from under the covers and there are a few small burns on the inside of each forearm.

"I'm sorry, I'm sorry," she keeps saying.

Without a word I pick up the lighter and the matches from the kitchen drawer.

"Do I have to take the cheese grater too? One more time, Anasztázia, and I take you back to the hospital and you can stay there until you are well enough to fly."

"You think I am crazy," she says so sadly.

"Sick is the word. Your doctor told me you needed those pills in Roma. You should not be travelling out of Italia even if it means cutting down on roles. And not crazy; you are very sick, more than you realise."

I ask her seriously that night can she manage, or should she be in hospital.

"No way, no way do I go to a Russian psychiatric ward, it will be horrendous," she says shocked.

"Are you going to be safe?" I ask her.

"Please just love me, Natalija, please," she says.

So I hold her and watch her sooty eyelashes gently close and I tell her that she is my fairy-tale princess, that she is forever.

I don't actually believe a word I am saying, but it calms her and she falls asleep. I am telling her about my father who was in and out of the psychiatric ward when I was a kid. He had bipolar type one. I remember a terrible August night he was psychotic; drawing on the walls with black magic marker, shouting, dumping cereal all over the kitchen floor. I was four or five years old, but I remember Lilla crying.

I remember taking him a blue balloon in hospital.

He was always manic in the summer. Then he slid into depression. He thought he didn't need pills.

Anasztázia is asleep. I am telling the story to myself.

The bruising is still obvious the day she leaves. I ask what she will say to everyone in Opera.

"That I slipped in my apartment on the marble floor. They all think I am in Roma. I can hide it with my hair."

"Okay, but I am worried...." I say. "Can you talk to Marina?"

As her taxi is arriving for the airport, she clings to me. "Please leave with me. Cancel your performances here. I need you. Please."

"Anasztázia. You can't expect me to walk out on a company. You wouldn't do it so don't expect me to and all this is too much for me. You need to get help, I can't deal with you like this."

"Oh, Natalija. What happened to us after we started so well?" She says.

What did happen to the magical beginning?

Now it has a dreamlike quality as I look back on the first few days, as I was on strong painkillers as well which heightened the unreality of it all. I had just been resurrected and this beautiful ice queen floated along the stage in a trail of blue silk after bringing the house down with her performance as Lucia di Lammermoor.

Only she is a real life Lucia di Lammermoor.

Her repertoire does not include happy endings. I sometimes think that no sane person would do what we do despite our immense talent, our powerful voices reaching for the heavens. She has died in every performance and now she will die as Nedda in *Pagliacci,* ironically stabbed to death for being an adulteress. I don't say this, no need to be cruel.

She says, "I am going now but I will wait for you to come back."

"I can't just forgive, don't you understand? And now you have this terrible habit which seems to be escalating. Get help now Anasztázia," I tell her. "This is destroying you. I will be back in just over two weeks."

"Natalija, please listen. I came all this way," she says. "Please come back with me."

"Anasztázia, you say I make you lonely, maybe I can't make you happy," I smooth her hair.

"Don't say that! I will never give up on you, Natalija."

"Anasztázia, promise to keep taking those pills?"

"Promise to forgive me then, Natalija." She traces my face with her hand. "Promise me?"

I say, *I thought I found an angel. I cannot promise.*

Maybe I should have lied. Saved her a sliver of hope as she runs down the stairs, hurt.

She said to live without love is to live in a world without colour. But her love burns with a murderous intensity like a greedy blazing fire.

She sends me a text every morning.

> *I will wait forever for you, Natalija. I am seeing the doctor, I am taking the tablets every day. I am sorting everything out for you. Your Anasztázia.*

She should be getting help for her, not for me. I never got treatment for bulimia for anyone else but me and my voice. It was all for me. And here is Anasztázia lighting candles all over Europe and praying to the Madonna for forgiveness.

CARMEN

November rains a lot that year. The year I am resurrected. I cry in the rain. Mainly I am crying because I think I have lost my wonderful voice which is my whole reason to exist.

Only a few tears are for her.

Marina has called me from Roma and screamed at me.

She thinks I hit Anasztázia. Everyone in the company thinks a man beat her. That is all everyone is talking about in the Opera House.

Who is he? The great Anasztázia being bashed around. How can she put up with it? Who is she dating; she is so secretive?

She says she fell on a marble floor in her home. Only Marina can put a face to the hurt. Every time she hears the Opera gossip.

I try to tell Marina the truth, that Anasztázia came to Latvia and she fell and hit her head.

"You are a nasty little bitch, Natalija!" she says. "You take it out on that tiny, fragile girl! She has that scar on her head which won't fade. She is depressed and you attack her! She has to hide it with so much make-up for her performances. You want to fight, lady? Because I will take you on! I wish you had stayed in Hungary in your dark world and never come to Roma! I feel responsible as I reassured her you were lovely when you are just like that bitch, Krisztyna. Is there something wrong with the Hungarians? Are you all so cruel?"

"Marina, why don't you believe me? Marina, listen, Anasztázia desperately needs help. I told you when you visited that night. I said to please talk to her......"

She has already ended the call. I send her a text to please help her; she needs medical help.

Marina doesn't send an angry reply back so she at least might listen to me.

I am so sad because in 6 months it has all turned into

such a nightmare. My insides are hurting because I am having to push myself with rehearsing and performances when I am still not ready. When my run in Riga finishes, the snow has melted and it is grey and I have a few days back in Roma in the sun. Marina is performing in Germany, thank God. She would hit me, I don't doubt that.

I even tried to call Anasztázia's parents when she left Latvia. I found their number in southern Hungary in her address book. I tell them, *I am a friend, their daughter had an accident and cut her head badly. She is also sick with depression, she is in Roma alone, she wants them to visit and I am not happy with her being alone. She needs them. She misses them.*

At first I thought her mother was listening until she said, *And why are you so concerned you call from Latvia?*

I am her friend. I care about her, she would love you to visit. I rent a room in her apartment when I perform in Roma....

She is not my daughter. I didn't raise her to be unnatural. And you are not just her friend, I know.

I never see my granddaughter because my daughter abandoned her own family. Please do not call here again. Leave us to grieve our loss in peace.

I tell her, *She is beautiful and famous and she needs you. How can you reject her? She is not dead, you don't need to grieve. Please visit her........*

But she has already ended the call.

What a bitch of a mother. If you had a beautiful world famous daughter, would it honestly matter who she dated? My mother would have given anything to have had more time on Earth with me. How can these awful parents honestly say she is more or less dead to them? It burns right through me as I want my mother right there and then, more than anything.

Anasztázia would be angry with me for calling but I was

trying to help. I am concerned she is alone in Roma.

When I arrive at Anasztázia's apartment from Latvia, thinking she is in Roma, I am hoping we can spend a few days trying to sort out her health. She is not there and I know she has nothing on at the Opera House. Her suitcase is gone. Where the hell is she? She would have said if she had a concert abroad? Her Opera website doesn't list anything for this week. She is down for some concerts in a couple of weeks. I was ready to tell her I can learn to forgive, I will help her with her self-harm issues. I will take care of her as much as I can. If I have to sacrifice a few gigs, so what. Right now my voice is weak and I am thinking of dropping out of Vienna, because I am not up to singing Mercédès and I am terrified of returning to the *Carmen* stage. I could say I had tonsillitis. I could then help Anasztázia. I have more or less made my mind up; I will drop the run, as long as she agrees.

Who am I to judge a self-harmer after what I did to my body?

I was lying on the floor vomiting blood in my father's house, for God's sake.

I had so many prescriptions for antibiotics for my damaged throat from the company doctor in Hungary, I lost count.

My heart could have stopped due to low potassium levels and I collapsed during rehearsals with chest pains. They told me I could have had heart failure in hospital.

I could have killed myself before someone else tried to.

So I am dolled up in a red dress, looking as good as I can and holding some pretty orange flowers.

Only she is not there. Worried she has gone off somewhere in a crazy emotional state, I go downstairs and ask the doorman.

He tells me that she has gone to Paris. *Didn't she tell me?*

I am angry now. She is with someone else already. She

didn't waste time.

Who is she seeing in romantic Paris? I could call her but pride stops me. I go back up in the elevator cursing. I take off the dress and put the orange flowers in the kitchen. Her pills are gone and they are not in the bathroom so she is still taking her medicine.

So I just go to Vienna. I don't know if I will ever have the voice to sing Carmen again, even if I get over this fear. I am playing Mercédès, which is one of my earliest Opera roles when I was so hungry for the big time. In Vienna it rains every single lonely day. I am too afraid to be hungry for the big time, afraid of this fated Opera now. My voice is lousy.

The rehearsals don't betray my weak voice so much, because we are in small rooms and not on the stage. I don't like anyone in the company or dislike them either. I am more focussed on trying to do my best, and too tired to do anything but sleep at the end of the day.

I am paranoid everyone is talking about me, saying how useless I am so I avoid the rest of the cast, in breaks and after rehearsals. If I see a group of them in the café on a break, I sit at the other tables. They then look at me and talk about me amongst themselves. Which makes me more paranoid. I am convinced I hear 'stuck up diva', 'lousy voice' and 'why the hell is she in this Opera?'

I probably don't hear this; they are just wondering why I am not friendly.

I hate Vienna and I hate it even more that November. If Anasztázia hated Latvia, I hate Vienna which was once home to my expensive eating disorders clinic. Everything that could go wrong does. The musical director even asks me why I am in the show as I am clearly not up to standard and he knows about my injury. He could have been nicer about it, but he just says I am dragging his production down. If it was down to him, I would be out. I am too broken to argue. I am definitely not the girl I was. The old Natalija would have told him to go to Hell even if it meant losing the role. At least I would have my dignity intact.

Instead I just go back to my inferior digs and cry, wishing I was in Anasztázia's beautiful place and not in hateful Vienna. Wishing I was in Roma where it is still warm, sitting on the balcony.

Even alone. Anywhere but here.

I also fall over some scenery the day before the dress rehearsal as some idiot turns the main lights out without warning. I hurt my wrist so it has to be bandaged up under my costume as it is sprained painfully. The fire alarm goes off half an hour before the opening night which sends us out into the cold street shivering, until it is discovered to be a false alarm and we start the show late. *Carmen* has turned into my unlucky Opera. I am convinced that it is fated, just like some actors refuse to have anything to do with *Macbeth*, even referring to it as 'The Scottish Play' as though the mention of the name will bring the chandelier down.

To crown the disastrous *Carmen,* one of the chorus girls gets bacterial meningitis at the end of rehearsals. We are all neurotic after this. She collapses, burning with fever and gets carted off to hospital and nearly dies. The fear is in my heart. What if I catch meningitis and die again?

I carry around antibacterial gel and use it so much my hands are raw. I swill my mouth in salt water, drink honey and lemon every night and take vitamin supplements.

I still get the texts every day from Anasztázia without fail.

She is waiting, she is waiting forever. She loves me.

I never respond. Not after her doorman told me about Paris. I can't face her lying again. Maybe she didn't realise I would go back to Roma for a few days in between gigs. She is a devious cheat after all.

The first time we are on for our dress rehearsal the stage

manager is showing me the props table and when I see the glint of the knife, I feel sick. The table sways and I feel dizzy. She puts the knife in my hand. It is blunter than the butter knives I left for Anasztázia in Riga.

"It is totally blunt," she says. "Are you going to be okay? You managed the rehearsals and were fine. I have every faith in you, Natalija. I know the musical director is not happy but he is very perfectionist and he has to understand the terrible injuries you had. You are struggling but most of the company know this and are very understanding. Can you manage the rest of the run without thinking of your last *Carmen?*"

"Yes, but this is so different. Rehearsals are so different to living the Opera and thinking about the ending...." I say.

"Johann is in charge of props and he will sit here every night of the run when that knife is given to Don José. I will make sure of it, Natalija. You will not even be near the stage when Carmen is stabbed. You won't see it. I promise. Wait in your dressing room if you want before the curtain call."

I am still cold with fear. There is no way I can even think about Don José stabbing Carmen. The only person to touch my back in that place has been Anasztázia. If anyone rests their hand on my back by mistake, I move instantly. I hate anyone to touch me there.

La Scala have been so understanding about this and Roma Opera and Napoli. They don't know about my bulimia but the stage death, or near death, horrified all of them. They held my schedules open and told me I could take months off. As long as I needed. But I didn't. They were prepared to wait until September or longer.

I just could do without being in Vienna. I hate the German language. I should not be somewhere unsympathetic with a hateful musical director, feeling lousy. I should be in Italia.

After the dress rehearsal I cry an ocean of tears in my

dressing room which is shared with the Austrian girl playing Frasquita. She is kind and keeps telling me I was fine, don't cry but I cannot stop. I cry as I was so afraid and I cry because my voice was lousy. She gives me chocolate but the tears don't stop. She is helpless as to what to do.

I tremble with fear when I know Don José plunged the knife into Carmen. I am waiting in my dressing room and not outside it even though I should be ready for our curtain call in the wings. I cover my ears when I hear the finale of the toreadors in the bullring and the applause. I can't drown out the backstage show relay in the dressing room so I put my coat over my head. I want to scream and I don't want anyone to see me like this.

I have to run out of the dressing room after the applause to get to the stage on time and I feel like I will pass out.

I need to call Anasztázia so badly it hurts after this first show. I forget about Paris and her cheating heart. I call her at midnight. She answers and she sounds sleepy, as though I woke her up.

"I'm so sorry it's late. I was so scared," I say. "I need to talk...."

"Natalija. I am so happy to hear your voice but I am in Paris. I was sleeping. I will talk tomorrow. Please, darling soon we will see each other but I am so exhausted now...." I hear a man's voice asking her something. I picture him leaning over her in the bed. She is wearing nothing but a red silk nightdress.

Lying bitch. Not only is she pretending to grieve over me, she is with a man. She, the Anasztázia who doesn't like the men, according to Marina. Not only is she cheating with women but men too. This is too much. I cannot deal with this little diva any longer. I want her out of my life.

"Damn you, enjoy romantic Paris with your man! What is this? Extending your operatic repertoire?" I hang up.

God, why did I fall in love with such a tart? I am so stupid and naive.

She texts me:

I am singing Marguerite in Faust. It is not romantic. Dear Natalija, I haven't smiled since I saw you. The man, he is an old friend from the Opera in Paris. He lives with his partner here. I stay in their apartment. You know I am never with men. I promise I will call tomorrow.

Damn her, what happened to the concerts in Roma?

I check her website. Sure enough, nothing else is listed except her role in December as Mimì in London for *La bohème*.

She calls me the next morning. She is performing in *Faust*. She had missed a week of rehearsals so she is really stressed but she has played Marguerite before in Paris, so when someone became ill, she was asked to step in.

"Please, Natalija," she says. "I should have called you to tell you but I knew you wouldn't believe me."

"I heard him, your lover asking who was on the phone. I heard him, you liar! I arrived at the apartment in Roma with flowers for you and your doorman told me you had gone to Paris."

"Natalija. I am staying at a friend's apartment. A male friend and his partner from Opera," she says. "I told you, I never, ever wanted a man in my life."

"You were married once so why was this mystery man in your bed?" I say.

"You know why I married and I hated every minute. And this friend in Paris wasn't in my bed. I fell asleep on their sofa, so tired after rehearsals and didn't hear my phone ringing. He was still awake and was worried it was late and someone calls me. He brought me the phone," she says.

"Damn you, Anasztázia! I was so worried about you since Riga. So worried about your head injury and your self harming. Marina thinks I beat you as the whole company is talking about your injuries! I am in *Carmen,* breaking my heart in miserable Vienna, scared to death of the stabbing scene, playing Mercédès badly.............."

"Natalija, please I told you ...."

"My voice is ruined. I was going to cancel this *Carmen* and I wish I had. I was going to cancel it and look after you. And you weren't even in the apartment. I was all set to do it, Anasztázia," I say. I am crying angry tears now for being such an idiot.

"Natalija. Get a flight tomorrow or today if you can. When are you on stage next?"

"Tomorrow and then not until Sunday. Today is Wednesday, is it? I can't even remember any more. It will have to be a Friday flight."

"I am performing again on Friday. Please come. It would mean the world. Come to see me in *Faust*. You can still get back to Vienna on Sunday morning."

I agree but I am not convinced about this man. Maybe it is better I see for myself.

Cheating with some hot female singer would still hurt, but I could almost forgive that. She didn't know if I would forgive her or when she would see me after Latvia.

On reflection I wish I had never said about cheating with some hot female. It turns out she is doing just that.

But as mad as I am with her, it breaks my heart that she hurts herself. How is she hiding it all with dressing rooms, costume fittings? After her head injury, most of Roma Opera think she has a violent partner and the plasters are covering bruises or marks someone else inflicted.

One day someone will work it all out. They will all hate me, thinking I beat her. She will be the innocent victim, I will be the violent tart who corrupted their Anasztázia. And my career will be tarnished, just like Krisztyna's was in Hungary. I will have to leave Roma Opera.

Everyone seemed to accept in all the theatres I worked in

that tarting around in dressing rooms, one-nighters, casual flings are inevitable. Gender is not so important.

But if they think we are together in Roma, it will become an issue.

I go online and see the reviews of *Faust* with a photo of Anasztázia, kneeling before the altar, gazing heavenwards with hands clasped in prayer, Méphistophélès laughing behind her. I read about all the praise for the Hungarian soprano who sang Marguerite with such soul-splitting intensity and emotion. '*Every last note quivered with tangible pain.....*' one review says.

'*She took the acting to the highest realms possible with her girlish fragility and innocence. Marguerite could not have been more believable or more haunting. She sings of true heartbreak with her sensational soprano voice.*'

I fly to Paris on Friday and I have a ticket to return Sunday morning to Vienna. I am risking it to get back for Sunday even taking an early flight. I shouldn't take time out but I do know *Carmen* inside out. I am supposed to be at a short run-through at the Opera House on Saturday but I will call in sick. Who cares if they fire me. I could sing every role in the Opera in my sleep. Let's face it; I don't need studying, I need a new voice. And if the worst happens and there is an air traffic control strike in France on Sunday, what the hell, everything has been a disaster about this *Carmen* run.

Do I really care if they kicked me off the show?

Maybe Anasztázia is trying to 'straighten out'; literally. Maybe she thinks dating men is a good career move. I cared for her in Latvia for nearly two weeks after she was hurt. I put myself out for this selfish diva. Luckily I wasn't in a major role and having to nurse her, care for her because of her accident. I still feel responsible because I pushed her. But I wonder would she do the same for me if I was sick. I can't answer that because I truly do not know. Her version of 'caring' for me would be me trailing around Europe with her to wherever she performed, she definitely would not cancel work for any reason even her own health. Which is why she has got to the place she is in. She is ruthlessly ambitious and would sooner risk her health for a role.

PARIS

I turn up at the Opera House in Paris and collect my ticket. I don't want to see Anasztázia before the show even though she asked me to. I just leave a big box of chocolates for her at stage door, tell them to make sure she gets them pre-show and text her to say I am running late.

I watch the show from the best box in the house. She is so haunting as Marguerite with her pain and those notes so beautiful and floating, I feel I could pluck them from the ceiling or more like the Heavens where they are drifting to.

But I am jealous. I am sitting there and seeing her in love with Faust and thinking, 'I bet she likes him too.' Her childish romantic delight at finding jewels is so believable. She sings as though she loves him. She kisses him coquettishly, declares her love for him. When she rolls on a bed with him, I want to leap out of the box and punch Faust in the face. I never had these feelings before, but then I never really watched anyone other than Krisztyna and her roles were more dramatic; Tosca, Turandot, Butterfly. There is something just a little too real about Gounod's delicate Marguerite especially as Anasztázia is so girl-like herself.

Despite the wonderful production, I am agitated.

I go to stage door post-show and tell them who I am. They are not expecting me, she forgot to tell them, damn her. I have never performed here so I can't just go up to see her. I show them my ID from Roma Opera and say my friend is expecting me, please can they tell her I am here. So one security man heads off and returns and says she will come out in ten minutes. This is a first. Usually she would tell them to take me to her immediately. I am convinced she is with Faust in her dressing room. The tenor, Robert in the cast list, is French and very handsome. This makes me worse. If he was like the Otello she played opposite in Bregenz, the fat sweaty eater of hot dogs, I could deal with it but to see her openly flirting on stage is new to me. I see

Robert leave the building and say good night to people round stage door and he has a sexual glow. A 'just been in someone's dressing room glow'. He doesn't notice me standing sullenly in the corner by the door. A dark angel.

Just as well for him.

I go outside. It is cold but I need to get some air. I sit on the steps brooding.

A man approaches me from the direction of the main entrance. "Weren't you on stage just now? You were terrific. Can I get your autograph?"

I sign his programme without a word and hand it back. He thanks me profusely and wanders off into the night.

Who the hell did he think he was watching? Was he staring at the surtitles all night like some moon-brain? I look nothing like anyone on the cast list. No one is dark and Marguerite is the only female lead. I get up and pace around to keep warm as the orchestra exit the building and some of the stage crew come out for a smoke.

Damn Anasztázia.

Anasztázia exits 15 minutes later and calls out to me. I am sulking on the steps. That was more like a 25 minute wait, long enough for some rolling around on her dressing room sofa.

"Natalija!" she cries out and she is delighted to see me. She is fresh faced and glowing beautifully. Even her pale complexion has a rosy glow around her cheeks which is more than just blusher. Is she glowing from him? This Faust? Or Robert as he is in real life?

She takes my hands and tries to embrace me but I am cold. She notices and holds me, studying my face sadly.

"Natalija, it is wonderful you are here, but why are you so sad and quiet? Did something happen? Is it *Carmen*?" She is concerned.

"I've been waiting nearly half an hour for you and I am cold. Why didn't you let stage door take me straight in? What the hell were you doing in there for so long?"

She follows me down the steps. "Natalija, I am sorry. I was so hot after giving everything in the show and I wanted to freshen up, change and look my best for my girl. I am overjoyed to see you, sorry I kept you waiting so long. I did it for you. What did I do, darling?"

"You and Faust! Acting a little bit too believable, maybe!"

"Natalija," she says quietly. "Please, I don't like men. I was acting, like you do, like we all do. And now you can come to Vincent and Yves' apartment with me. I really wanted to look perfect for you, reapply my make-up, put on my dress and perfume."

She does look like she made an effort and has slipped on a pretty purple lace dress.

Her scar is fading as I gently look at it under her loose hair.

"It's healing, Natalija, don't worry," she smiles. She is holding my chocolate box tightly to her chest. She is so pretty it is hard to stay angry with her.

"Marina thinks I beat you. Everyone thinks you have a violent partner. Only Marina thinks it is me. Do you know how terrible that makes me feel?" I say.

"I will talk to her. She only saw me for a few minutes in Roma. I promise I will tell her the truth," she says taking my arm. "Are you hungry? We can go home and eat something. I am so sorry I wasn't in Roma to see you for those few days you were back. I was longing to see you but I got called here. I should have left a note. I am sorry, but I really didn't think you wanted to see me after I was so crazy in Latvia. I was ashamed, Natalija."

"I was hoping to see you, Anasztázia. And you should have told me. I was all ready to give up Vienna for you, to look after you."

"That is so caring, so caring, Natalija. I never thought..." She smiles beautifully.

Just as I soften and help her into her coat and think I

overreacted about her tarting around in Paris, how it was clearly due to *Carmen* stress, an Italian beauty exits stage door. Her burgundy dress accentuates her curves and she has high-heeled shoes the same colour. I stop to look at her as she throws her long dark hair over one shoulder to light a cigarette. She sees us and smiles. She is totally a Krisztyna type. I can't help staring.

She saunters straight over to Anasztázia and looking directly at me, wraps an arm around Anasztázia and asks her is she coming to eat? "Please, darling, we are all so hungry. Bring your hot little friend here too, this pretty dark angel......and I am really hungry for....."

Anasztázia stiffens and says, "Sara, I can't. This 'dark angel' is Natalija. My girl from Roma."

Sara drops her arm from Anasztázia's shoulders without any shame and with one hand grasping my waist, kisses me on both cheeks. Her perfume in her warm hair reminds me of Krisztyna's heavy scent. She looks like a glamorous news anchor. She wasn't in the Opera so she must be performing in something else and has come to watch Anasztázia for obvious reasons.

"Natalija... well, I have heard a lot about you. All good." She puts her head on one side and eyes me up. Prime meat. I feel so cheap. I do not like this woman one bit.

She turns to Anasztázia and whispers in her ear. Anasztázia doesn't smile as she can see my mood and it isn't good.

"I will leave you two to enjoy the night. Have fun. See you soon, beautiful."

She slaps Anasztázia lightly on the ass, gives me a final lusty pout and laughs as she heads back to stage door, shimmering along carelessly and blowing her cigarette smoke into the night.

"Natalija...."

"Save it, baby. I do not want to hear you lie. For an actress, you do it so badly. Must be your guilty conscience." I open the door of a waiting taxi and climb in. Anasztázia gets in, gives the driver the address and looks at me with hurt.

I haven't even hugged her. She reaches for my hand. "That was my stage manager. She's on the desk. She's very good. She's Spanish and very tactile."

"Yes, I could see that, Anasztázia. I could see that when she hung around your neck and slapped your ass. I don't doubt she is very good. I presume she is not so tactile with the rest of the cast. Stage manager? Tell me, does she wear that tight dress and killer heels on stage? Have you already....."

"No, she doesn't. She wears theatre blacks on stage, but she likes to look good outside work. And Natalija, I don't want to lie. I was so lonely.....I didn't know if you wanted me at all after Riga...Sara was there for me. I told her I was missing you so much, my heart was sad."

"For God's sake, your heart was sad! That is a novel approach. You are such a little tart!"

The taxi driver looks in the rear-view mirror with surprise.

He can't understand Hungarian but I am shouting a lot.

"I was lonely. It means nothing, I missed you. Please understand that I didn't think you'd be here, you never called or answered my texts. I was so crazy last time I saw you, I was ashamed. The medicine, it is working better now."

I look out of the window. I should have known she couldn't keep this up. Well the medicine is working at least. Too bad there isn't one for tarts.

I imagine her looking at Sara with those huge innocent blue eyes saying she is missing her girl, she is very lonely in Paris. Sara looks like a predator of the highest order. More even than Krisztyna. God, Anasztázia is so naive. Or more like her little girl act is just that; an act to get people to want her.

I feel her hurt gaze on me and she says nothing until we

are nearly at the apartment.

"You came here not to see me but to see if I lied," she says. "You didn't want to see me, just to see if I was cheating."

"No Anasztázia, I really did want to see you. I wanted to see you in Roma. I dressed up and brought you orange flowers, was even going to cancel *Carmen* to take care of you," I say. "And here you are tarting away, baby. That angelic little body slides into a lot of beds and dressing rooms."

"That hurts. I came to Latvia because I loved you. And as for being with Faust, that is so crazy. But you seriously were going to drop *Carmen* because of me, to stay in Roma and look after me?" she asks. "Natalija, you would have done that?"

"Yes but I am so glad I didn't sacrifice anything for you now, however shit my voice is. You are happy with Sara. She looks like she seduces everyone in sight. Anyway you are the crazy one and a lying little cheat. I was willing to overlook all that just to help you get well."

"Wouldn't you have done the same, Natalija? I was dying of loneliness. And you cheated on Krisztyna with that Sicilian girl, Fiamma. You also cheated on Fiamma with Krisztyna. So don't judge me as Krisztyna was really hurt and you broke Fiamma. She slashed her own wrists! She left Opera because of you! You did your fair share of cheating, Natalija! And I am not crazy!"

I think back to the situation and I was a bit of a bitch. I hurt them both because I just didn't care.

"I guess Krisztyna told you all this because I sure as hell didn't," I say.

Anasztázia turns away from me, sulky and silent. She is angry over the crazy comment.

I shouldn't have said that. I would never have thought of my father as crazy. He was sick.

My mother was too. Maybe I will be; two parents with

bipolar. Maybe I will end up really crazy.

It shuts me up. I reflect more and more and I am just as bad. I will end up on a funny farm.

I am poison. I am a love cheat too. Madness is waiting in the distance for me too. I am sure of it.

I begin to feel lousy. I look at the glistening lights of Paris flying by and it reminds me of Budapest, these golden lights.

Vincent and Yves, her gay friends who work in the costume department of the Opera are kind and sweet. I am not friendly. They are generous and hospitable. Things are not right between me and Anasztázia. We lie in bed after eating some light snack. As the show is long it is midnight before we arrive home. We are unable to sleep and I feel so totally alone next to her. She still cannot believe I came here and accused her of being with someone she performed with. She says if I was performing with Don José she would never think I was with him in reality.

"You dated men, I have more reason to be jealous but I am not, Natalija. It is a role, and the more believable, the better we are. It is our job to act as well as sing or you might as well be watching a concert."

"I didn't care about the men I dated, but you already went with this tarty little Spanish piece," I say.

She sighs. "You are right. You saw Sara and I know that made you upset and I am sorry. I see why you would be mad."

Then she goes quiet.

"Anasztázia, I turned up in Roma really wanting to see you, only the apartment was empty. I cared for you in Latvia, even when I was so tired rehearsing. I was ready to give up a role in *Carmen* to try to get you well. You didn't push me away with how you behaved in Latvia, baby. You might have pushed others away, but I am not most people. It is your lying and cheating that I can't deal with."

She sighs and stares at the ceiling and looks so miserable.

I think, *Why are we together? Have we crashed and burned? Because it feels like the end.*

I cannot deal with this. Both of us opera singers, stressed and our volcanic emotions are exhausting.

For the first time I want to throw up all my emotions, just like the old me. I want to stuff my face with all the rich food in Vincent's fridge; fatty French cheese and foie gras and white bread and throw up because I can't bear feeling anything right now. I sit up in bed. "I need to throw up," I say swinging my legs out of the bed.

"Darling, are you feeling ill?" she asks concerned. "You didn't eat much this evening, are you sick?"

"No, I need to stuff my face and throw up because I can't deal with my emotions. I have done it since I was 14," I say. "I'm going to the fridge and then the bathroom and you can sleep while I just get on with it. Call your hot stage manager if you want but I am sorting out my head in the kitchen, then the bathroom."

She holds me and says she will not let me. She will not let me ruin my voice because I can't deal with my emotions.

"Please let me," I say. "It won't take long. You sleep and I will be quiet. I am an expert at this. You cut your feelings out of you. Well I throw them up."

She pushes me back into bed.

"NO! You do it once, you will do it again. I cannot watch you end your career hanging over a toilet bowl! I mean this Natalija. Listen to me; I am having help for my self-harm, I am taking meds. I have seen a shrink here in Paris, so don't you dare go to that fridge tonight!"

She wraps herself around me. I would have to drag her along the floor to reach the fridge. I give up trying and pull at a bandage on her wrist. So much for having help over her self-harm.

"Please don't," she says. "I fell leaving the stage the other day."

"Anasztázia. You cut yourself again, I know you did."

I am losing it, I am losing my mind too. Carmen, Vienna and now all this.

"I would never have gone with Sara if I thought you would come here. I haven't cut myself since I saw you, I haven't."

The urge to binge and throw up is easing.

"I am sorry, I should have called you from Latvia, Anasztázia. You didn't know what I would do. How can I be angry about Sara when you thought I hated you. Does your head still hurt?"

I look at her and touch the fading scar on her hairline.

"No, I had headaches only in Latvia, it was just bruised. The scar is healing, I will always have it; a memory of you." She says this sadly. Not accusing. But I still feel horrible.

I turn over and think about everything.

If she had just thrown her hands up and said, "Go, stuff your face!" I would. I would have done it. I need to start seeing the eating disorder specialists again. I thought I was cured but I am never cured. If I do it tonight, I will do it again and again until I destroy my career.

"You could be with me all the time, Natalija. You are not safe at the moment. In a month maybe, your voice would be ruined."

"Anasztázia, the truth is you need me. You need me there to stop self-harming. Did Sara see your injuries? What did she say?"

"I don't want to talk about her," Anasztázia says.

I lie there and watch her sleep.

So she has cheated again although she swears if I am with her all the time she wouldn't. I can't believe that. I was in Roma and she did. I can't give up my life to travel Europe with her. She is getting to the point where she shouldn't be working out of Italia. She should take La Scala, Roma, Napoli, even Sicilia and stay in one country, at least until she gets well. All the travelling, the different digs and languages are not helping her. She has done it for over 20 years and no way should she have gone to New York. I can't help thinking it pushed her into the meltdown she had in Latvia.

I am starting to see her behaviour as symptoms of her illness. It all goes together, making her so captivating on stage, and yet so exhausting off it.

I wonder if I could love someone enough to care for them. My voice might never come back so would I then? Scratching around for tiny roles, washed up diva at 29, as I will be in December. It is already looking bleak with my voice nowhere near as good as even when I first sang at music academy. It is lacking any sparkle.

I am studying my notes for *Carmen* on Saturday morning, determined to sing Sunday night's show better than the last and Anasztázia is having to go into the Opera House. They need to run through extra rehearsals before Sunday night.

"Come with me and sit in the theatre café," she says. "Please."

"I am busy," I say. "And I do not want to see that slutty Spanish stage manager slapping your ass."

"Please, Natalija. Bring your notes, write them up. Sit in the café and wait for me. We can have something to eat after." she says resting her hand on my shoulder.

"No," I say. "You go and I will stay here." I don't look up.

Vincent tries to talk to me too, but I am not receptive.

"Natalija, she is upset. She is hurting."

"It is none of your business!" I snap. "Sorry, but I am not in a good place."

He sits at the table watching me write. "Please go with her to the Opera House." He lowers his voice. "I am very concerned about her self-harm, she is cutting again, Natalija. And her head? Was that really an accident?"

"Fine," I say. I gather up my books and shout to

Anasztázia to wait for me.

Anything to stop this man quizzing me. So she always did self-harm. I didn't want to believe it.

"I knew you would," she smiles as she waits patiently by the front door with her bag. "I am so glad."

But getting to stage door and seeing Sara having a smoke outside makes me mad again. She is tarted up in full sexy Spanish news presenter outfit; emerald green dress and shoes and a ton of make-up. She kisses Anasztázia hello and moves to do the same to me but I step away and say, "No thanks, I don't know where you have been."

I stalk into the Opera House as Sara laughs.

"There was no need for that," says Anasztázia sadly as she follows me in.

"There was every need for that," I say signing the visitors' book.

I look back. Sara is watching me as she finishes her cigarette and her lips are in a beautiful pout. She looks at me with big dark eyes and I see the hint of a smile. The male crew smoking outside stare at her and she stares at me. Why the hell does she arrive in those tight dresses and high heels like she has to prove her femininity? She only has to change when she is working on the stage. She just wants to look as good as possible to pick up vulnerable people. Just like Anasztázia.

She has had Anasztázia and now she is craving new blood. She is beautiful but I do not want anything to do with her. She reminds me so much of Krisztyna with all her flirting and pouting.

Anasztázia joins me after a couple of hours as I am drinking my third cup of coffee.

"Well, you do get around, Anasztázia, I have to say. And it won't bring you happiness, you know that yourself."

"Please, I won't go with Sara again. I promise."

"Save it for confession, Marguerite," I tell her. "And Sara is not going to take no for an answer."

Anasztázia says she needs to go to the bathroom, wash her face, do her make-up.

I ignore her and then there is someone leaning over the table. I think the waitress is taking my cup, so I say, "Just wait, I haven't finished." I grab hold of my cup and stop writing.

It is Sara, not changed into her seduction get-up, still in crew outfit, her long hair tied back but she shimmers with vitality. She leans over the table and her dusky perfume is so familiar, so Krisztyna.

"What the hell do you want?" I ask looking at her smouldering dark eyes, full lips and see that underneath her make-up and attitude she is naturally a very beautiful girl. I feel a sense of déjà vu

I notice her white teeth, how her dark skin and hair are truly Carmen. She looks like a Mexican beauty who should be centre stage, not on the desk, out of view.

She must bleach those teeth given the cigarettes she smokes.

"I am returning to Teatro Real Madrid after Paris, early next year. Heard you were down for *Don Carlo*. I will be on the book for that, so I will be seeing you again. A lot more of you, Natalija, I hope."

"How would you know, Sara? And why would I care if you are stage manager?"

She leans closer and says, "I looked at your website, honey. Impressive, especially your seductive *Carmen* photos. Take my card and call me. You know it isn't so bad to have desires. We all need desires." She puts the business card on the table in front of me, tracing her fingers lightly across my hand. I don't slap her away. The touch makes me shiver and suddenly I want Sara. I want her dusky exotic beauty, her vitality, her curvaceous body in an anonymous hotel room right now with absolutely no feeling or love. Just like old times in Hungary. Like the greedy Carmen I was.

"You remind me of someone," I say as I look at her more

closely. "Someone I lost."

For a moment I see Krisztyna flicker in her eyes. The quiver of old magic, the lively sexy woman who was so forward, so careless but so intoxicating.

Her beautiful pout splits into a smile and she says, "I'm sure I do. Sorry about borrowing your girlfriend. She was lonely. Sure you understand, but I can make it up to you, Natalija."

Then she is gone.

What a tarty little bitch, I think after she has left the café. She is so brash, so confident. So determined to have anyone she wants. Just like Krisztyna. Or maybe, just like I was too.

I think of ripping up the card and throwing it in the trash but as I go to do it, I hesitate. I put it in my bag just as Anasztázia returns.

She sits next to me. "I've been thinking, baby. Why don't you stay with me, get the help you need. I won't hurt you, I swear on my life."

"You'd love that. My career dying and you at the top of the world," I say.

"No, it isn't that. You are still not well, so let me...."

"Forget it, Anasztázia. Forget it because I am not your toy and you need me as your nurse, that's what this is about. I was going to drop *Carmen* because I wasn't ready and I thought five weeks to take care of you in Roma would be nice. Not following your career around Europe, no fucking way." I let her hand drop to the table where she was resting it on mine. "Let's just get out of here."

I refuse to come out for dinner that night.

Her friends must think I am such a bitch. So what. I have seen enough of Paris. I hate it.

Anasztázia gets into bed as I am lying there pretending to be asleep. She has brought me some food. She places the tray on the table. Despite myself, I reach for it and eat the snack. I am hungry.

She has the sense not to say anything as I eat. I gulp down the milk and then settle back in the same position.

I feel her wrap her arm around me and she sighs. When I turn around in the night she has been crying as usual, as the candles are still burning in the room casting a glow over us. She looks so unhappy and she is wrapped tight in her silk gown, determined I don't see any damage. Anasztázia needs physical passion from anyone who will give it to her. She is a greedy lover, throwing herself at people. Then they hurt her and she hurts people she really loves. I am tired of her constant demands, but as I trace the scar next to her hairline I know every passing month she is getting sicker. No doubt the role of Marguerite is not helping. I feel crazy when I watch *Faust*. We could have both done without our respective Operas this November.

I try to pull the silk sleeves away when I wake up but she sighs and stirs and moves deeper underneath the sheets. She looks at me, hair draped over her lovely face. So sweet, so innocent and freshly beautiful as she sits up from her deep sleep. Then I think of how she seduced me the very first night. She is not innocent. Krisztyna was right; she is a greedy lover.

"What are you thinking?" she asks me sleepily.

"When I met you I thought you were angelic like a lost fairy-tale princess. You are not who I thought you were," I say.

"What did you want me to be? A china doll you put on your dressing table and just look at? You keep referring to this all the time," she says hurt. "I know you are angry about Sara but she is nothing to me."

"That's right, baby. Just a bit of passion in your dressing room, right?" I say.

"Yes, she was," she says sadly. "I'm not lying to you, Natalija."

"Show me you haven't cut yourself. You surely haven't needed to with your stage manager paying you so much attention," I tell her. "Can you just at least show me your wrist under that bandage."

It is a sprained wrist, so she says. Anasztázia stares at the ceiling silently after she tells me this, probably looking for that heavenly place I thought she came from. My hopeless and impossible dream of a magical creature from some mystic land.

"I thought you were pure. You were so fragile, delicate and lovely. I thought you had fallen from the Empyrean the night I met you," I say remembering the first evening with Anasztázia.

"I am still the same Anasztázia you met. I am sorry that I never lived up to your dreams. You saw an angel when you met me, maybe because I was still in a role. I was Lucia and you saw what you wanted to see. I was never going to live up to your dreams, Natalija. I am not a fairy-tale elf or an ice princess, I am real!" She taps her chest. "Real! And you hurt, Natalija. You always do." She glances down and stares at the floor.

"Love hurts, baby," I say. "And you are hurting yourself. Sara would take anyone beautiful. Just don't take it out on your skin when she throws you away. And you are wrong, you are an ice princess. You always will be."

She gives me a gaze of absolute desolation.

I am chilly as I leave that morning to get my flight back to Vienna.

"Please don't leave like this, Natalija," Anasztázia says. "You hardly spoke yesterday. You seem so troubled. Are you still worried about *Carmen* and your performance tonight....and if you are worried about Sara and me......"

"I have to go," I say cutting her off mid-sentence, getting into the airport taxi.

She kisses my face and tells me she is still waiting for me. "And Natalija, I promise I will not go with Sara again. And I am getting help over my self-harm...."

"Okay," I tell her. "Whatever you say, but I don't believe the faithful line for a minute. Go back to Sara if you want. I hope she devours you for breakfast. I have had enough." I shut the taxi door.

I am here for you. I am waiting for you wherever I am. Always. You are the One.

BLACK MAGIC

Throughout the *Carmen* run, I don't get the applause I want. Carmen does. Don José does but I am just a supporting role and without the power in my voice, because it still hurts to sing. Lucky for me I take my curtain call with Frasquita, my gypsy buddy or I would be so ashamed.

I am worse than I have ever been as a singer. If I were watching me I would wonder what the hell I was doing in this production. The musical director was right to question my being here.

'Mercédès was smouldering, beautiful and a very fine actress but her mezzo voice simply lacked any kind of power or seduction, with her notes falling flat into the orchestra pit instead of floating into the Heavens,' says one reviewer.

That hurts. That really hurts because it is so true. If he had softened it by mentioning I am recovering from an injury, it would be better. Now everyone who reads it without knowing what happened to me just thinks I am a pretty girl, hired for her looks, with a weak voice. I am angry and I write to the newspaper informing the critic if he knew anything about the Opera World he would have known what happened to me in March in Budapest. I nearly died, for God's sake.

I send the link for my website which is full of good reviews, photos and videos of me in leading roles. It is my first bad review and it really hurts.

The reviewer surprises me by emailing an apology the next day. He says he is very sorry but never saw me in anything before. He had never heard of the horrible incident in my last *Carmen*. I am disappointed that he had never heard of me; I thought everyone in Europe linked with Opera knew of my talent. I feel more depressed despite the critic being thoughtful enough to print an apology in the newspaper under his next theatre review; *'Natalija who played Mercédès had been in a serious stage accident in March in the title role of Carmen. She has only just returned to performing and is not yet fully recovered, which explains her reduced vocal capacity in Carmen last week'.*

Stage accident. More like attempted murder. But then I realise he has to be careful, he could be sued for writing the truth.

Every day I have a text from Anasztázia.

I am never giving up on you. I am waiting. Your Anasztázia.

She is now in London. She has to stay through until 10th January. She has to perform on Christmas Day and she is horribly lonely there. She hates England. Like me, she is fine in the Opera House, but finds the city overwhelming once she steps out of stage door. She rents some extortionately expensive place nearby as she cannot negotiate the metro, which is why she generally avoids London. She calls to say happy birthday to me early in December.

I feel bad for her out in London, so I speak to her for half an hour.

She gabbles on like a glove puppet. She misses me like crazy, she was so sad the way I left in Vienna. Was afraid she had lost me. Because of Sara.

"No," I sigh. "I am still calling you now, aren't I? Besides everything is in your apartment."

"Oh," she says sadly, realising I am still staying there as it is a beautiful place and no rent to pay. "I'm sorry you don't want to live with me for the right reasons."

"You could always make it right, Anasztázia."

She then says excitedly that she has a gift for me. She knows I will love it.

She can stuff her gift. She can have lovers in her London

dressing room every day for all I care. And given it is a long, lonely Christmas run, she will be.

I tell her I will try to get over for Christmas but I cannot promise as I am seeing my father and stepmother and my brother Levente. I haven't seen them since I nearly died.

"I understand, Natalija. But please don't use 'dead' and 'death' so lightly....but when will I see you? I need you."

"Honey, you are dying every night of your run. You die in every Opera you perform in. You should be an expert on death by now. I know I am. I see my near death experience as enriching for future performances, to act the dying better."

"Natalija, please, this is horrible."

I don't see the big deal. I have learned a lot about dying since I was resurrected. Next stage death will be perfection.

I promise her that I will get over before La Scala rehearsals open on 3rd January and I will try to make it New Year as she hates New Year. I feel bad for the way I behaved in Paris.

She reassures me she is being good, not cutting, taking her pills every day.

Then after she hangs up full of love and affection, I am angry with her.

She is so gentle, so sweet and I am despising her because she is sick and needy and won't give up on me. I must be twisted, not to be flattered by this superstar's attentions but she is tiring. I am still walking in the shadows.

I also cannot deal with any more jealousy. *La bohème* and I will be jealous, not of Rodolfo, but of some sexy stage manager or anyone around. I have seen photos of the handsome Italian singing the role but he isn't a threat. In fact, they are all good looking, the alternate cast too. So she has plenty to choose from. Especially a Christmas run. Especially Puccini. I have lost count of how many singers I know who say they met playing Mimì and Rodolfo. I have lost count of how many singers say they left their husbands, wives, lovers for their co-star on this heartbreakingly sad production.

It is more likely she will be cheating with Musetta. Musetta is performed by a very pretty English rose of a girl, actually called Rosa in Anasztázia's cast. That fits. Yes, Musetta the incorrigible flirt of *La bohème,* will be the one Anasztázia is with.

All that stuff she told me the night we met about being very shy and needing Marina's help to find a date is just lies. She only has to flutter her eyelashes, say she is very lonely and probably bring on a few tears. She knows exactly what she is doing.

The fact she is lonely is my fault but I am not doing anything about it. I am ignoring all my feelings as the old Natalija would. I knew of many opera couples who suffered similar such feelings. One Hungarian tenor said he couldn't bear it, to watch his soprano wife with another man.

"I just go mad," he said. "Crazy jealous, Natalija. I cannot figure the reasoning. I perform with women in the same way and it is acting. I know that but I just cannot control the jealousy. Part of me knows she would never cheat but the other half of me is totally irrational. I think it is because we met on stage. We were lovers in an opera and so I think if it started with us, she could have those feelings on stage with someone else."

He met his wife when they performed in *La bohème.* As Mimì and Rodolfo.

There is no difference whether we are men or women. We all suffer jealousy and irrational emotions. Falling in love on intense, long runs is so common. It happens as your emotions are so powerful and concentrated so much on the rehearsals and performances. I had many men and women fall in love with me when they watched me on stage, or performed in the same Opera. I had affairs with people I never really cared about. I especially chose the guests who would be gone after the run finished.

I pretend Rodolfo is you so I am with you
every day. I am still waiting for you. Your
Anasztázia.

I have to perform in a concert in Budapest so I go straight
from Vienna, since it is a couple of hours on the train as
there is no point flying back to Roma for two days. I am
surprised given everything I said in the Italian media about
my near death in the Opera House that I am wanted. I do
not even want to sing in concerts as a rule. I find them dull.
And my Budapest memories are still raw. They stay raw as
everything is wrong here. First of all I argue the whole time
with my father. We don't stop.

He is angry with me because I have spoken critically
about Hungary to the Italian media. It has been translated
into Hungarian and he has seen it.

"It is your country, Natalija. You criticise your own
people. What happened to you in the Opera was terrible but
you have gone too far. You have talked to every news outlet
in Italia. One of the most famous young opera singers from
Hungary who has turned her back on us."

"Hungary is no longer my country or Anasztázia's. We
are exiled because we do not fit the mould.

And if you turn your back on people here they stick a
knife in it!" I am angry with my father, years of anger never
expressed.

"Natalija, your mother was not Hungarian and she
wasn't alive long enough to become a full citizen. She would
not be happy about all your hatred. This was the country
she loved."

"I have met her many times since I died," I tell him. "She
said she had watched me and regretted every day she didn't
spend with me but she never mentioned you! What did you
do so wrong?"

He covers his face. "Where did you meet?"

"In my sleep. Since I died and first met her in her beautiful red wedding dress and she sent me back to Earth," I tell him.

He is emotional and pacing around. Talking about my mother is something he always avoids and it drives me mad.

"She never comes to me because she is not in our world, Natalija. She died. You were dreaming. Morphine gives you wild dreams. You just wanted to see her, it's understandable....."

"I'm not lying and I have had many dreams since then, István. You think she is somewhere, not a load of ashes. You refuse to believe she is dead. And why do I call you by your name? All my life; never dad, never daddy. And you never noticed my bulimia when you were a dentist. You never noticed why my tooth enamel was always damaged. I was throwing up when I was 14! You never talk, damn you!"

He walks out of the room. He cannot bear to talk about my mother. He loved her more than Lilla.

I am so angry with him.

We have never argued before. Only me and Lilla. We would cat fight like girls even when I was 25 or so. We hated each other but now it is reversed. Lilla is the understanding one. He drives me crazy.

As I leave his house, he is sitting under my mother's portrait of her in the red dress on the living room wall. He stares at the lovely dark eyed sad creature she is. Beautiful and haunting. Next to it is Lilla in white, so similar in appearance yet with a vacant gaze; an immature 18 year old child bride. He took the image of my mother as his wife, 28 years younger than he was, plucked from a Budapest street when she was only 17. Lilla was just a girl. She would never be the person he wanted her to be. I hate my father right now; he knew nothing about women. Thinking he could replace his lost love. I actually feel sorry for my once hated stepmother. If she became cruel and materialistic, he is to blame.

We are all deeply fucked up really.

He has already told me I will lose Anasztázia. My behaviour towards her is beyond cruel.

"Hot-tempered arguments are okay but not this," he says. "And to be jealous of her on stage? It is a role, Natalija."

Anasztázia was one of his favourite singers when he used to go to the Opera. Ever since she joined The Royal Hungarian Opera at 22 until she left 14 years later. He is angry with me because I am with someone he admired. "Someone so beautiful, with exceptional talent, adores you. She is offering you the world and you walk away. Your stepmother was so jealous I liked Anasztázia and started refusing to go to Opera when Anasztázia was on."

"Interesting," I say. "But you are not her type."

"Don't leave it too late, Natalija. I would understand if she were a tempestuous diva but she thinks the world of you."

"Wait," I tell him. "She has the face of an angel and the body of a demon. She cheated with Krisztyna in Roma. Krisztyna was her old flame from Budapest from years ago. She cheated with Krisztyna during Butterfly, in Bregenz and when Krisztyna was playing Tosca in September. Anasztázia admitted it. Even when I went to Paris to see her, she was accosted by some slutty Spanish stage manager right in front of stage door. She claims her heart is true but that flirty little body is not. How can I deal with her, István?"

He looks sympathetic.

"Oh," he says sitting down at the table. "Oh, Natalija. I am sorry." István is thoughtful, then he says.

"But she is human."

"And then the tears, the 'sorry' a thousand times a day. Gifts, texts, calls, begging," I tell him.

"Natalija, you probably knew about me and your stepmother. I cheated, she cheated and we broke each other. But now I couldn't do without her."

"She is sure to be cheating now, my Anasztázia. She is so desperate for love. Krisztyna was her first love in Hungary. I still can't forgive her for that betrayal."

I push my coffee around in circles. I never talked to my father about relationships. It is probably the first time.

"Yes, I see it hurt you with Krisztyna. But you cheated so much in the past, and knowing you, you probably will again."

I glare at him. He thinks I am a serial tart.

"Don't throw somebody so beautiful away, Natalija. You will regret it forever, I can promise you this. Listen to me. If you don't take any more advice, take this from me."

"She cries all the time and she self-harms. When I first met her, she hadn't done it for some time but she is worse. She is sick, she has been for a long time. In Latvia, when she just flew over to see me and was crazy, I had to hide all the sharp knives in the snow. She split her head open on the coffee table and I had to take her to the emergency room. I think she is really ill, István. I had to call her doctor to give her a shot of Valium in October. She has a cocktail of meds. The doctor said she should not be alone, or work out of Italia right now."

"Natalija," my father says taking my hand. "If she is sick, please help her. You know I was so ill I needed support. I couldn't have done it alone, without Lilla."

I say nothing.

"And don't forget what you did with your bulimia. Cutting seems worse to you, but I saw patients you would never believe would do it; attractive and successful women of all ages. I saw it when I was a dentist under those bright lights. Anasztázia needs help, just like you did."

"I am so exhausted by her dramatic needy behaviour."

I sigh. I realise I am crying. I don't look at him.

"Natalija, she is depressed and hurting. Don't leave her because she is ill."

"I don't want to sacrifice my career."

"You might have to sacrifice a concert here or there, but not your career. Natalija if you live purely for yourself, you will be alone. As you said, it's lonely at the top. It will get lonelier."

But he doesn't realise what it is like. Anasztázia wants so much of me, more than any human could give. Now I begin my demanding schedule, it is impossible.

The concert I am performing in is not in the Opera House but a concert hall, together with some other singers and it is paying me well and no one mentions the negative comments I have made in the Italian media. Except one older musician comes up to me afterwards, his violin tucked under his arm and says I should be ashamed of what I said. I tell him to shut the hell up. I am brittle and I am angry. I leave soon afterwards. I checked into a hotel for the few days before as I still like to have my space. There is room in my father's house, but I still have this need for my own space when I am performing. And after me and my father argued, I am tense around him.

Still the old Natalija who never admits to any feelings.

I haven't been back to Hungary since the stabbing and I haven't seen my apartment since I left in April. It was such a pretty one overlooking the Duna in the XIII district and it is where Krisztyna is still living.

The day after the concert when I am due to fly home to Roma, Lilla says she needs to go and get the money from Krisztyna for bills. "You know, Natalija, you should come with me. You should see your apartment. I would like you to see Krisztyna. It is Christmas and I am worried about her," she says pulling on her coat.

I tell her I don't think it is a good idea.

"Please, Natalija. Just come with me. Just ten minutes."

I just don't want to tell the whole damn story so I decide it is easier to go with her. Just to see the apartment one last time.

Lilla rings the bell and there is no answer. We wait and Lilla unlocks the door and goes ahead of me.

"I told her 2pm. She must be on her way. She won't mind if we go in. She has told me to do that before if she is running late. She knows I am coming."

I think, *She will mind if I am here. I should not be here.*

It is neat, way neater than she was when I lived here when I forever picked up her stuff she carelessly left all over the apartment. Lilla wanders into the kitchen and says she will make some coffee.

I pad cautiously into the master bedroom and as well as a spotless, obsessively neat room, I see a large collection of photos all of me next to the bed, in silver frames. I pick one up; it is of me as Amneris, my first role with The Royal Hungarian Opera, just before I met Krisztyna. I am standing like a princess, my arms held aloft dressed in black and gold, looking like the world belongs to me. There are photos of me from virtually every Opera I have been in. All these pictures look like the room of someone who adores the person in the photo, like a goddamn shrine. There are even candles. Some are red, some are black and looking closer there are spells written out next to candles and I feel uneasy. Some candles have pins in, there are pieces of paper bound with red ribbon. She has been performing black magic on me. One spell written out carefully is entitled 'Dream of me' and is pinned to one of my photos next to a red candle. I am freaked out. I don't know if I believe in black magic but I am still uneasy that I discover this. I have done nothing but dream of her. Without wanting to. She is a witch. I find the lock of my hair she tore out in the summer bound with red ribbon and step back, afraid. She did keep it to perform spells on; to perform spells on; she is using witchcraft to control me. I need to get away from this.

It is scaring me.

I drop a photo to the floor with a clatter.

KRISZTYNA

I wander into the living room and have a shock as there she is; sensual, beautiful Krisztyna stretched out on the sofa, deeply asleep. Her face looks gentle, almost like the girl I knew. I step closer cautiously, waiting for her to open her eyes and see me and spit her venom at me.

Lilla is in the kitchen. I am safe.

Krisztyna will wake up any minute and ask me what the fuck I am doing here. Either that or laugh like a wind-chime and say, *Couldn't stay away, little girl?* In her mocking way.

Lilla shouts loudly, *Do you want a coffee?*

Krisztyna doesn't stir. That should have woken her up.

I step closer.

Her long dark hair spills over the pillows.

Then I notice on the coffee table, there are two bottles of empty sleeping pills next to a glass and an empty bottle of champagne on the floor. There are also some travel sickness pills and I realise why; they can stop you throwing up if you take them before an overdose.

"No, Krisztyna, you wouldn't," I say. My head spins. "You wouldn't do that. You take your anger out on everyone else, you are a cobra. You always loved yourself......" I lean over her where she sleeps so serene, her face so peaceful and I touch her hand; she is still warm but her lips have a blue tint and her dark complexion is very pale.

"Krisztyna! What have you done?" I scream. "No, Krisztyna, you didn't! Tell me you didn't! Wake up, please!"

I feel for her pulse on her wrist but I can't find it.

Lilla comes running in and asks me why am I screaming. She sees Krisztyna and she rushes over to her and holds her. "God, Natalija, what has she done to herself?" Lilla touches her neck and she can feel a weak pulse.

I call the emergency services and tell them my friend has taken a massive overdose, *She has a pulse. I don't know how much, how long ago. Please help.*

Lilla says, "Krisztyna can you hear me? We are getting you to hospital. It's all okay, darling. The ambulance is coming. Stay with us."

As Lilla holds Krisztyna, reassuring her help is coming although she is as floppy as a rag doll, I am looking at a bit of paper in front of me on the table. It is folded and on the top she has printed my name.

I open it.

Natalija. I am so sorry for everything I did and didn't do. I loved you so much, I hurt you so badly, I messed up, I couldn't move on after Carmen. I hope you forgive me for hurting you all those times, if not now, one day. May God forgive my soul. Please never forget me. Forever your Krisztyna.

I sink to the floor holding the paper. Lilla is crying over Krisztyna as she knows all about trying to die. She took an overdose as a teenager and permanently damaged her liver.

I can't move. I bring suffering to everyone around me, like a bad luck charm. I am poison.

"Krisztyna, you didn't need to do that....."

"It's okay, Natalija. The ambulance will be here." Lilla holds Krisztyna in her arms and says, "Why did you do that, Krisztyna? Why didn't you ask me for help? Why, darling? What was so terrible?"

The apartment is suddenly full of activity. Lilla has let the paramedics in and I am dazed and sitting on the floor holding this note. The paramedics are working on Krisztyna with urgency; she has a pulse and her breathing is shallow but she is still alive.

"This is my fault!" I cry.

"No, Natalija, don't ever blame yourself," Lilla hugs me.

I show her the note. "The bedroom is like a shrine to me, Lilla. I never knew...."

"It's okay, it will be okay now. We found her."

The paramedics take the note out of my hand and the empty pill bottles and Krisztyna is rushed out of the apartment.

Krisztyna took a massive overdose. The hospital found quantities of cocaine, MDMA as well as a load of prescription pills in her body, washed down with champagne. She was only just alive. Did she do it as a cry for help or did she really want to die?

I will never know the answer. The next day passes as she is in a deep sleep. The hospital have worked to try to get the drugs out of her but a lot has been absorbed already. They tell me they are not sure if she will make it. Which means she took the pills long before she thought she would be found. She meant to die. She knew Lilla would come that day and she would be found in eternal sleep. She never knew I would be there.

I knew Krisztyna feared dying alone and no one finding her body. She had once told me this was her greatest fear; lying rotting away for weeks, no one caring.

I am standing with a bouquet of roses. Red and velvety. At the hospital I cry in the December greyness. They take the roses away, because Krisztyna is too fragile to have flowers in her room. My father tries to hold me. I push him away and curse him.

My once lovely Krisztyna. I cry tears I never thought I had left.

I forgive what she did to me in Roma.

Being in our old apartment has brought back nostalgia.

I despise Anasztázia right now. She messed Krisztyna's head up by cheating on me with her. It hurt all of us. I sit in my father's house wondering what to do about everything. The hospital call me that evening; Krisztyna is awake which is very good. It means the damage should be limited. *Do I want to see her? She is very weak but she has been asking for me. She heard I was with Lilla.*

I am saddened when I see her.

Outside Krisztyna's room, on the desk of the nursing station, there are flowers from her family, my roses in a vase. She is surrounded by confirmation that she is not alone. There are people who care.

She looks so delicate; her dark hair seems dusty and dull, her golden skin is parched dry white, lips cracked and slightly blue, like Mimì on her deathbed. I sit down and she looks at me. At first I am afraid her brain is damaged as her eyes are so dead, so dark and there are black circles underneath them. She looks very sick. A drip is inserted into her left hand.

Then a tear slides down her face. "You should have let me die," she says so quietly and turns her face away from me. "Just like I wanted. *'Con onor muore'.*"

"Krisztyna, listen to me. Lilla would have found you. I was with her."

"I didn't mean her to find me alive. I didn't know you would be there," she says still avoiding my eyes.

"Krisztyna, I will tell you this now. You don't have to listen, but someday you will be glad you didn't die. You will find someone who really loves you, you will be a success, you will get well....you could play Mimì right now looking like that." I touch her right hand lightly and it is cold. She turns to look at me, but a tiny smile flickers in her eyes at the reference to Mimì. Her fingers close gently around mine.

"You have so much to live for. But I have to go now, Krisztyna. I have to go and you have to let me go. Please get well. Krisztyna, *Un bel dì* still exists for you. I promise you this. The beautiful day will come."

She stares at me without speaking.

I get up and lay her hand gently back on the bed. I have nothing more to say. At once I have forgiven her. I don't need to tell her. She knows.

"Natalija," she says as I walk towards the door.

I turn around.

"I'm so sorry," she says quietly. "For everything, please say sorry to Anasztázia too. I never meant to hurt you, or her. I couldn't live with myself after how I treated you. You know I never ever had anything to do with the *Carmen* incident. I loved you."

"God has forgiven you, Krisztyna. And I know about *Carmen,* I knew it could never have been you."

I leave and close the door.

It is the last time I will ever see her.

I sit through Christmas depressed. I can't face going back to Italia yet. Lilla, Levente and my father try to get me to go to eat with them, but I refuse to eat. I only drink liquids; loads of coffee because I don't want to sleep. I am having nightmares. They ask me to sit at the table at least.

I don't feel so well myself. For the first time in my life I am well and truly depressed. My father has given me antidepressants which help me sleep but the nightmares are horrendous. He said I am a wreck. Lilla is not doing too well either. She is traumatised. Apart from Levente, no one is talking much. Lilla pushes food around on her plate.

My brother Levente brings me a wrapped box; his Christmas and birthday gift to me.

I open it without heart. Inside are white figure skates. I look at them and want to cry. I was the Hungarian National Junior Champion when I was 13 and 14 and took the silver medal in the Junior Europeans. I was going to the Olympics until a bad accident in training knocked me unconscious and I gave up. That was when I channelled it all into Opera. One door closed and this abyss of theatreland opened and swallowed me up.

I might have had a happier life as an ice-skater, but by now my career would be over unless I moved to ice-dancing.

"I thought it might help. You were so good, so good,

Natalija. It might help to skate just for you with no competitions to stress over. The blades are already sharpened ready to go."

"Levente, she won't," my father says angry with him. "And she can't risk injury now. She is an Opera star."

But I look at my brother and I smile. It is the best gift I ever had.

But I do not eat, I won't talk. My father says me and Lilla will end up on the psychiatric ward. She looks up at him from the kitchen table with anger and says, "You stupid, selfish fucking man. You know nothing so shut up! Don't forget you were virtually holidaying on the psychiatric ward when I was only 18, bringing Natalija to see you with her balloons and I told her you had flu. Don't you ever forget that, you idiot!" She looks away.

Levente looks up in surprise. He missed all of that happy childhood I had. It was much calmer for him. He knows our father is a bit strange but he never saw the intensity, the craziness.

My father pushes his plate to one side and leaves the room. He doesn't want to be reminded of the bipolar illness which ravaged his life and cut his career short.

I look at all the messages from Anasztázia on my phone, the last one on Christmas Eve. Her daughter is visiting her for the 28th December show. *She is so delighted at this surprise but she is very sad that I am not there. She would love her daughter to meet me....*

She wonders how I am. If I am going to make it to London before Milano....

I hope she is tarting her way through the London Opera House up and down stage, in the wings, on the fly floor, in the dressing rooms.

One opera house I guested at, the staff had an unspoken competition who could get the most and in how many locations, the riskier the better. The winner was the technician who had sex on the grid, right up in the fly tower above the stage during a very moving performance of *Madama Butterfly*. I told him I thought that showed a complete lack of respect for Puccini. *Never during an Opera. An Opera is sacred.*

My father hands me a plane ticket. It is morning but I don't know what day it is. Some day after Christmas anyway.

"What the fuck is this for?" I ask.

"London. It is New Year's Eve," he says. "In case you forgot."

"So what," I say. I look away. "Besides I am supposed to be in La Scala on 3rd January. I was going to fly straight to Milano tomorrow."

"Get on that flight and go to Anasztázia," he says.

"She is a cheat and a liar!" I shout.

"Shut up, Natalija! She loves you! Forgive her. You are so cold, little girl! You push everyone away, you always did. You were always the centre of the universe. No one else mattered, only your success. I called her on Christmas Day since you didn't and I told her how you and Lilla had found Krisztyna. She should have been told too and you just didn't think. She was so sad but she told me, 'Please get Natalija to come over for New Year, it would mean the world'."

"You fucking interfering idiot!" I scream. "How dare you!"

He hauls me off the floor and I stick my nails in his arm, scratching him, fighting him.

"Natalija, she is your responsibility! You are callous and unfeeling. No wonder she is hurting the way you behave! I promised her I was sending you there. How would you like to be alone in London longing for a selfish little diva to visit? How did you turn out so cold? We are all sad about Krisztyna but you have someone who is longing to see you. Pack your bag!"

"No!" I scream. "Anasztázia, the great diva self-harms! I can't deal with her!"

"You self-destructed and nearly lost your voice and could have killed yourself. Krisztyna called me when you were ill and we got you to the eating disorders clinic. She drove you there twice. She didn't walk away, Natalija! You were dying in front of her but she didn't walk away!"

I do not need reminding of what I did to myself.

"Get off me!" I scream. He drags me to the bathroom by my hair and I am fighting with him hitting him, shouting curses but he is much stronger. He shoves a towel in my hands and turns the water on. He is waiting for me in the living room and he will pack my suitcase. He will put my opera gown in that I wore for the concert; black and elegant and beautiful.

He hasn't packed my ice skates when I am ready to leave and I am mad. I grab the box from the table and he tries to pull it away but I am ready to hit him. He sees the look in my eyes and waits while I unzip the suitcase and fit in the white, beautiful skates.

He drives me to the airport, sulky and resentful. It is snowing. I hate him.

I call Anasztázia in the airport, waiting for an espresso in the café and a slice of cake because I will pass out any minute. I tell her I am coming, like my father said. It is morning so I will be there in plenty of time.

"I knew you would, darling. I know you are feeling terrible. Your father called and I understand you couldn't speak to me. I perform tonight, you can see me and stay with me. I will leave your ticket....."

"Krisztyna tried to kill herself, Anasztázia. Don't you care? Me and Lilla found her. You said ......"

She cuts me off. "Natalija, I know. Your father explained; you didn't call me because he said you and Lilla were traumatised. I cried so much thinking of the pain she must have been in. I am so sorry she was so depressed. Look I am in the Opera House and I need to do something so I will call you in an hour, okay?"

"Whatever," I say. "What do you care? You are so selfish....."

She has already ended the call.

Anasztázia calls me back again when I am wandering around the airport. I am buying a lot of stuff because airport money isn't real money, so no guilt. I have bought her some perfume I know she likes. I also buy jewellery; matching rings except one is sapphire for her, ruby for me and two more rings in white gold. She will like that, hopeless romantic she is. She hates my spider poison ring so I don't wear it these days. It is also an unlucky charm. I have put it away in its box.

"Natalija, is Krisztyna damaged?"

"She's not brain-damaged but she is a wreck. She wanted to die. Why didn't you leave us both alone in Roma? Why couldn't you just do that, Anasztázia?   Thanks a lot for wrecking our lives!"

I realise just how angry I am with Anasztázia.

"Because it was you I wanted, Natalija; for so long. Krisztyna said you would throw me away. I should never have listened, I am so sorry."

The line is silent.

"Natalija? Did you go back to Krisztyna?"

"No of course not, I was with Lilla to see the apartment. And send that poor girl some flowers. She was your first love." As if I would have gone back to Krisztyna after how she had behaved.

"Natalija, I already ordered some after your father called. I would have told you but he said you needed space. Blue roses, they should have reached her by now. Please come to London. I don't want life without you. Whatever has gone wrong since October, we can fix it. I promise you.

I need to prepare now. Just be there."

And she hangs up first, damn her.

FIRE AND ICE

I think about Anasztázia waiting for me all through December and now it is New Year's Eve. I am a bitch. I am heartless. I destroy everything and everyone around me. I thought I had become a better person but the truth is I haven't.

Krisztyna's mother ripped into me at the hospital as I stood there with the velvety red roses I had brought.

I was a cruel and heartless diva who rejected her beautiful daughter. Broke up the family and then I leave and go to Roma. Krisztyna turned up to find me with the girl she had loved, Anasztázia. That Krisztyna had broken her heart. I am the devil diva. Her beautiful talented daughter is now lying sick in a hospital bed, lucky to be alive. And I am to blame, devil diva.

Obviously Krisztyna had edited the true version of events. I said nothing to her mother. She seems to forget how me and Lilla saved her daughter's life.

I sit on the plane all the way to London feeling angry with the world. Anasztázia is sick. I think I am the bad luck charm. I make people crazy. Or maybe I just attract this kind of person; the flamboyant, beautiful but damaged divas. I just don't see it at first.

Maybe Anasztázia is too old for me. 16 years is a big age gap and her daughter is only 7 years younger than me. But then Krisztyna was 11 years older and I thought nothing of that.

I hope Krisztyna doesn't hurt any more. May God forgive her. I hope someone takes care of her. I hope she finds some inner peace.

And I pray there is not a flake of snow in London because I have to fly to Milano on 2nd January. One flake in Britain and everything stops. I cannot miss any rehearsals for *Aida* and they start on 3rd January.

In London, I arrive at the Opera House, collect my ticket and go to stage door as it is one hour before the show and Anasztázia asked me to quickly call and see her before the show and there is plenty of time. I had to change into my opera gown and get ready in a café bathroom. At stage door, I show my Roma Opera ID and they are bitchy about letting me up to see her. The men are not familiar to me as I have not performed here for a long time. They don't even try to help when I say she is waiting.

"For God's sake she is my girlfriend!" I shout, mad at their officious attitude. "Anasztázia is my girlfriend so let me in!"

The three men on stage door are so surprised one takes me straight to her dressing room. The others just stare at me like I am a zoo animal.

I don't know why I said that. Even if it is true.

It says **Anasztázia** on her door. No surname. Just the great Anasztázia.

As she opens her dressing room door with such delight, I remember that I did love her and maybe I still do. I see her through my old eyes, the light of spring and wonder. She looks so well, not hysterical and desperate. She drapes herself around me and I inhale her sweet perfume. *My snow queen, my beautiful sweet Anasztázia,* I think.

The stage door man is still hovering around staring at us. She gives him a strange look and shuts the door.

"Why is he looking at me like that?" she says.

"He got his eyeful," I say.

She smiles so beautifully at me. I give her the flowers and perfume I brought and she accepts them with such happiness, arranging the roses in a vase. As I watch her looking so calm and delighted to see me I think, I will forgive her sins. She is sick after all. She has a tender heart.

"This is for your birthday, Natalija. I have been wearing it hoping it will bring you back. It is too beautiful to keep in a drawer. I wore it here this evening because I so wanted you to wear it tonight and you will look a million dollars with that flowing black dress."

She smiles, a gentle lovely smile and takes off the diamond necklace and the rainbow of colours catches the light. Anasztázia fastens it around my throat and turns me to face the mirror.

Only a diamond will cut through a diamond.

"It's amazing, so fitting for a diva, but why are you always trying to buy my love? These diamonds must have cost thousands of euros, Anasztázia," I say. She should not be the sweet Anasztázia she is now as I have virtually shut her out since Paris last month. And she shouldn't be spending like this on jewellery. I might get robbed if I wear it in Roma or Napoli. It is way too expensive.

"I can't accept this, really it is too much. I got you something but I will save it for later. Christmas isn't something I do but I thought you might like this so later, when we go to your digs."

"You are what I wanted, not gifts tonight and I don't try to buy your love. I want you to have it because I want to show you how much you are worth, how beautiful you are and it is a thousand times more than those diamonds."

She gazes at me in the glittering jewels and rests her hand on my shoulder as I admire myself in the glass.

I look at myself more closely in the mirror. The jewels sparkle at my collarbone as they imprison the light and I notice my skin is smooth, my hair is now back to shiny raven black ringlets. It is the first time I have noticed the reversal of the damage caused by my eating disorder where I looked deathly pale and ill; even my hair was dusty and dull.

I look a million dollars and it has made me vain. The dress is an 'upstage every female in the Opera House' kind of dress. I had it in my father's house unworn for a year and I wore it for the concert performance on 15th December. To upstage everyone else in the concert, to say, *Fuck you, Hungary.*

"Did you get in without too much hassle at stage door? Security is so strict in London, worse than anywhere. I can't believe how it is here but I guess they are worried about terrorism. Strange how you never had to think of that in Hungary and not really in Italia. Did you get your ticket at box office already?" She asks powdering up with the stage make-up.

"Yes but I had to tell them I was your girlfriend for those miserable men to let me in."

Her hand stops with the powder puff. She looks at me in the mirror. "You said *what*?"

"Just that. They had to let me in because I am your girlfriend," I shrug. Really I was just trying it out. No big deal, what are they going to do? "That's why the security man was staring at you."

I feel the chill as she looks down and says nothing for a few seconds.

She whirls around to face me and says, "How dare you, Natalija! How dare you say that! Do you have any idea how much damage this could cause to my reputation? Why the hell did you say that? Now everyone will know about me!" She is furious. She goes back to slapping on the make up, banging the cases on the dressing table. "Everyone will be talking by the end of the night!"

"I better go front of house," I tell her. I see how mad she is and I don't want her more upset before her performance.

"Just get out! Get out before my costume lady comes in!"

I wander round to the main entrance, forgetting Anasztázia and instead enjoying the attention as I flow through, my midnight blue fur coat in one arm, my black dress trailing behind me and the diamonds glinting around my throat. People stop and stare and so they should. I am the diva, I am the star who will take the stage of La Scala next month. I inhale the admiration and unlike 6 months ago, there is no pain standing around in high heels.

I have left my big suitcase in Anasztázia's dressing room. I didn't think. All I have is a small purse.

Now she might not let me in after the show and I will be stuck.

The way she was I wonder if I will need to go to a hotel tonight. That will cost a fortune on New Year.

No, she will just scream and cry all night. She will probably take me home. I know her address, it is a tiny overpriced place round the corner as she is agoraphobic.

The stage door men just let me straight in post-show with knowing smiles. I see everyone in celebratory mood for New Year.

I knock on her door. "Anasztázia!" I call.

First of all I think she won't open it. She will lock herself in.

She does open it, but her costume lady is still there.

Anasztázia steps aside and lets me pass without looking at me. "You were wonderful, really heartbreaking," I tell her as I hug her. I mean it. She was.

"Thanks," she says but her body is stiff and she glances at me with beautiful eyes full of deep rage before looking away again.

After her costume lady leaves Anasztázia's smile turns to ice as she shuts the door.

She turns her earlier rage back on me as if she went out, entranced the audience as hauntingly fragile Mimì, died so tragically people wept including me, and now picks up our quarrel where she left off. "I still can't believe you, that was so stupid of you!"

"They won't even remember by tomorrow and I was hoping you would still be in Mimì role," I say. "Are you ashamed of me?"

"No. But I don't want people to know about my private

life," she says so frosty and cold.

"You would sooner the entire company of Roma think you are bashed around by some boyfriend than a hint of being with me? Everyone talks about you in an abusive relationship after you split your head open and are always covered in sticking plasters. Do you want to be seen as a pathetic victim? And do you want to lose me? You really think you could do better than this?" I say pointing at myself in the mirror. "You really think so? Because I don't!"

Before she answers someone knocks on the door and waves a bottle of champagne. It is the singer who played Colline. "Anasztázia! Come and drink!"

"I will. Just give me a minute, I need to finish up here." She smiles at him and shuts the door.

Then she turns icy again. Her look says everything. *I hate you, I don't want you here.* She turns away from me and finishes getting ready.

"Give me your apartment key, I am leaving you to it," I tell her taking hold of my suitcase.

"Since you are so ashamed of me. You are old enough to be my mother, you ageing tempestuous diva."

After this remark she throws the key to the floor and turns away in angry silence.

I pick up the key from between my shoes and stalk out dragging my case.

Fuck her.

I am asleep with the lights and TV on when she comes in. I am curled around her silk gown as it smells of her sweet perfume, the diamonds still around my neck. I was so tired. I didn't expect her to come home at all, given she is not performing on New Year's Day and since she was so mad at me. I was nasty calling her an ageing diva. I hear her trip over a chair and curse. She obviously drank more than a glass. She crawls over the bed and the soft paws pad gently over my body like a big cat.

"Natalija, my darling girl," she says sweetly. "My love, my life."

Even by this I know she is drunk. "Natalija, wake up, my angel." I feel her kisses on my neck and stir. I turn over. She leans over me so beautiful and radiant and full of champagne. "I am an idiot," she says stroking my face. "I am so stupid, I wanted you here so badly. So what if you told them, so what," she slurs. "Let the world know. I will paint it on the Opera House walls if you want. You are mine after all."

She really is drunk if she is saying that. She shouldn't drink on those pills she's on. She will be on a real downer tomorrow too, which will not be nice for me or her.

"Anasztázia sorry for being a bitch. You're not ageing. You froze time, it is powerless under your spell. You are so young."

She smells of her new perfume and stage make-up as her hair hangs like silk tickling my face.

"Shhh, baby. Don't worry. I am old enough to be your mother. And you thought I wasn't proud of you. You looked so devastating tonight, more than ever. You are so beautiful, the most beautiful in the world," she says tracing my collarbones and the diamonds with her fingertips.

"You are so right to say what you did before, about Roma Opera company thinking the great Anasztázia is a bashed around victim. Bashed by some cruel man. Better they all see that the great Anasztázia is with the most beautiful girl in the world. I saw you tonight and I wanted to be with you forever," she says. "Forever, you and me." Her whispers are so soft, her skin so warm and I close my eyes and let myself drown.

In the morning she is shy and quiet. I ask her is she mad at me again?

Her down mood has kicked in after the alcohol wiping out the medication. She will be good for nothing all day.

"No, I was so stupid, overreacting. After all, American English uses 'girlfriend', Hungarian would, many languages. It's not like you said 'lover'," she says. "And you were hurt. No wonder you called me an ageing diva."

"That was nasty. And it's so not true. But one day, Anasztázia, someone will figure it out," I tell her. "Neither of us dating men. You said yourself better the great Anasztázia is with....."

She cuts me off. She either doesn't remember or doesn't want to remember what she said.

"My head hurts, I had three champagne flutes but I felt so wasted. I forgot to eat. I never have more than one," she says. "My throat feels like shit. Alcohol is not good for the voice. And it mixes so badly with my medication. I feel depressed."

"I wasn't invited for some reason. And you know what happens with alcohol and meds. One glass after opening night is okay, baby, not three," I tell her.

But I am glad she is still taking the antidepressants and benzos. It should be levelling her out a bit by now.

She says she is really sorry. She is not ashamed of me. She is so proud of me, just it will affect our work if people know.

"And they haven't figured out with all your tarting in dressing rooms all over Europe? Who did you spend Christmas with? Musetta?"

"Who told you?" she says from under the duvet. "How do you know?"

"God you are so easy to trick, baby. Rosa good was she? Or is she good, more like?"

"Not Rosa, the Musetta from the alternate cast, Simona." She hides herself under the covers.

"My head hurts. Please stop, Natalija...I had to borrow the spare apartment key last night. You took the only one I had."

"Oh of course, the pretty young Italian girl. God, she is

about 25 years old. You are such a predator. Just like your Sara in Paris." What is wrong with Anasztázia? She hasn't changed a bit.

"Romanian, Natalija. I was so lonely, so was she. After Paris, you more or less walked off, said you didn't care if Sara devoured me. I didn't know if you were ever coming back. I was in Roma for three days after Paris and I came straight to London. You were still in Vienna. We are so far apart in our schedules and I thought I was too crazy for you. I am sorry." She hides herself and her shame under the duvet.

"Don't. I have heard it all before. And I will hear it again and again. Seeing your body, you haven't been cutting which is something."

I try to pull the duvet off her but she buries herself under more, rolling herself in it tight.

"I didn't cut this whole run. The costume for Mimì, I could never have hidden it. I am getting help here too. There is a good shrink," she says. "But Musetta, Natalija...."

I sigh. Honestly, what else would I expect? Musetta is a tart. I get out of bed and make the fucking breakfast as she is not up to anything. Selfish little tart. So much for last night.

I insisted on going to the outdoor ice rink on New Year's Day. Anasztázia says I am crazy with my insides still healing. I tell her she doesn't have to come. I need to do this for me.

"What if you break something, Natalija? You are so reckless. You start rehearsals for *Aida* in La Scala in two days. You have a death wish. Why did you buy ice skates?"

"You know I was a champion when I was a teenager, and my brother bought them as a gift," I say as I remove the plastic skate guards and step onto this perilous surface. I am afraid but inhale the ice and feel such nostalgia.

This is the arena I once flew on, leaping so high into split leaps and death-defying triple jumps. My body was as supple as elastic as I performed spins like a whirling tornado with my skate blade pulled so high over my head with both hands. Now and then I cut my hands but I didn't care. I was in the eye of the storm and it was an incredible rush.

Your brain begins to stop feeling dizzy. But I know that once you have a break and try to spin, you are dizzy; your brain and the inner ear crystals are telling you it isn't right. And my body is not so bendy any more.

The rink is half full as it is morning and the whole world is probably hungover. I skate cautiously at first. Then I turn backwards and build up speed. There is no way I am going to risk jumping, not even one rotation. But I am feeling like I am flying again; no fear only stupidity. If I fall, my internal injury might tear, I could break a wrist.

I remember my father asking what was it like to skate, as I was so young when I started I had no fear of the ice or trying jumps and spins. He watched me as I fell over and over again one training session, sprawling on the ice as I was learning a new jump. I never cried. Not once.

"You try it then," I had told him. So he hired some skates one day and stepped out. He couldn't stand up even holding the crash barrier. He was like a bear on skates and after half an hour he gave up saying how could anyone balance on knife blades, it was the worst experience ever.

So unnatural and dangerous and wrong, he said.

But adults have fear.

I work in the centre of the rink alone; I skate, cutting through new ice. I love the scratching sound as I make figure of eights on edges, backwards and forwards and arabesques, pulling my skate over my head. Then I try a spin. And another. I do more spins but I am sick and dizzy. It is going to take time. But it feels so good leaving the ice rink, the frozen air, the wonderland of ice. It is so good to lose myself in something which is not the Opera. Now and then I fall off my edge and onto the ice but I have gloves, and I just bruise my ass.

Instead of being impressed like the other people floating around the outside of the rink who stop to watch me spinning and circling in the centre of the ice, Anasztázia has her arms folded and sits in her white fur sullen and clearly disapproving of my circus tricks. She is miserable as she is cold, tired, hungover and angry. She says nothing as we go back to her tiny studio.

I carefully removed all the ice with a towel from the gleaming silver blades and placed them in their soft soakers to protect the steel at the rink. Now I am checking the blades and screws like I used to do ritualistically and polishing the white leather. Anasztázia watches me silently with the TV on some English New Year's Day trashy film.

"What is wrong with you?" I ask. "You have hardly spoken to me. Is that film really more entertaining?"

Anasztázia gets up and opens the fridge. She doesn't have much food in either.

"You could have really hurt yourself out there, didn't you know how fast you were going?" she asks me. "That was so dangerous, I was afraid for you. You fell a couple of times."

"Yes, but I didn't do any jumps, so what's the big deal? I split my head open on the crash barrier falling in training when I was a junior champion. I was exhausted training and took off too close to the edge and knocked myself unconscious. Lost my memory."

"You are so self-destructive, that is your problem," she says and sits back in front of the TV.

And so is she. She is the most self-destructive person out. If Krisztyna was destructive, she had nothing on Anasztázia apart from the suicide attempt. And Anasztázia thought about it, albeit half-heartedly climbing the Szabadság híd aged 22, the very same bridge my mother jumped from. Easiest to climb, everyone says. And symbolic for its meaning of 'freedom'. Free in death if not in life. I don't think she ever wanted or wants to die. She just can't deal with life.

We say very little to each other that day. She orders some takeaway Italian food and we hardly speak. She is in some weird mood, I hope she doesn't drink three glasses again as the whole day is shot to hell for me too. I suggest she orders some Hungarian food as I noticed a Hungarian restaurant fairly near as I passed in the taxi the day I arrived. She tells me she hates it, always hated it, hated those fatty heavy lumps of lard her mother hurled in everything.

I hate that cuisine, Natalija and most of all the horrible breakfast with nasty cheap salami, rubbery cheeses, pig everywhere. I was made to live in Italia. I was born in the wrong country and definitely to the wrong parents as they hate me.

I am not a lover of my country's food, but it isn't all pig's foot soup and lard and cheap salami.

I was trying to make her feel better. I get it wrong as usual.

I have told her she is making a mistake to accept *Lucia di Lammermoor* in Palermo. It is rehearsals starting early June and finishing beginning of July. She told me who the hell am I to tell her what not to take, I am not her agent.

Your agent doesn't know how ill you are. When you performed in May in Roma, your performance scared me. You said yourself that role was dangerous. That it was like staring into a black hole, Anasztázia, and this time you might fall into it. It is the last role you should be taking. Marguerite didn't help either in Paris. You need Puccini, Verdi, but not madness. Do you want me to be visiting you in a psychiatric ward in Sicilia? This is not the way to get well.

She sits on the floor staring at the TV, hunched like a vulture in a deep sulk.

You give me no choice, baby. You are not going to Palermo

alone. I am going with you.

Fine, she says. You do that, Natalija. You do that and be my little nurse.

Isn't that what you wanted, Anasztázia? Me looking after you and your crazy moods?

She doesn't answer.

Later, I asked her casually about the flowers for Krisztyna. I didn't want to make it a big deal since everything else is a big deal in London clearly. But she has hardly mentioned the poor girl she once loved too. Doesn't she care?

Of course I did, Natalija. I told you on the phone, I ordered blue roses. Blue are beautiful and rare and it is very tragic. I am so sorry for that girl. I am too sad to talk about it. But your father he was so nice, so nice to me when we spoke, said he would love to meet me. Your parents are so liberal, Natalija. Mine would tell me to burn in Hell if I took a woman to visit them........

She lost it. Krisztyna stared into that black hole for too long, Anasztázia.

Don't, please don't. Please stop talking about madness, Natalija. I don't feel well. Please stop.

The jewellery didn't help. It was a dumb idea. I gave her the box all wrapped up on the breakfast tray when she finally emerged from the duvet and she seemed happy. She ripped open the paper with childish delight and then looked so thrilled. Inside was a sapphire engagement ring and a white gold wedding ring. I got myself a box with a ruby engagement ring and the same white gold ring. I said they weren't so expensive unlike the diamonds she got me. Not cheap but now we both have them. Then I placed her rings on the ring finger of her right hand. Her smile faded as she looked at me. She looked more unhappy when I did the same with mine.

"Natalija, what are you trying to say? These are wedding rings?"

"I thought that was what you wanted. And if you don't want people to know, they won't. In Italia they are worn on the left hand. Oh, for God's sake. I can't do anything right. I thought you would like the idea. Paint it on the Opera House walls you said only last night. Better the great Anasztázia is with the most beautiful girl in the world than some violent man you told me. Forever, you also said."

She doesn't take them off but she said very little after breakfast and the rest of the evening, she is sulking, not speaking to me, because of the rings, the ice rink or God knows what.

Well that was a waste of money.

I have to focus. I need to throw myself into rehearsals. This time, I will not return to Roma during the rehearsal period like I did in September. I rent an overpriced place near La Scala in Milano.

Aida is going to take everything I have got.

"Please forget about me during the run at least, Anasztázia. The way you were since I have been in London has been so weird. First I get thousands of euros of diamonds, then the cold treatment, then affection and then silence. I don't care that you cheated with Musetta. I would have done too. Okay, I was a bitch in Paris, but I come first in my world now. And you were so unhappy about those goddamn rings. Give them away if you feel like that."

It is 2nd January and my legs are aching from ice-skating yesterday, using muscles I haven't used for years and I am about to leave for the airport.

"I'm sorry, it was a lovely gift, really it was. I was just shocked because it was such a big gesture for you. And no one knows, it is just for us. I won't let you go, Natalija. I am in London until 10th January and I am coming straight to you. I need to see you just for a couple of nights," she tells me. "You know you have made me yours now. I am yours forever."

She says that like she means it and I wonder what the hell I have gone and done.

It was a really stupid idea. What the hell was I thinking in the airport buying those rings?

"Anasztázia, I am going to be really busy.....the rehearsals will be so tough.... I am poison so please just let me work," I tell her. "Go pick up with some new flesh if you have to. I told you I cannot deal with your drama......"

"Natalija, no, it was a lovely idea, the sapphire and you got the ruby, I was just so surprised. I need to see you, Natalija. Soon. You know my daughter will only be visiting for a few weeks in Roma."

"Have your daughter live with you. I will find somewhere else for a few weeks," I say.

"No, Natalija, please listen. I told her that *Il Trovatore* would not be a good time for you. She will visit when you are away afterwards in Madrid. I have a few days before going to La Scala for *La Traviata* and then she can stay in the apartment when we are both away. I need you...."

The taxi is waiting outside her apartment as we go out. She is performing tonight. She is hanging on to me trying to get me to agree to this visit in Milano when I will be stressed, tired, bitchy and mean.

It won't help us. She looks at me trying to read my soul then at her right hand which is gripping my arm, at the sapphire rock which I chose to match her eyes. She studies it for a few seconds.

"Oh for fuck's sake," she says and in the cold daylight of the busy London street she kisses me passionately in full view of everyone walking by. "That's what you wanted, wasn't it? That was what this is all about, fine. There. Now everyone saw that. Happy?"

I smile. "Well that was a nice change."

She has already gone back upstairs, ashamed that the whole street saw.

So fucking what. I don't care who sees, I am done with caring.

I get in the cab.

"Can you do that again, love?" says the driver adjusting his mirror.

"No, it was a one off show," I tell him. I stare out of the window.

She also seems to believe my career comes second to hers and this is making me mad. I am fighting so hard to be the outstanding mezzo I was. She has 16 years on me. Of course she is more famous but she has a big head start and it is easier to be famous as a soprano.

Am I turning back into the bitchy careless Carmen I was now I can sing again?

I want this annoying, clingy diva to give me space, with her moods still spiking up and down. I have told her over and over.

Yes I think I love her but she drives me mad.

She won't leave me alone.

Her show finishes 10th January and she arrives in La Scala when I am rehearsing. The rehearsals are the most intense and arduous I have ever had. Even if I was 100%, La Scala has raised the level way higher than I am used to. The director is very demanding. I am shattered. The heavy role of Amneris, the stress of reaching the level demanded by La Scala and the rehearsals are taking everything from me. My voice is lacking projection; I notice, the directors notice, the other singers must notice and I am worried they will cut me from the production if I don't improve. The quality is the same, but I haven't got that power I had. I am not going to reach that chandelier and I will be cat-called off stage and axed from La Scala forever.

No one says anything though, unlike that musical director in Vienna. Bastard.

One of the stage managers tells me my Hungarian friend

is waiting for me in the café as I finish my rehearsal. He sighs as he says, 'the beautiful and wonderful soprano, Anasztázia'.

He tells me how touching this famous diva is my good friend.

He is obviously in awe of her. He breathes her name as if she were a goddess.

All these men who would kill to spend just one night with her and here am I, half-hearted and heartless. She doesn't even notice them which I think makes them more obsessed.

They don't even know why. Why would they?

I just smile at the stage manager and tell him we share our nationality, that helps.

Everyone seems to revere Anasztázia here. She has performed a lot in La Scala. What is she here for? *Oh, just to see a friend, my Hungarian friend from Roma.*

Liar.

What is adding to the stress is the amount of lying we have to do. I lied about Krisztyna but people either knew, didn't care or didn't ask. There was a lot more secrecy in Hungary and I miss that. Here the first question in Italia is, *Are you married?*

I don't want to keep up the old lie of the Opera World makes relationships difficult forever. Maybe I should have made her wear her fake wedding rings on her left hand. I chose the right because it is Hungarian but also Spanish too, thinking of Sara, who thinks she can have me. I will tell her I am promised to someone else.

I hurt Anasztázia probably because deep down I do not want to be this person who needs anyone.

I am pushing her away not just because she was unfaithful, but really because I cannot accept being needy myself. So what I told the stage door men in London I was her girlfriend. So fucking what. She made it a big deal. They probably have already forgotten.

It would hardly tarnish her reputation.

I wore a wedding dress for Krisztyna to her performance and the company women were so bitchy. But I only did it just to shock them all and nothing else. I didn't do it for the right reasons. I was just greedy, wanting attention whether it was good or bad. I loved being hated.

I go to find my sad princess in the café. She is toying with her espresso cup and she rises up to meet me, with that lost dreamy look in her eyes. She is so beautiful, I can't throw her aside. Where would I find another to equal her?

Later that evening I am bitchy and mean from lack of food and tiredness after rehearsals for *Aida*. Angry because every muscle in my body is screaming from the demanding role as my voice is being stretched to the limit. Angry because I am not as good as I was.

That maybe I am done for.

That maybe my career has been well and truly stabbed through the heart.

"Why are you so angry? Do I make you like this or is it *Aida*?" Anasztázia says pathetically.

I am banging the plates on the table, dishing up ravioli bought from the trattoria below my apartment. I am still mad at Anasztázia for cheating in London with tarty little Musetta.

She always fiddles with her bracelets when she has cheated. Little girl hurt look and then she looks down and plays with her bracelets. Now she is fiddling with her wedding rings I gave her. At least she is wearing them. I thought it would keep her faithful for a bit but it hasn't worked for more than ten minutes.

Always the same whine, *I was so lonely. I missed you. I didn't know if you still wanted me.*

A pity as she has dressed up so beautifully for me. Taken time out of her busy work schedule to be here.

I could at least make an effort for two nights. I am so ungrateful. Thousands of euros of diamonds on me and I can't be nice.

"Natalija, I am so sorry as you are in pain again after singing, but why do you act like you really hate me?" She touches her forehead, the scar faded but still visible.

It always makes me so guilty when she touches her scar.

"I don't hate you, Anasztázia. Is your head hurting?" I say.

"No, it is okay but please don't blame yourself. I was crazy in Latvia, I was really fucking crazy.

And don't blame yourself about Krisztyna either. Natalija, after *Carmen* she wasn't the same. You and Lilla saved her life."

"Listen, Anasztázia, I am sorry if I am bitchy. I am worried my voice……. And you are just so goddamn needy."

"Where is that girl I first met because I don't see her? Natalija, you are so tense and unhappy. You said you always cheated, so why are you so angry with me? How much do I have to tell you how sorry I am. Especially about….." She doesn't say the name. I can forgive her for Sara and Musetta and whoever else, but not Krisztyna. She was so devious, calling Krisztyna before she even arrived in Roma. And that is the worst excuse ever, *I cheated because I missed you. Because she told me you would throw me away.*

My eyes start to tear up. She thinks it is her but really it is my voice. I am afraid it has gone. That is really what is troubling me, not this damaged diva who can't keep her clothes on for more than five minutes.

I turn away and stare out of the window, trying to hide the tears, wiping my face with my wrist.

She notices and gets up as I am crying. "Come here, baby, come here." She wraps her arms around me. Easier to let her think it is her and not even to articulate this horrible feeling that my Opera career is in tatters. If I say it, it will come true. I will be finished.

"Old enough to be your mama, Natalija," she says softly.

"I want my mother," I say.

"Let me be for tonight. Please don't cry, Natalija, I hate to see you cry."

"Everything ends, there is nothing lasting in this world," I say. "Maybe I will have myself a few flings just like you do." I cry more.

As if I had one iota of energy. I have nothing left to give as I am more exhausted than I have ever been in my entire life.

"Come on, honey. We can make it okay," she says stroking my face. "I promise you."

Let her feel guilty. She touches my ruby ring and entwines her hand in it.

"That was so lovely of you to buy those matching rings, it shows you really wanted to be with me. It was so romantic and you are not a romantic type; the exact opposite. I just behaved like an idiot on New Year, worrying what the world would say."

I seem to own her now. A moment's airport spending when I was stressed, buying loads of stuff and I have married myself to the girl.

I want to take it back. I never wanted to be married to anyone, never wanted to be anyone's possession. I am impulsive and reckless and stupid.

I want to throw food at the wall, or better still smash some plates.

"Don't think everything ends," she tells me. "And cheating is no fun. It is horrible."

"I broke everyone's hearts once and that was no fun, no one was having fun, not even me," I tell her.

Broken their hearts so carelessly. And still at it. Angry and lashing out at the world.

"Natalija. Just because I was in Paris with that tarty Spanish stage manager. And Sara dates everyone." She throws her arms in the air. "Everyone."

"Good reason not to be with her then," I say.

"You fell in love with my photographs. I can never live up to that," I tell her.

"And you do live up to it, Natalija. And you fell in love with Lucia di Lammermoor. Only I don't live up to what you needed. I know I am sick." She looks down. "I have thought there was something wrong for about 20 years. It has got so much worse the last couple of years. I am frightened, Natalija. I am very frightened."

"I know," I say. "At least you realise it. We need to work on this."

She nods. We both push the pasta away. Neither of us is hungry.

"And you are Lucia di Lammermoor, no wonder you played her so well."

"You think I am crazy?" she says anxiously. "You told me I shouldn't take the role in Palermo in May."

Dinner is fucked anyway. What are a few tears in the cold ravioli. I am not hungry.

"You can reach the depths of madness because you feel it. Anasztázia you are not crazy but since you last performed that role you are much sicker. You have got much worse in the 8 months I have known you. You scare me, Anasztázia."

"I know," she says. "I know, Natalija."

"Tiramisu," I say dropping it in a bowl. "None for me, I don't trust myself with it."

She eats her tiramisu even though I know she isn't enjoying it. She can't look at me. I watch her. I feel sad for her. I take her hand. Maybe you shouldn't tell a person they are getting sicker.

"What if you don't come back out of that black hole, Anasztázia? What if Lucia takes you over and you don't come out of 'Il dolce suono'? Please reconsider. Take Puccini, take Verdi but think so hard. I told you I will come to Sicilia, for the whole time. My last Opera finishes early June. I will keep those five weeks free since I have shows in July and August. I need a rest break anyway. I told you in

London."

She nods and says quietly, "Thank you. It means a lot."

"I am not having you alone in Palermo performing *Lucia di Lammermoor.*"

The feeling still hangs between us, heavy and sullen; the madness waiting for her, shimmering ever closer.

I look at her, so fragile and gentle, admiring her porcelain beauty. But so easy to break, porcelain. This famous diva, the beautiful Anasztázia who has chosen me and wants to give me the world.

Yet I am forever pushing her away and she is tarting around. Then she self-harms. Then she tarts around more and I push her away. It is never-ending.

We are dying. In endless yet graceful circles we are dying, like the aria 'Il dolce suono' when Lucia spirals around the stage before collapsing in death.

I thought I had found my new life, love and everything.

Really it is all fragments of dust.

I am trying to sleep. Even her delicate as crystal voice has started to grate on me. Tonight I am not hearing tinkling glass, just *-ek, -ek, -ek.*

Using the Italian language so much now, I am becoming aware of what I don't like about my native tongue; the backward formation of sentences, the insane grammar, all those endings with -ek, -ek, -ek. I see and hear it from a foreigner's point of view.

We always speak Hungarian with each other. All I am hearing tonight as I am wanting sleep is *-ek, -ek, -ek.*

"The Opera World has contaminated everything about the way we see reality. There are no happy endings in performances, but this is our life."

"Please stop talking, Anasztázia. I am tired."

"Why are you so full of darkness? I want my Natalija back, the one I met at my première in May."

"Didn't anyone ever tell you that you are so exhausting, baby? I need to focus on my rehearsals, so just shut up!" I punch the pillows and flop further away from her. I need to sleep.

"Natalija! Please look for these beautiful lights which shine in the distance. You are still walking in the shadows." She ghosts her fingers along my arm, tries to hug me but I do not move. I stay with my back to her. "I'm sorry for being so needy, Natalija."

"It is an illusion, Anasztázia. Light. Just like the stage lights or the beautiful lights at night in Budapest or Paris. The city draped in gold like a wonderland and in the morning the magic is gone," I murmur half asleep. I am seeing the golden lights of Buda Castle in my head.

Anasztázia sighs. She rests her hand on my back, on the scar which has healed but I haven't. She leaves it there gently and I fall asleep without turning round as I feel the gentle spidery caresses round and round my skin.

I wake up to her holding me tight, her fingers wrapped around mine.

I am in rehearsals all day and once I return, we manage to spend an evening without strife.

We go to eat in some overpriced, overrated stuck-up restaurant near my apartment. The waiters are rude, the food indifferent and it is full of Milanese businessmen shouting on cell phones. I really hate this city at times like this. If I lived here I would go insane. She pays. She pays for everything and I feel guilty. I have money but she won't take a euro from me.

I manage to tell her what I needed to say in the restaurant. A neutral place makes it easier.

"Anasztázia, I am really happy you are here. I was so ill with bulimia, I was dying. I had to be forced to get help. I haven't behaved well towards you. It is just so hard because I am in my rehearsals and so tired and stressed. But I will try to help you get well, I really will." I look down.

"Natalija, that means so much. You didn't have to say it,"

she says.

"I wouldn't say it if I didn't mean it," I tell her. "But I will never truly understand you. Maybe nobody ever did and that is the problem. No one ever tried."

"No, they didn't," she says quietly. "They all walked away."

She has to leave the next morning. She has work in Roma, some concerts to perform in but she will return for my opening night. It seems sweet but I tell her, *No need, please.* I really mean 'please don't.'

I really don't want her to come to opening night or any night. This was fine. I am in rehearsals but I can't deal with any more of her until I finish my *Aida* run.

LA SCALA

I am back to where I was in the Opera World, taking on major roles and returning to the old me which is splintering through the good girl façade. The sweet, softer Natalija is falling away as layers of the chrysalis unravel faster and faster and the pushy arrogant diva is re-emerging to take the limelight. The ruthless Natalija who has to be this way to stand in front of 2,000, 3,000, 4,000 people and sing at her absolute best. Who cannot share the glory with another diva. *I am, I am, I am,* I tell myself in my dressing room mirror as the stage manager gives the half hour call. My eyes are made up with gold and black and my face appears as a mask as I look in the mirror.

Amneris, I say. *Amneris, you Egyptian wonder. Beautiful, ancient, exotic. You are, you are, you are.* The transformation is complete.

I am.

The role of Amneris is so tough on opening night in La Scala and my nerves are so bad because I am not sure I am going to manage to hit some of those notes. So far removed from my early Opera days when I felt full of power and positivity. Now my body is struggling to make transitions from the notes, aching as I try to project my voice with the effortless grace of only a year ago, even when I was damaging it with bulimia. Only my crashing great ego pushes me on, forces the sound out.

A few people shout from the gallery when I do not hit the notes with the power I need and I can visibly see the sound flopping into the orchestra pit. I was fine in *Rigoletto* singing a minor role a few months ago but this demands so much. Just two or three of the loggionisti, those pigs who sit in the cheapest seats in the house and ruin it for everyone else who might have paid up to 500 euros to see *Aida*. But it is a few uncouth people and not the whole house. I thought I would scream 'Go to Hell!' as some singers have, and walk off because it throws me. No one ever shouted out during an Opera before even when I was not 100% or others in the cast were hopelessly short of the level they should have been. But then this is La Scala; the arena, the Colosseum of Opera.

The respect I get from the rest of the auditorium when I finish my aria is overwhelming shouts of *Brava!*

They even have printed in the programme this is my first major role since I nearly died in a stage accident in Budapest. The audience who do buy the programme, who read this have nothing but respect and I am cheered the loudest at the end. The musical director holds me alone for a minute and the whole orchestra and company, even the veteran soprano who played Aida turn to give me such applause. I bow with tears in my eyes, hold my hands to my chest. So unlike the arrogant young Natalija who raised her arms in success after singing the role of Amneris to a crowd of 4,000 people in the open air festival in Budapest. The one who thought she was invincible.

Afterwards, there is one person who wants to see me so much. Who had a bouquet of blue roses sent to my dressing room before the show. I have put the roses in a vase as they are pretty. Blue roses are so symbolic of mystery and some emotion I feel but yet I just cannot articulate. But blue roses fit Anasztázia and her layers of mystery. She sent them to Krisztyna in hospital. She loves them herself and hates it when she has to have them sprayed blue if the flower shop doesn't stock them. But these are real blue, brilliant and rare. I look at them and think of her every time. She joins me in the dressing room as soon as the curtain is down. There is no première for this show and I am glad. Hungary has too many as does Roma and I am too shattered to face anyone. There are autograph hunters around stage door but I cannot deal with anyone tonight, even myself.

I could really do with being completely alone.

Anasztázia is performing in La Scala as Violetta in *La Traviata* when I am in Madrid in March and April. I will have two weeks off after Madrid so she is hopeful I will come to watch her in La Scala. The same stage she has sung on so many times to magnificent reviews. There is never a bad review of her. Anywhere. She is always perfect. On stage anyway. Off it, she is far from perfect.

Anasztázia looks lovely in a silver embroidered dress which trails with a metre of rustling fabric although I think she has overdressed even for La Scala. She wears her white fur, and her dark-honeyed hair rests on her shoulders styled and set. She has more eye-liner on than usual, giving her the effect of looking even more unreal. My china doll.

She hangs around my neck and says I was wonderful. I am soaked with sweat and feel anything but wonderful. I feel the exhaustion bite and I collapse on the chair by the mirror. Anasztázia locks the dressing room door and smiles at me in the glass and I see all her lovers flash before her eyes in that look.

She is beautiful but God, she is a terrible flirt. Look at her. She will cheat again, Natalija. Make no mistake. I wish she were a china doll tonight and would just sit where she is placed and let me get on with getting ready to leave. Sleep is really calling.

"You don't need to lock that door," I tell her. "No one is coming in, I have already given my costume to the girls to be cleaned."

I am wearing a black backless dress for some unknown reason. I am not going anywhere. I try to get the gold braid out of my hair which is wound around the strands of black. I give up. I am too tired.

"I do have to lock the door," Anasztázia says slipping off her coat and hanging it up. She steps towards me and kisses my neck as I am sitting down and massages my shoulders which ache, as I begin to wipe off the heavy gold and black eye make-up with my cleansing wipes. There is so much make-up, I need a good shower. I feel grimy and sticky and irritable. I do not feel beautiful and I do not want to be touched.

Her hands move down my bare back into my dress, softly travelling down and she kisses my spine.

"No, baby, no," I tell her. "Not now. Can you just help me get this gold thread out of my hair, it is wrapped so tight?"

She ignores me and carries on caressing me and I see her expression in the mirror; her look says, *Don't you want me? I will make sure you do.* She wraps herself around me as I struggle to wipe my make-up off.

She is trying to seduce me in my dressing room.

Tired, emotional and angry, I turn on her.

"No! I told you no!" I shove her away from me. She steps backwards against the wall and slides down it with a look of total despair.

"Anasztázia, just stop it! I don't want this! Just leave me alone! You are such a little slut!"

I never forget her look that night. Her silver dress sparkles in the light like the goddess she is and she is so beautiful, but I am so tired my insides are screaming. I wish I had been softer, said that I was in pain from singing. *Please just hold me instead,* is what I should have said. *Hold me as I am so exhausted.*

I didn't need to insult her so brutally. But I was not kind and it had nothing to do with my insecurity and everything to do with not caring about her feelings. I am the diva tonight, not her. Neither of us speaks for a minute. She sits there and I carry on removing my make-up.

"You know, I had so many lovers in dressing rooms and they were just passion, short-lived and meaningless. It kills me that the girl I love doesn't even want to touch me. The person I love most in the world. I can't do this, Natalija. I love you, but I can't take your moods." She doesn't move from the floor where she fell like a broken toy and holds her head in her hands. "Didn't you even notice I was wearing a wedding dress? You wore one for Krisztyna. Now I am wearing one for you. Doesn't that tell you something? And didn't you notice my arms, I have been getting help, I have not cut." She holds out her bare arms to show me.

I look closer at her sitting on the floor in the silver embroidered lace and fitted bodice. Not so obvious as white but now she tells me it is pretty obvious. Too obvious.

"It's just you are too much, Anasztázia," I say quietly. "And wearing a wedding dress to come and see me? What the hell are you thinking? Are you supposed to be my bride or what? You are never sure what you want and you are very demanding at the wrong moment, like tonight. I cannot deal with your needy nature, always wanting to be the diva. Forever wanting love and attention. It is all about you and your demands. No wonder you are dressed like that. You wanted to upstage me in every way. You just wanted to be the star tonight."

Even said quietly this is deeply hurtful.

"Too demanding!" she screams and leaps up from the floor. She hurls the box of chocolates one of the directors gave me across the room. "There, stuff yourself with those but don't come crying to me when you throw up! You make me feel dirty, as though I am just a one off tart! You think I am just after a quick dressing room roll-around? What is your problem?"

She is full of rage and throwing everything around the room, anything she can get her hands on, even her beautiful blue roses and the vase shatters against the wall. She grabs some other flowers, sent by my family, and I get mad and tell her. "Don't you fucking dare, Anasztázia! I mean it!"

I grab hold of the end of her dress, this rustling silver concoction.

She puts the flowers back and looks around for something else to throw.

I tell her, "Sit down, please. Stop acting like a goddamn

child."

"No! You are the child, Natalija! You are the spoilt little diva and you love it!"

"Anasztázia, why did you throw your flowers at the wall? They are so pretty."

I get up and rescue the blue roses, wrap them in their paper and pick up the pieces of vase which has smashed into big hunks of glass. "Please, just sit down. Look at this damn vase. It isn't even mine, Anasztázia. God, you really are a petulant diva. Just because I was on stage tonight and not you, you throw a tantrum."

I sit down again. I want her out of my room, out of my life. "Just get out, Anasztázia. Get out and leave me alone. Just go back home to Roma, I don't want you here, I never did." I put my head on the dressing table hoping she will leave.

"No! It's always going to be about punishing me for my mistakes, Natalija. You have made me beg every day since I hurt you and you will never let it go!"

"Anasztázia, that is so unfair. I am exhausted and I am the star tonight, not you," I am too tired to shout.

I look at myself in the mirror. I look as drained as I feel.

Neither of us moves and I don't look at her.

She has stopped shouting, which is good. But in fact she is gearing up to scream at me.

"I feel I am never good enough!" she screams "Never good enough for you! You are the little diva way more than I was. Krisztyna was right! You are the most arrogant prima donna I ever met! You love yourself, you can't get enough adulation on that stage! You worship it! I saw you for what you really are after tonight's Opera and it is not the Natalija I knew! All I do is love you and buy you everything in the world! And you only love yourself!"

It is the first time I have seen her really lose it. Scream and shout and hurl stuff around, yelling that she never feels good enough for me. Her tears are angry and she starts to take her coat and put it on. I get up and hold her and tell her I am sorry.

She tries to shakes me off but I hold her wrists.

"Let go of me!" she screams louder. "I give you the world and you throw it back at me! I would let you have everything; fucking diamonds, five star hotels, my apartment free. I would buy you anything you wanted, anything you desired only it's never good enough! I admitted I cheated, but I am human, Natalija. How many more times do I have to say I am sorry? Until the day I die? I don't want anyone else! This has become twisted and cruel and you are the puppeteer!"

She is so hysterical and fighting so hard and screaming so much and so loud, I am afraid someone will think I am killing her. I am afraid as I have never seen someone lose it like this. She is crazy tonight. Worse than she was in Latvia, way worse.

I slap her face, not to hurt her but to stop her terrible screaming. It is incessant shrieking and everyone will come running any minute and break the door down. The shock stops her and she says, "You hit me, you hit me." She holds her hand to her face and cries. "You hit me, you really hate me, don't you?"

I pull her towards me. "Anasztázia, I'm sorry. You are hysterical. I don't want to hurt you but please stop screaming. Someone will think I am killing you in here. This is terrible."

"Let go of me, I hate you!" she says crying. But she has stopped her awful shrieking.

"No!" I hold tight. "Come on, darling. Come on, let it go, give it to me." Her soft white fur coat makes me feel like I am trying to control an angry cat, claws scrabbling, twisting to free herself but I am stronger and she gives in. She just turns her face into my chest and cries, her hands clinging to my long hair. "I hate you, I really hate you!" she says.

"You are right to hate me. I am Natalija the diva on that

stage. I have to be, you just never knew me when I was," I say. She just cries as I hold her tight and the terrible demon which possessed her dies down.

"You just kept leaving me or ignoring my calls, Natalija; in Latvia, in Vienna, when you were in Budapest last month. It made me crazy! I know I am a wreck, I know I self-harm but I just want you to love me! Please just love me! Love me!" She says into my chest. "Love me because I am sick and I am so scared I am losing my mind!"

"But I do, I do love you," I tell her into her hair. I stroke the silken strands away from her face and let her just cry into me, hoping the demon has left her body. "And I am sorry, that silver dress is really beautiful on you. You look a million dollars. You are sick, but you won't lose your mind. We can get you better. I promise you."

We can make up, I can take her home. I will make it all up to her.

"I am so sorry I upset you, please don't cry," I say. But when I let go of her for a second to get her some tissues, she grabs her bag, unlocks the door and runs out without a word. It is just too late for sorry.

I chase her down the corridor. "Anasztázia! Come back and do what you want. Do anything! You can have all of me. You are forgiven!" I hold out my arms to her.

She whirls round so angry that I am calling out down the dressing room corridor. She looks and makes sure no one is listening to her. Faces me with her deep blue eyes, furious that I am shouting when people could hear. Her mascara has run into spiders down her cheeks and she says quietly, "Shut up, Natalija. Everyone knows me. They will guess, maybe someone is Hungarian here, so keep your voice down. The last thing I need right now is gossip about my personal life. Maybe you don't care but I do."

My anger ignites again. I look at her and say coldly, "Ashamed of me are you, just like in London? Why? You're the one crying, cheating, and cutting yourself not me. You're the one making a scene in La Scala, wearing a wedding dress as well. You are the one begging me for love like a little child. You are the one so desperate for me to forgive you. You are right; this relationship has become sick or maybe it always was. You and me; we are so, so bad for each other." I fold my arms and just look at her, my heartbroken princess.

She looks at me shocked that I am so cold. She shakes her head and holds the wall, leaning against it for support.

"It is always going to be like this, Natalija. I love you but you do not love me. Marina was so wrong when she said you would never hurt me. I thought you were sweet. I am sorry I wasted so much time on you, sorry I cried so many tears over you, sorry I told you I would wait forever. You are not the girl I fell in love with."

She grips the wall and is silent.

"Anasztázia, you are not that elfin princess I first saw in May on the Opera House stage, like something from a fairy tale. I thought you were magical only you are not. She never really existed. It was an act. I was lying to myself. I loved her, not what you have become."

She holds up her arms. "I have begged you to forgive me but it did no good. It's over, Natalija. We are finished, because I am broken. Totally broken. You won." Her hands drop to her sides and she looks down as tears still glide down her face. She cannot even look at me. "You are right; we are so bad for each other. You are making me sicker, Natalija."

I take her hand and suddenly I don't want her to go. I am about to promise her that I can try to love this Anasztázia, the real Anasztázia, the one no one ever tried to help or understand.

That however broken and damaged, she can still be the one.

"Anasztázia, please look at me....." I say.

She doesn't pull her hand away, but she still won't meet

my eyes. I reduced this beautiful, delicate star to this; crying in a dressing room corridor over a heartless diva. I have learned nothing about love in the last year. I am ashamed of myself. I was careless with her heart. If she is sicker, I am to blame. I kept walking away all the time, I never helped her and now she is really ill.

Some people behind me in the corridor distract us momentarily. We stop talking immediately. I turn round and watch as they go laughing into a dressing room with a bottle of champagne, not even noticing us. They close the door and the corridor is silent again and only the sounds of the stage crew working on the lighting rig are audible. It is dark and eerily quiet. When I turn back to Anasztázia, she has gently removed her hand from mine.

She has slipped through my fingers.

She is gone.

"No! Anasztázia, come back!"

Maybe she really has gone for good this time. I run out through stage door into the street but there is no sign of her. It is bitter and cold outside after the warm shell of the Opera House.

She has disappeared into thin air, vanished, this fairy-tale girl. Into the cold night air.

"Anasztázia!" I shout. "Anasztázia!"

But she has gone. The dark street is empty.

"Anasztázia, please come back to me," I say to the night air and the street swirls around me. I throw up on the frozen ground; all the pre-show nerves and post-show stress. My ribs ache. The street is deserted. Almost everyone has left as it is such a cold night with swirls of fog in the January blackness; Milano and it feels like Siberia. I am shivering in my thin dress, aching with exhaustion.

I go back into the cocoon of the theatre and I ask the stage door keeper did he see Anasztázia leave? The one in the white fur coat? He did but she ran past so quickly. He called out to her, he knows her well but she just ran past him.

She is feeling very ill tonight, I lie. *She has a bad migraine.*

I ask him to call me a taxi and I go back to the dressing room. One of the stage managers sees me and asks am I okay, I look very pale and anxious.

I tell him it was just so tiring, I need to sleep after my first major role back. That is all.

Good girl, he says. *You'll be perfection by Thursday night. Go and rest now.*

I will, I say. *I know I will.*

I go back to my dressing room and I stuff my bag with everything lying around except the chocolate box, now dented and misshapen. I try to form it back into shape and give up and place it by the mirrors. I leave the pieces of the broken glass vase on the table. I pick up Anasztázia's beautiful roses, hand the key back to stage door and go back to my tiny apartment alone. I place the flowers in a tall glass on the table as there are no vases and go to bed drained of all life and hope. They are the only bit of colour in this overpriced tiny studio. Miserable Milano.

I lost the most precious thing in the world. More precious than the stones she gave me which are glittering on the bedside table. I send her a message but I know she won't reply.

> *My dear Anasztázia, please understand how much I love you. I am sorry I hurt you. I was tired after Aida. It is not over. I forgave you a long time ago. Just call me. You don't have to be perfect, far from it. I only want you just as you are.*
> *I promise you this.*

She doesn't answer. I don't know if she has gone back to

Roma already.

I send some flowers a few days later but I hear nothing. I have to focus on my work. The *Aida* run over the two and a half weeks stops me from thinking. I have to concentrate on the show. I sent the white roses to her apartment when I knew she was in Roma to receive them. She is lost to me. I half thought the flowers I sent could win her back, but it runs too deep for that. She can't be bought with a few roses if I cannot be bought with thousands of euros of diamonds.

I channel it all into Opera, reaching depths I never did before. My final performance as Amneris brings so much applause in the sold out La Scala it goes on forever. Even the soprano singing Aida is not jealous and I feel she was every bit as good as me, better even. But she knows, like the others how hard this has been to come back.

And each night on my hard bed in miserably cold Milano I look at my favourite photo I always take with me when I travel; Anasztázia draped in red velvet sitting across a stage somewhere in Europe, gazing up to the Heavens. This photo is from *Tosca*, as she has on a silver crucifix and tiara. So I go to the Duomo in Milano one Sunday and pray for Tosca to come back to me. It doesn't work. God maybe is tired of all my theatrics. Tired of both of us. He has had enough of my requests.

Every night I dream of my mother. She looks so sad. I ask her to please help, but she doesn't speak.

She just watches me and doesn't reach out to hold me.

I wake up one morning and Tosca's crucifix is on the pillow next to me. It was a gift from Marina years ago when we first met in London. I haven't worn it for some time as it is more stage jewellery than anything everyday. Marina was performing as Tosca and she handed me the crucifix for luck.

I wore it to my audition at The Royal Hungarian Opera when a director noticed it and noticed me, thought I was the ultimate Carmen. One who would drag everyone to Hell, the underworld, or some similar words.

And in a way, he was dead right.

Only Marina's second gift of the beautiful Lucia di Lammermoor that glittering night in May, has not been so fortuitous. Marina didn't know that when she handed me this princess, Anasztázia.

"She's yours now, look after her," she had even said to me as if she had given me a precious jewel. An object, not a living, breathing human. Marina only sees an elfin otherworldly creature, she never saw reality either. No one could live up to that image everyone always had of her; Anasztázia the fairy-tale princess of the stage.

It is lonely, so lonely at the top of the world, she had said.

I stare at the ceiling and think of the other diva I know. I wonder if Krisztyna will ever light up the stage as Puccini's heroines again. Lilla has called me to say she visited her in hospital. She is better but they have moved her to the psychiatric ward as she talked about killing herself. She is heavily medicated, Lilla says, an empty shell of the smoky sensual beauty she was. I lie there thinking morbid thoughts before getting up to go to the Opera House.

"She will get better, Natalija. But it is best for you not to see her," Lilla tells me. "I found all those photos of you and the black magic. I boxed your photos as I was packing up Krisztyna's stuff. Best she doesn't have them. Your father will sell the apartment. Krisztyna needs her mother to care for her. It was thoughtful of Anasztázia to send those lovely blue roses. I saw them in the hospital. I think it helped the poor girl, she was admiring the colour."

I say nothing to Lilla. It is all too complicated.

I should be happy that Krisztyna is better but it saddens me she still wants to die, she doesn't want the life we saved.

I will return to Roma for *Il Trovatore* and the most

demanding role of Azucena. Then I will be going on to Madrid for Princessa Eboli in *Don Carlo* and after that, after a break of two weeks, after turning down *Carmen* in Napoli, I will be La Principessa di Bouillon in *Adriana Lecouvreur.* So I am fully booked until the beginning of June. It will be September before I am resurrected in my signature role, *Carmen* in Riga Opera. I have offers from many places, for roles I have not performed before. My voice is stronger every show I sing, but I am sad. I wish Anasztázia were singing opposite me as Adriana in a self-reflexive opera about theatreland. She would be the one poisoned at the end, who collapses and dies.

I am always interested in the self-reflexive operas such as *Pagliacci* and *Tosca*.

I promised I would not let Anasztázia go to Palermo alone for *Lucia di Lammermoor*. I will not take anything for those five weeks of June and early July. Even if she hates me, I am going to Sicilia for that time. I am a selfish diva; I come first but I am not having her alone out there to go insane. I am afraid of receiving a call from Palermo hospital to say she attempted suicide or has been sectioned.

I have open air festival arrangements for July and August in Italia. But I am leaving those five weeks free. Two days after *Adriana Lecouvreur* finishes she is due in Palermo.

It is lonely, so lonely at the top of the world.

I wonder if I should even start doing comic operas. I wonder if tragedy is dictating my moods.

I think it has done with her. In 16 years I will be going crazy too. Sick, not crazy, I remember.

She is sick, Natalija. She never got the help she needed 20 years ago. She has been ill for a long time.

I picture myself as Cherubino in *Figaro* hiding under skirts and feel worse at the thought of the fake laughter and the stupid jokes as well as the idiot costumes and meandering plotlines. No, not that. I can't. My spirit is not made for comedy. I would sooner die every time. I would go crazy. Sitting through *Così fan tutte* for Krisztyna one dress rehearsal, I lay down in the box across three chairs, out of sight. I hated it that much I felt ill. Another time I fell asleep as she performed in *Die Fledermaus,* one New Year's Eve with my head on the edge of the box. But I was sick with tonsillitis.

I dial the number and wait for her to answer. She picks up on the second ring.

"I am very happy you called, very happy, Natalija. I thought you would. You anywhere near Paris? Or Madrid from next week?"

"No, I am performing in *Il Trovatore* in Roma. I am in Madrid in March. You should know, you saw my website."

"I know you are but thought you might be coming earlier, just to see me," she almost purrs.

"No, my career comes first, Sara, so don't flatter yourself. You just remind me of someone who was very special."

"That's what they all say. Well…….. maybe I will make it to see you in *Il Trovatore.* Yes, I think I can spare a couple of nights one weekend." She laughs, almost like the wind-chime laugh of Krisztyna, only throatier as she is a smoker.

"*Il Trovatore* is not a good idea, Sara. Anasztázia is performing at the same time in *Romeo et Juliette.*"

"I don't want to see her. She bored me very quickly, too much wanting love. Are you still in Milano or has your run of *Aida* finished?"

"Last night of the run is tomorrow," I say.

"You know I have nearly a week off right now if you fancy romantic Paris." There is a quiver of mischief in her voice.

"No. I don't believe in romance, Sara. And neither do you. You have to come to heartless Milano if you are hungry enough. I am here for two days after tomorrow night then I return to Roma."

"Well, see you when I see you," she says carelessly. "I

might if the flights are cheap enough. We'll see."

Since Krisztyna is long gone to me, I am calling her Spanish double. Sara, slutty stage manager from Paris. Once with Anasztázia, now thrown her aside and hungry for the next roadkill. Only I am better at this than Sara is.

Why should I live like a convent girl? I have to move on. And maybe a meaningless fling is what I need to unravel after *Aida*. I don't like Sara's personality one bit, but she is beautiful, sexy and smouldering. I don't want to talk, I just need a tarty fling. I hope she makes it over just for me to have some fun. Anasztázia is anything but fun.

As I travel on the flight back to Roma, there still exists a deep emptiness in my heart. Emptiness for that lovely, ethereal girl who captured my heart at her glittering première. So fragile and I have torn off her butterfly wings and lost her. Anasztázia.

The memory of Sara makes me feel cheap now. Her kisses linger on my neck, her warm dusky perfume clings to my skin. Passion for two meaningless nights in my apartment in Milano. Just because I could.

Just lust with the promise of more in the future in Madrid.

The jewels Anasztázia gave me sparkle cold on my neck and across my collarbones.

Sara gently removed them, softly calling me sweet nothings in Spanish. They were sweet but they were nothing especially as I don't speak Spanish. And so was she; nothing, reaching for her packet of cigarettes carelessly as I turned over and tried to sleep.

"I knew I would have you," she said arrogantly as she blew her cigarette smoke out of the window, selfishly not caring that the cold winter air rushed in and turned the already cold studio into an icebox.

"Milano is overrated, La Scala especially but you are good, way hotter than your girlfriend. She was gorgeous but so goddamn needy and the self-harm was horrible. Don't need that shit, it freaks me out. I always have whoever I want."

"Me too," I had said. I thought it was kind of cruel to refer to the self-harm.

But do I really care what Sara thinks? I am not with her for conversation which is pretty smutty at best. She says the theatre is a brilliant place for meeting hot chicks. And then they are gone. It seems to be her main agenda for being a stage manager, although I don't doubt she is good at what she does.

She sounds so much like the old Natalija in Hungary. Tarty empty flings with whoever walked through the Opera House stage door. Sara gets who she wants because she is beautiful and pushy. Like Krisztyna was. Like me.

Maybe I had better return the necklace to Anasztázia since we are over. I cannot keep mementos of the dead.

DIAMONDS

I am back in Roma for *Il Trovatore* and Gounod's *Romeo et Juliette* will alternate with my Opera. This means Anasztázia is in Roma for the whole time I am in *Il Trovatore* as Azucena. Not such a good thing under the circumstances, our schedules colliding. She is playing the lead as Juliette. Our roles are polar opposites; sweet Juliette and angry, vengeful Azucena. Like me, Anasztázia has hardly any German language roles on her repertoire apart from some roles very early on in her career. She hates the language but she is a soprano and has so much more versatility. She can even sing Carmen although she never does, so her roles are not limited unlike my mezzo roles. Puccini loved sopranos which is a pity. I always longed to be one of Puccini's feisty heroines such as Tosca or Turandot.

I have heard nothing from her since our argument in La Scala. None of the texts she always sent, full of love and longing. She has given up on me this time. She didn't wait forever.

We both fell in love with illusions, clinging to impossible dreams, chasing shadows this way and that across Opera stages failing to see the reality. She fell in love with Carmen and Amneris. I fell in love with sadly, madly beautiful Lucia and melodramatic Tosca.

I murdered her love. I destroy everything. I will just have myself some flings, like I did with Sara. Better than living like a nun. My phone pings with a text from Sara. She will see me in Madrid in March.

> *Wish it was Carmen. But you can be Carmen just for me, beautiful.*

What is it with everyone wanting Carmen? I write back:

> *I am Carmen. I am her. You'll see.*

The day I arrive back from Milano I am anxious that Anasztázia will have changed the locks so I am relieved when the keys work but she is not at home. The white roses I sent her are still on display in her bedroom. I touch the petals. Her suitcase is there so she must be at the Opera House.

I check in my lilac room and am relieved she hasn't thrown all my clothes out of the window. She is not vengeful anyway. Krisztyna would have definitely thrown my clothes into the frenzied heart of Roma to be run over by scooters and stolen by the fortunate; all my beautiful Opera gowns.

I need to de-stress so I grab my skates and go straight to the ice rink and skate until I feel I am flying, trying to complete more rotations in my spins until I am dizzy. I am exhausted after La Scala but it is so good, so good to fly again. I feel reckless. One fall at speed and I could put myself out of performances again, but I feel like being reckless, like spending the last two nights with Sara. The guilt has gone. The old bitchy diva has completely cracked through the shell.

The doctors would not be happy about the skating either, given my insides are probably still not as they should be. I have only just got back from the ice rink and I am polishing my skates in the kitchen when I hear the door. I am worried about seeing my broken ice princess. Will she scream, sulk, cry or just blank me? I hear voices and Marina is with her. Marina just looks at me and says, "What are you doing with goddamn ice skates? Honestly, Natalija you are not of this world. And I don't mean that in a good way. And skating when you are a singer? You are very stupid with *Il Trovatore* rehearsals opening tomorrow."

"I was junior champion, twice in my country and second in Europe until I knocked myself out and lost my memory for a bit. I was going to be the best," I say.

Marina looks at me as though I am crazy. "I think you

still have memory loss since you forgot someone."

Anasztázia walks into the room and watches me silently, standing behind Marina as though Marina is her mother. She gazes on mournfully like a child I hurt who cannot forgive. I say hello but she doesn't answer, just pulls at the sleeves of her long black sweater and looks away. Marina taps me on the shoulder, "Natalija, I need to speak to you. Stop with those fucking skates and come with me."

Anasztázia watches me as I get up. I move to touch her but she steps backwards as if she is burnt, her big sad eyes telling me *you are so cruel, you hurt me*. I follow Marina to the living room.

Marina was my first Opera crush. I had lots of fantasies about her; twenty years older than me when I was performing in my very first opera in London aged 23. She was a diva then and still is. She is a complete Tosca.

But I knew then she wasn't on my wavelength, romantically speaking.

Pity. She is still gorgeous. I wouldn't say no.

But there are a million reasons to say no. Even without Anasztázia. More than anyone, Marina would be breaking plates and hurling my clothes out of the window. We would strangle each other. Better she is happily married and I don't even have to give it a thought.

We sit in the living room and Marina is hostile.

"Anasztázia is crying so much I am in despair. She will lose her voice before her Opera rehearsals open. What did I say in April? That she was fragile and you just hurt her. I am ashamed of you."

"Marina, you know she needs help and I was so stressed. My role in La Scala was the most difficult to date. Loggionisti catcalled me from the gallery when I didn't hit a few notes. It took everything out of me and....."

Marina interrupts me. She has no time for explanations, which is kind of rude since she had told me about how stressed she always got when performing in La Scala. She called it the Colosseum. She doesn't want to listen.

"She said you cannot love her. She is back to the sad Anasztázia before you arrived in April. In fact she is sadder than ever. But her heart does want you although God knows why. I am so worried about her. I don't know what you did in Milano because she won't say. She came back from watching you in *Aida* heartbroken. She was so proud of you, so happy to go and admire you in your first major role in La Scala."

"Marina, she is ill and she needs more help. I didn't make her sick. I had to call the doctor for her on emergency in October. He told me she was very sick, that she shouldn't go to New York for that concert," I tell her. "Marina you have no idea what it is like."

I say nothing about Marina's angelic friend being a serial cheat. That she is not the fragile little elfin beauty whose heart is true, but someone who betrayed me. I say nothing. Besides, I am a cheat too.

I am the devil diva to Marina.

Anasztázia's heart is true, I don't doubt that.

I can feel Marina's anger as she flicks her long black hair over her shoulder. She looks at me with disgust.

"Marina....." I touch her arm. "Listen to me..."

She shakes my hand off her. "She's been cutting, Natalija. I find out she started again; she lied many times. I asked her and then she broke down. I was so shocked she could do this to her body."

"She needs treatment, Marina," I tell her.

"Natalija, you can hold yourself accountable, because this is the first time I have seen it in years. Only when she arrived so sad from Hungary all those years ago did I think I saw some marks on her, but not since then." Marina looks at me with such contempt as if I did it. As if I sliced Anasztázia's beautiful skin.

And she has done it since she first arrived in Roma. She

has just hidden it so well.

"She's so beautiful, Natalija. Please do something."

I say nothing. Because I am as helpless as anyone else.

Marina softens. "Please, Natalija. And her head injury, did she do that to herself? I am very sorry I blamed you for that…….." Her dark eyes look at me pleadingly. "And the whole company still talk about who is her violent boyfriend? Who is hitting the great Anasztázia? When I hear such talk I get very sad for her."

Marina sighs. She is Italian and Hungarian darkness scares her, scares the hell out of her because she doesn't understand us.

"Marina, her own doctor said she should not work out of Italia. She is taking medication but the doctor nearly hospitalised her in October. I don't know if I should even be here because she said it was over."

Marina pats my arm and she is calmer.

"Look, Natalija. I know you are under a lot of pressure but don't walk out on her, I beg you. This apartment is big enough to have your space. Anasztázia is hurting but she will be better in a day or so. If she was anything like me, she would have chopped all your opera gowns up. I would have done. When I found out my first husband was having it away with some little tart at his workplace for God knows how long, I chopped the crotch out of all his Gucci suits before hurling all his possessions into the stairwell and I threw his designer shoes into the fountain. I stabbed the tyres dozens of times on his sports car, painted 'STRONZO' on the windscreen and then I changed the apartment locks. Hearing him scream with rage outside the door was the best sound ever."

She laughs loudly at the memory and then says cheerfully she has to go. Her vengeance story seems to have lifted her spirits.

I hear her talking to Anasztázia in the kitchen. Then the front door slams.

Yes, Marina would be a nightmare lover. Chopping clothes up, smashing plates. I would go mad if someone chopped up my designer clothes. Krisztyna once took a knife to a wedding dress because Fiamma gave it to me. The beads and sequins were all over the closet floor.

I was mad enough then.

"You came back not because you wanted to, but because you were made to by Marina. You do not love me," says Anasztázia. She stands in the living room, looking so petite and hurting, holding her stomach as if it is physically painful.

Instead of being kind, I tell her, *I can still sleep in the lilac bedroom or the pink one, if that is how you feel. And pay rent. You did tell me it was over. If it is over then I pay my own way. But this is my home too. That is why I came back, Anasztázia.*

Still cruel and bitchy Natalija. I look at her with coldness, face hard and defensive.

She angrily spits back at me, *Fine you can sleep in your lonely room and think about what you really want, Natalija. And don't you dare offer me money! Don't insult me like that. Stick your fucking money, Natalija! I cheated with my flesh and blood but never with my heart. I was weak, Natalija, but I am real, not some china doll! Look at me, I am fucking real!* She clutches her chest with both hands as she says it for emphasis, as though she were on the stage, trying to reach the people at the back of the auditorium. Drama queen.

She furiously slaps the 500 euros I am holding out of my hands and the notes flutter to the floor. She is so angry.

"At least take these back, Anasztázia. I cannot accept them now," I say and remove the glittering stones from around my neck.

I hold them out to her. She snatches them from my hand and her blue eyes are ice. She pushes me in front of the mirror and fastens them round my neck digging her nails in as hard as she can as she fastens the clasp. She is cursing, crying angry tears, *Ungrateful little bitch, you are unreal you are so cold.* She makes me face myself and jabs at the glass in front of us.

"Surprised you are still wearing your rings," I say noticing her right hand as the sapphire glints in the light.

"So are you!" she says grabbing my hand. "So are you!"

"The rings are nice. I bought them for Christmas, for myself just as much as you."

"Nice, Natalija? Nice? You married yourself to me! And now you are stuck with me because I am not getting divorced again in my lifetime. You should have thought about it if you didn't want me. It is too late for regrets. I am yours forever now."

"They are just rings, Anasztázia," I tell her. "Only jewellery."

"No they mean way more. I belong to you and it's too late to throw me away. You are stuck with me for life. I don't care if you hate me but you can't ever get rid of me!" she says turning to face me again. She taps my collarbones hard with her fingertips and I sound hollow.

An empty shell of a diva.

"Don't insult me with your money and trying to give my necklace back. I would sooner you threw the diamonds in the garbage!"

She says, *You need to pay with solitude.*

"I do not want you in my room right now, Natalija. You stay in your lilac bed. It is a healing colour, help mend your cold heart."

"I'm not surprised you need to sleep alone, Anasztázia. You wore yourself out tarting around Europe. Anyone would be tired after all that."

"You are so horrible, Natalija. If this is the real you, I don't know if I would have wanted ...." She sighs and turns away. She would still have wanted me, because she fell in love with my beauty, not the real me.

When I try to hold her, just to give her some comfort, she pushes me away. I see a bandage underneath her loose black top when she raises her arms.

"Anasztázia.....please stop self-harming. Even if you hate me, please get more help. You are ruining yourself."

I try to hold her again, but she pushes me away, pulling her sleeves down over her fists which are clenched tight.

"Get away from me! You hurt, you always do!"

A real life Carmen you are; cold and uncaring. Making everyone fall in love with you because you are so beautiful and waltzing off without a backward glance. I really hate you so much!

I lean against the wall. "Are you finished now?" I ask.

She points at me and lets all the hurt fly out.

"Don't you ever, ever leave again, Natalija. I will drag you back by your hair through the streets of Roma if you leave me. Why did I have to fall in love with you? I am at the top of the world and I fell in love with a heartless girl. Every day I regretted how I hurt you, every day I swore forgiveness, every day I have been kneeling at the altar asking God to forgive me."

"Didn't work then, did it?" I say honestly.

"Fuck you, Natalija!"

"God is not listening, baby. You have to want to stop," I tell her. "Same with your cutting. Dress rehearsal is in a few weeks. Your Juliette costume has no sleeves, I've seen it in the costume department. Stop for that if nothing else."

She hates herself way more than she hates me.

"Anasztázia, you are sick. It hurts Marina that you do this. She cares about you and it sure as hell will hurt your daughter when she visits. What will you tell your Mária?"

She says nothing.

"Fine, go ahead Anasztázia. Just tell everyone all the same lies about falling over, slipping in the shower when you get your next costume fitting. They all think you're being bashed around which is bad enough. They all wonder who is beating you, how do you think that makes me feel?"

My God she is messed up.

Maybe my heart healed into ice. Maybe I have become crueller than ever if this is how people end up over me. Everyone ends up hurt over me and I don't even try to hurt. I just do.

She should tell me I am ungrateful. She is right. A diamond necklace around my throat and an expensive apartment. She offers me the world and I behave like this.

She told me it was over between us. *Over.* I follow her as she tells me to come to my lilac bedroom.

I have arranged an altar for you and your dead heart, she tells me. *Your church is right here.*

She shows me that she has set up a crucifix and a statue of the Madonna surrounded by candles. *For you to pray for your soul,* she says. *You need to be saved. Pray for your sins.*

"I've already eaten, you can help yourself. It's up to you if you eat or starve or throw up. I really don't care," she says as she walks out of the bedroom.

"I have work to do. My rehearsals start tomorrow so please stay out of my way tonight. This apartment is big enough," she calls out as she goes down the hall.

The living room door slams. I hear her singing the sad laments of Juliette. Her soprano voice slices through the apartment walls with such haunting melancholy as she plays the piano.

My rehearsals start tomorrow too for the demanding role of Azucena. Damn her. She thinks she is the better singer and this makes me resentful.

I want to sing *Stride la vampa* in the hallway as loud as I can until the neighbours complain. Azucena the vengeful gypsy, overpowering Anasztázia's delicate Juliette with all the power a mezzo can unleash, soaring over the orchestra and chorus.

But no need to mess up her rehearsing. It is her

apartment and we don't need more arguments.

Azucena can wait.

I go and get some toast and coffee from the kitchen. The fridge is full of my favourite food I notice.

She knew I was coming back from Milano today and filled the fridge just for me.

On one shelf is a note on the buffalo mozzarella; PLEASE EAT ME. I almost smile.

But I am not hungry. I just go with the toast.

Her pill bottles are on the table. She is still taking the medicine at least but it doesn't seem to be doing that much. She probably needs stronger pills.

I creep into her bedroom when she is in the living room and light candles. The room looks like a shrine. I roll on the bed in black silk and try to look seductive. This is what she wants after all; she wants my body not my wild personality and erratic behaviour. If I make it up tonight, I will feel much better for my stressful role and *Il Trovatore*. I lie there looking at my music sheets, going through the Opera in my head. I will make up for my sins by being sweet to her and I will be saved.

Just be the temptress, her little Carmen whore. She cannot resist you.

"Natalija! You will burn the place down, what are you doing?!" Anasztázia blows most of the candles out. "Please be careful and get off my bed. Go back to your own room. Please leave me alone."

"Does *Un bel dì* exist for you?" I ask. I lie on my side, try to look as sultry as possible, twirling my hair.

She looks at me and the hate has gone for now. She sadly says, "I don't know, Natalija. ....for me to hold that shard of hope I was clinging on to....I hurt you...but you were, you are the only one I.......I don't know...."

Her voice is so quiet, so broken and she cannot finish

what she was saying. Her words fall off the edge of our world. She is so unlike the Anasztázia I met. She gazes at me for a few seconds, almost inhales my black beauty with a sigh as I see myself through her eyes; the seductive, smoky Carmen. I think she will change, take my hand and tell me I am beautiful. But it is not going to work.

She just turns around and goes off to shower leaving me lying there, a siren for nothing, my long black hair draped over the edge of the bed, scarlet lips hungry and unkissed. She locks herself in her bathroom. She never locked herself in showers before. She is determined not to crack and she doesn't want me to see what she has done to herself.

"You better not be cutting yourself in there!" I yell before she starts the shower water. "I will find out!" Then the sound of running water drowns out everything.

I am still lying across her bed with my music sheets when she comes out and she is so incensed she doesn't speak. She shoves me aside like garbage, as I am lying on her silk dressing gown. I see her bandaged arm as she encases herself in the lilac silk. I sit up and hold out my arms for her. She hesitates for a moment then she pushes me back onto the bed roughly and there is no tenderness. She pulls on my hair, her hands are not gentle, her teeth graze my shoulder and her nails cut into my back deep enough to leave marks. She has no sweet whispers for me only an angry blaze of fire.

Afterwards she closes her eyes and sighs, stretching her arms and I gaze at those impossibly long black eyelashes, her delicate porcelain features profiled in the candlelight for a moment. Her dark blonde hair is spilling over the pillow; she looks soft and peaceful and at rest.

"You are so beautiful, Anasztázia," I say thinking I have won her over as I ghost the fine white line of the scar on her head which has faded so well. My gift to her, forever branded as mine.

But she opens her eyes as she feels my fingers gently run

through her hair and turns to look at me with absolute hatred. She rolls out of bed and fastens her gown, turning away as though I am a dirty little whore she got pleasure from and now she is disgusted with herself, with me.

Without a word she opens the bedside drawer and leaves a 50 euro note on the table.

Then she leaves the room. No shouting, no talking, no nothing. Just that.

I feel horrible for a few minutes, like a cheap hooker she just paid for sex. She wanted me to feel bad. Leaving money on the bedside table.

So much for romance and I was in the mood. Well it was better than nothing. I get up and I am about to leave the money lying there, then I take it. I want her to see that I don't care. No emotions involved, just like the old me in Budapest. She probably expected a reaction, for me to chase after her and shout, *Don't you dare treat me like a whore!*

Maybe I should have just laughed and said, *Is that all I get? Make it a hundred, at least.*

That would make her so mad.

I go back to the lilac room, unfeeling and cold and stare at myself in the mirror wondering what is the meaning of life. My life. Why I am so careless and cruel. Why I bring out the worst in everyone, it seems. The mind games, the screaming, the tears, the volcanic domestics. I am the catalyst.

Always have been. Ever since I was a kid; bitchy and cruel in ice-skating class, telling them they were all fat and useless, I was going to be the champion. A five year old sociopath.

It worked. I had private classes and did become a champion.

I say to myself. *You should just leave, live alone. She hurt you and begged for your forgiveness. But she is not cruel. You are, Natalija and you always were. You are breaking her heart. And her self-harming is not your problem. She is 44 years old, for God's sake, she needs to deal with it.*

She is sick and she will drag you down when you want glory and fame. She doesn't have to be your possession forever. You don't need to own damaged goods.

Maybe I should have moved on to the next love interest. There are plenty more out there as I search with my restless smouldering Carmen eyes.

Sara the stage manager for one. I don't even like her, but she is smokily beautiful and I don't want heart to heart conversations and pleading and tears and 'I love you'. I want passion and emptiness in soulless hotel rooms, dressing rooms, rented apartments.

I am thinking about everything when I see a photo in its silver frame on the window ledge. I go and pick up the photo; me as Carmen, dressed in sensual, sultry red and black and smoking hot. Carmen, the fiery careless gypsy girl. I look at it for a long time. She embodies the free spirit everyone tried to possess and no one ever did, the true heartbreaker.

It touches something deep within me. Anasztázia cannot let go of the girl she fell in love with. I am the only one she ever wanted. That is why I am here even though she is lost in her own world, one of self-destruction and hurt. She only ever loved her Carmen. She only ever will.

I pad along the corridor to the living room where Anasztázia is sitting at the piano, playing softly, singing but quieter now as it is late. Her role is not a happy one but she looks so sad. She doesn't see me leaning in the doorway at first watching her, but she senses I am there because she stops singing and the piano is silent. She looks down at her hands and won't look up.

"Anasztázia, I just want to say that whatever it is you are going through, you are not alone. I am just down the hall if you need me. You don't have to suffer alone, I don't want you hurting for any reason. Please."

She says nothing, only sits there and stares at her fingers which are motionless on the black and white keys, in place ready to continue.

I turn and go back to my room and I hear her close the piano lid. There is silence.

For, God's sake, Natalija, I tell myself. *You can still live this life of illusion. Illusion is your life, so lose yourself once more in the Opera World. Chase those beautiful shadows, however fleeting across the stage and don't ever cross back into the land of mortals. Stay high on this mountain peak and don't look down. Help Anasztázia, don't leave. She is sick, it is not her fault.*

I resolve to try.

I look out of the windows where the lights of Roma glow gold through the delicately twisted iron of the balcony. I am offered the world and I am still restless and empty. Then I sit on the chair in front of the dressing table and examine my reflection. The diamonds around my throat sparkle rainbow rays of light. They speak of infinity. But yet I do not.

I look at the cold beautiful girl in the mirror and begin to remove the make-up. Like Turandot, I am like ice yet I burn. Burn right through to the bone. And I feel nothing as I stare into her dark eyes as the last traces of smoky eyeshadow are wiped clean.

I get up, close the curtains on the night city below. I place my Carmen photo next to the bed and the music sheets for *Il Trovatore* under my pillow, a ritual I have always followed the night before rehearsals, confident that the music will seep into my head as I sleep.

Tomorrow I will be the best again. I will.

I am Natalija, Queen of the Opera World.

I am now resurrected.

I turn off the light and darkness swallows the whole of me.